Life, Part 2: Lydia's Story

Life in Palmyrton Series, Volume 1

S.W. Hubbard

Published by S.W. Hubbard, 2019.

LIFE, PART 2: LYDIA'S STORY

First edition. October 15, 2019.

Written by S.W. Hubbard.

Chapter 1

Lydia entered the foyer of Hennessy's and waited while the beautiful young woman at the maitre'd's desk dealt with a couple. The man wore a checked shirt and scuffed loafers; the woman a flowered knit dress tight enough to reveal the outline of her bra. A knock-off Louis Vuitton bag hung from her shoulder.

They did not have a reservation.

A furrow formed in the hostess's smooth brow as she earnestly scanned her book. A slender, pink-manicured fingertip slid down the page.

Hennessey's did not use a computer for reservations.

Never had, never would.

Finally, the young woman looked up at the couple. She gave a small, sad shake of her head like a surgeon delivering a death sentence.

Nothing could be done.

The couple turned and left.

Lydia knew what was passing through the young woman's head. People like this must be turned away, even if there were empty tables. Even if they insisted.

Especially if they insisted.

Lydia knew because twenty years ago, she had been that young woman. Elegant...well-spoken...gracious.

But firm. The greeter at Hennessey's was trained to never waver.

Lydia looked down at her Ferragamo pumps as the rejected couple passed her. The smooth black leather stood out against the subtle navy and gold pattern of the carpet, the same pattern that had been there twenty years ago when Lydia had seated the man who would change her life.

━━━━◉━━━━

Then

THE MAN WITH THE BAD comb-over and polyester tie leaned over her desk trying to see the reservation book. "There's plenty of tables. We'll take that one right there."

Lydia withdrew from his scotch-soaked breath. The manager of Hennessey's would fire her if she seated this lout and his equally drunk friend in a prime table in the main dining room. She'd been trained to make eye contact, smile sweetly, and lie consistently in these situations.

"I'm sorry. There's nothing available until 9:30."

The lying never came easily. Despite a year of practice, some slight hesitation always gave her away. The drunk sensed it the way a cat senses the one person in the room who's allergic.

"Oh, come on. We'll eat quick and—"

A man in the next party stepped forward. "Excuse me, but the young woman has given you her answer. Those of us with reservations are waiting." He spoke in a firm, calm voice. The boor opened his mouth to protest, but wilted under his opponent's patrician glare.

"Screw this," he muttered and clomped away.

Relief mixed with concern as Lydia turned to her savior. "I'm sorry you had to wait."

The man's face softened as he smiled at Lydia. He had hazel eyes flecked with gold just as his rich silk tie was marked with tiny gold fleur de lis. He was older than she, but younger than the man who'd hassled her. "Maybe I shouldn't have interfered, but you seemed like you could use a little help getting rid of those two."

"I did. Thank you." He was one of four men, all dressed in expensive suits. Clearly, a business dinner. She glanced at her book. "And your reservation...?"

"Eastlee. Charles Eastlee."

Of course, this wasn't the very same carpet that had covered the floor the night she'd met Charles, just the same pattern.

Hennessey's managed to replace the carpet every few years during the eighteen hour period on Mondays when the restaurant was closed.

Paint was retouched, chairs reupholstered.

There should never be any signs of shabbiness.

Nor should there be any signs of change.

The young women who greeted diners also never changed.

Yes, they had different names over the years—Catherine, Elizabeth, Emily, Lydia—but they were essentially the same young woman. A graduate student from Drew University or Farleigh Dickinson—undergraduates were too flighty and unreliable. She would be a scholar in the humanities—scientists were too brusque. And she would stay only a year or two, until she finished her degree and moved on with her life, replaced by another beautiful young student.

The position of greeter at Palmyrton's most exclusive dining establishment was not meant to be lifetime employment.

The greeter must remain perpetually twenty-three, twenty-four tops.

Lydia had been perilously close to the end of her reign when Charles had rescued her. Limping through her master's degree two courses per semester, regretting she'd started but fearing completion, begging for extensions on papers, dating a feckless poet/songwriter, creeping ever closer to her twenty-fifth birthday.

Twenty-five.

It had seemed like the end of the road at the time.

"Good-evening, Mrs. Eastlee." The greeter smiled, revealing her perfect teeth. "Mr. Eastlee and the others are in the Peacock Room. Follow me."

Lydia hardly needed a guide to the private dining room at the back of the restaurant. She'd walked the path countless times as both employee and guest. But she fell in behind the slender young woman. Together they navigated between the widely spaced, white linen-draped tables, several of which could have accommodated the rejected couple.

Lydia didn't know if the girl leading the way was Caitlin or Anna or Renee.

Charles always learned their names. It paid to be on good terms with the greeter if he needed a last-minute table.

Lydia didn't bother.

She never came to Hennessey's without Charles. This place contained too much baggage for her. Not that the current greeter had any inkling that the distinguished Mrs. East-lee had ever held her job.

Only two of the longest-tenured waiters recalled Lydia as a colleague, and they were too discreet to acknowledge their memory of her as a confused, unhappy grad student drinking with them at the bar after closing.

These days, Raoul and Anthony took her order for grilled sea bass or poached salmon with a polite nod. Charles Eastlee was well known as a generous tipper. No one wanted to get on the wrong side of that.

The greeter reached the Peacock Room, opened the door to a wave of animated chatter, and stepped back to allow Lydia to enter.

All conversation halted.

"*There* you are, my love! Did they make you work overtime on your last day?"

Charles Eastlee crossed the room and kissed his wife on the cheek. He looked as crisp at seven in the evening as he had when he'd knotted his Hermes tie at seven this morning. His gold-flecked eyes had tiny wrinkles in the corners, his forehead was a little higher, but other than that, Charles had barely changed from the night they'd first met twenty years ago. Taking her hand, he drew her into the group sipping from champagne flutes. Lydia's heart still quickened when Charles held her hand like this.

Was it arousal?

Or the thrill of knowing she was cherished?

"Darling, we've been lo-o-onging for your arrival," Betsey von Maur gushed as a waiter placed a champagne glass in Lydia's hand. "How was your last day at work?"

Lydia endured the double air kiss without coughing in the overpowering cloud of Betsey's perfume. "Wonderful. There was a catered lunch at the office. The copywriters wrote new lyrics to 'Here Comes the Sun', and the entire staff sang 'There Goes Our Lydia' to me."

"Of course, everyone's so *clever* in advertising." Betsey scanned Lydia for the presence of a gold watch. "And did you get a gift?"

"Yes, a lovely crystal bowl." Lydia edged away from Betsey to greet the other guests. The bowl still rankled, and she didn't want to discuss it with Betsey or anyone else. Eighteen years she'd given to Imago Advertising and they sent her off with a bowl. Baccarat crystal, but still.

A bowl.

"Here's our girl!" Tom Schilling crushed her in a bear hug. Of all their circle of friends, Lydia liked Tom and his wife best. He had the true salesman's gift of gab and an entrepreneur's reckless optimism—totally different from Charles's stiff law firm partners. His wife Madalyn was a reserved woman who observed him with quiet bemusement. "Are you ready to start your life of world travel and endless adventure with the birthday boy?" Tom released Lydia and clapped Charles on the back.

"Ready as I'll ever be." Lydia hoped her smile was sufficiently enthusiastic. They were gathered to celebrate her husband's sixty-second birthday and his retirement as managing partner of Eastlee, von Maur, Finn and Morrone. Charles had been talking for several years about retiring at sixty-two. But it was only recently that he'd made it clear he expected her to quit working as well. He wanted to travel, take really long vacations instead of two-week excursions. And they didn't need the money from her position as Creative Director of Imago.

"We leave next week on our Mediterranean cruise," Charles said. "A month on a small luxury ship with other Harvard Law School alumni. We get lectures on art, architecture, and history from Harvard professors in every port of call. There are even cooking classes from famous Italian and Greek chefs."

"Isn't that lovely," Madalyn said.

"Fabulous," Tom boomed.

Lydia nodded. "Can't wait."

It all sounded so, so....claustrophobic. Trapped on a boat. Every minute of the day planned. Every conversation highminded.

She caught sight of the waiter in the corner as he transferred weight from one foot to the other. His shift had started at four and wouldn't end until after midnight. You wouldn't catch him complaining about lying on a cruise deck for a month.

You're lucky, Lydia. Remember? Lucky, lucky, lucky.

The party buzzed on, and eventually they sat down to dinner. At the large round table, Lydia drifted off into her own thoughts as the conversation bubbled around her. Her mind dissected the scene this afternoon at Imago. She didn't know what she'd expected on her last day at work, but it was more than the tepid gathering around deli sandwiches and lard-frosting cake in the office conference room.

Her career was over. Did anyone care?

When she'd started at Imago, she'd been a directionless young woman with a practically worthless Master's degree in English Literature. Charles had gotten her the interview, calling in a favor from the owner whose ass he'd saved in a lawsuit. Charles had believed she was clever enough to write ad copy. Or maybe he just believed anyone who could write a forty page master's thesis on Feminist Tropes in Victorian Fiction could surely produce four sentences of BS extolling the virtues of shaving cream. She would never have had the nerve to apply for the job herself, but Charles had pushed her, and the president of Imago had given her a chance.

The rest was history.

She loved writing ad copy. And she was good at it. She'd worked her way up from copy assistant to creative director. Now, twenty-two-year-olds came to her begging for an internship, a chance to prove themselves in advertising.

Or they had. Now, those people would be knocking on the door of Bryce Salazar.

Because Imago had already hired her replacement. A twenty-eight year old guy with a man-bun and ultra-skinny jeans who said the words *actionable insights* more than any human could endure. A guy who had shoved aside with a cursory glance all the detailed reports she'd prepared on every client.

The president of Imago had accepted her resignation with regret and gratitude.

But he hadn't begged her to stay.

Everyone wants to feel indispensable. But tonight, Lydia suspected she hadn't been indispensable at all. Imago would get along fine without her. Maybe while she was here at Hennessey's celebrating Charles's birthday and their joint retirement, everyone at Imago was knocking back Moscow Mules at South Main Tavern celebrating the arrival of a new creative future.

A future without Lydia Eastlee.

A roar of laughter brought her back to the party. The wine had been flowing during dinner and even Charles's uptight partners got into the spirit of delivering toasts. One after the other they rose to tell stories that were amusing only to other lawyers, but the group had been loosened with expensive wine and good food, so it wasn't hard to get a laugh.

Finally, all eyes turned to Lydia.

She realized with a clutch in her gut that she too was expected to stand and offer a toast. She wasn't like salesman Tom or litigator Regis—extroverts who didn't hesitate to speak in front of a crowd. Lydia was an introvert who only felt comfortable with public speaking when she was totally prepared.

Charles looked up at her with shining eyes. He raised his hand to his throat and tugged on his tie.

She couldn't disappoint him.

Lydia stood and raised her champagne glass. Somehow the words flowed off her tongue without any processing from her brain. "Happy birthday and happy retirement to the man who has always been my knight in shining armor. May we ride off on many new adventures together."

Then the waiter wheeled in an elaborate birthday cake with sixty-two blazing candles. The couples cheered and broke into song, led by an off-key Tom Schilling.

....*Happy Birthday, dear Charles.*

Happy birthday to yo-o-o-u!

All eyes turned to the birthday boy.

The candles flickered and sizzled.

The scent of melting wax filled the air.

The waiter glanced nervously at the smoke detector in the ceiling, waving off the rising vapors.

"C'mon man—make your wish and blow out those candles," Tom shouted.

Charles's mouth twitched.

In slow motion, he tilted to the left.

What was Charles doing? It wasn't like him to milk drama from his moment in the spotlight.

Lydia watched her husband's right hand claw the tablecloth.

Charles Eastlee fell in a rain of shattered crystal and china.

Chapter 2

The days after her husband's death passed in a blur.

Lydia and Charles had been Christmas and Easter Episcopalians, but Charles had contributed generously to the St. Peter's stained glass window restoration fund, so the rector had come calling promptly upon hearing the news of Charles's stroke. Together they'd planned the memorial service, while Regis Morrone took care of notifying all Charles's business contacts and Fred von Maur wrote the obituary. Someone at the firm cancelled the cruise and got all the money back.

It paid to have lawyers for friends.

They didn't have much family—Charles, a brother in Chicago; Lydia, a sister in Australia. Those calls couldn't be delegated. Lydia had to dial and speak the words: Charles is dead.

Charles's brother, his wife, and kids would fly in from Chicago. Lydia's sister had offered to come from Perth, but Lydia assured her the long trip wasn't necessary.

Then she called Kathleen.

Her best friend started chatting the second she answered her phone. "Hey! I was just going to call you. So much going on here, but I miss you every day."

"Charles is dead."

"What? What did you say?" Kathleen's voice shot up an octave.

Lydia knew she shouldn't have dropped the bombshell so harshly, but she'd run out of self-control. She went for shock value because she wanted sympathy. Lydia pictured her friend sitting in the kitchen of the house in Pittsburgh she'd just bought with her boyfriend. They'd carried on a long-distance relationship for nearly a decade, a decade in which Lydia had complete access to her friend. Two weekends a month, Kathleen and her boyfriend flew back and forth between Pittsburgh and Palmyrton, but the rest of the month, Kathleen was always available for lunch and shopping expeditions and silly chick flick movies. Lydia had relied on Kathleen for that part of her social life that didn't revolve around Charles or work.

But then the inevitable had finally happened. Kathleen had gotten engaged last month and moved to Pittsburgh. It still felt like Kathleen was away on vacation. Lydia hadn't reconciled herself to her best friend's relocation.

She spent half an hour tearfully telling Kathleen every detail of that horrible night at Hennessey's. "The funeral is on Thursday," Lydia concluded.

She waited for her friend to say she'd hop on a plane and be right there.

Silence hung between them.

"Oh, God, Lydia—I have some news, too. This is such a terrible time to be telling you."

"What?" Dear lord, surely Kathleen hadn't gotten a cancer diagnosis? Lydia wouldn't be able to bear that much loss.

"I'm pregnant. Three months."

"Three months? And you're just telling me now? I mean...I didn't mean it that way, sorry." Lydia managed to change her tone. "Congratulations!"

"I was going to tell you this week. At my age, I wasn't sure the pregnancy would, you know, last. But I had all the tests and I'm fine except for puking constantly, and the baby is healthy. But I'm still considered a high risk pregnancy. Advanced maternal age."

"You can't travel. I understand." Lydia felt her lip trembling. She'd saved the call to Kathleen for last so she could let go of her composure. All she wanted was for Kathleen to come and hold her and tell her she'd be there for her. Instead she took a deep breath and spoke. "It's okay. You don't have to come. I'll be fine."

Fine as long as she could distract herself from replaying those awful final moments of her husband's life.

Madalyn Schilling had been the first to spring into action. "Call 911," she barked at Tom. "See if there's a doctor in the house," she commanded the waiter.

Madalyn had trained as a nurse although she hadn't worked in a hospital for thirty-five years. Now she knelt beside Charles, loosening his tie and turning his head. She placed two fingers on his neck and watched the seconds tick on her elegant gold watch.

"Do you know CPR?" someone asked.

"His heart is beating. It's a stroke." Madalyn spoke in a calm, steady voice.

Lydia dropped to her knees beside her husband. A stroke was fixable. People lived through strokes all the time. Charles's eyes were open, and his gaze met hers. She'd never seen him look so apologetic.

"You'll be all right." She gave his hand a reassuring squeeze. But Charles didn't squeeze back. His hand lay in hers, flaccid and clammy.

Lydia felt a wave of panic rising within her. She directed it at Madalyn. "Do something! Help him!"

"Palmyrton Hospital has an excellent stroke team. The paramedics are on their way."

A bitter cackle escaped Lydia, bordering on hysteria. She pictured the greeter turning them away.

They wouldn't have a reservation.

The waiter returned with a young man in a blue blazer and penny loafers.

Penny loafers!

He claimed to be a doctor, and had left his dinner to help. He didn't look old enough to rent a car.

While he crouched over his impromptu patient, a spasm passed through Charles.

The doctor grunted and sat back on his heels, head hanging sheepishly like a teenager caught with a beer. "I'm sorry. He had a second stroke."

Lydia glared at him, demanding a better outcome. This man wasn't qualified to pronounce her husband dead.

People sometimes said the dead looked as if they were sleeping. But even in sleep Charles had exuded a mastery, a dignity that rest didn't diminish.

The body lying on the floor of Hennessey's was blank, empty, an obscene relic of the man Charles Eastlee had been.

Lydia screamed.

———◦—◦———

AFTER THE BURIAL ON Thursday, people came back to the house for the repast—Betsey had arranged the caterers, and Madalyn Schilling came early to help direct their work. The guests milled through the expansive first floor of the Eastlee home having conversations that echoed those toasts at the birthday party.

Except now all the verbs were past tense. Charles had been a great lawyer. Had been a loyal friend. Had been a savvy manager. Had been an impressive golfer. When Lydia drifted into a group, conversation dried up. They patted her, reassured her, complimented her fortitude until she finally eased away. Then they returned to their cocktail party chatter.

A contingent from Imago came to the funeral, including Bryce Salazar, who wore black skinny jeans and a sports coat so tiny it seemed he must've gotten it for his middle school graduation.

Some of the copywriters and graphic artists hugged her awkwardly. Lydia realized she'd always thought of them as friends, but they thought of her as their boss. Their sympathy was genuine, but the distance between her and them couldn't be bridged. Only Eleanor, the oldest of the copywriters, seemed to know what to say. She pulled Lydia into a tight hug. "This sucks," she whispered in Lydia's ear. "No one deserves this, least of all you."

But the cluster of Imago mourners were conscious of being out of place. After all, most of them hadn't known Charles at all. They nibbled at the food, checked their phones repeatedly, and then like a flock of migrating birds following a leader they couldn't even see, they all moved to the front door and left in a flurry of hand squeezes and air kisses.

Lydia wandered into the dining room, feeling like an awkward party crasher in her own home. There, Madalyn Schilling picked up ravaged platters of food and carried them back to the kitchen. She paused to put her arm around Lydia. "You're exhausted. I'm putting the food away as a signal to everyone that it's time to leave. Take an Ambien and get some rest."

"I don't ever take pills," Lydia protested.

Madalyn turned to a tiny purse she'd left in the corner and produced a blue pill. "Make an exception. I'm going to call you next Wednesday. We'll go out to lunch."

Lydia shook her head. "Thanks, but I won't be good company."

"I'm not expecting good company, silly girl. I'm coming to get you out of this house. No arguments."

Madalyn disappeared into the kitchen with another tray. Her strategy worked because within the half-hour, all the guests filtered out.

Lydia stood in the foyer listening to an endless litany.

"So sorry for your loss."

"If there's anything we can do, let us know."

"Don't hesitate to call."

Tom Schilling was the last to leave.

He placed his large hands on her shoulders. "Are you going to be okay here all by yourself?"

Lydia glanced away from his bright blue eyes, unused to seeing them solemn instead of creased with laugh lines. "Yes, I'll be fine. Thanks for staying until the end."

"I'm here for you, kiddo. Charles would want me to take care of you. That's what friends are for."

"Thank you," she whispered as she closed the front door behind his broad back.

Lydia looked around the vast foyer.

She was a widow.

She was unemployed.

She lived alone in a five-bedroom, 6,000 square foot house.

She was forty-five years old.

She slid into a heap on the floor.

She cried.

Chapter 3

Alton Finn, the partner who specialized in estate planning, waited a few discreet days before summoning Lydia to his office to review her husband's will.

"Apart from some charitable bequests, Charles left the bulk of his estate to you," Alton said, leaning back in the dark red leather chair behind his vast, empty desk. "I always advise my clients that they should discuss their plans with anyone who might be expecting to inherit to avoid nasty surprises after the passing. I want you to know that Charles and his brother both agreed that neither needed the other's money. So there will be no objections from that quarter."

David was seven years younger than Charles, an investment banker. They'd never been close, but neither had they been acrimonious. It had never dawned on Lydia that Charles's brother would make a play for his money. But she supposed Alton Finn saw a lot of bad behavior in his line of work. "Of course," she murmured.

"So let's go over the bequests first." Alton tapped a pen on the desk and drew the single document closer to him. "Charles felt that Harvard didn't need his money, so he set up a scholarship at his prep school to help deserving young men from modest backgrounds to attend."

"Yes, he mentioned that to me."

"So that's one million dollars."

Lydia jerked in her chair. She had no idea Charles had been that devoted to his high school alma mater.

Alton continued talking, choosing to ignore her reaction. "And he left $250,000 to the Rosa Parks Community Center since he sat on their board." Alton rustled his papers. "And there's a small annuity to the woman who worked as his mother's housekeeper and caregiver until the time of her death."

Alton looked up just as Lydia sipped from the sparkling water Alton's secretary had brought her. "And the rest comes to you. $16.7 million dollars. Not counting the house. And the cars."

A spray of water shot from Lydia's mouth and spattered her silk blouse. "Excuse me?"

Alton clicked his tongue against the roof of his mouth. "I take it you were unaware of the extent of his assets?"

"No, I...I—" Lydia made an effort to pull herself together. She didn't like looking like some dumb bunny housewife in front of Alton Finn. Charles had managed their finances. She had her own accounts, of course. Charles had always encouraged her to keep all the money she earned at Imago in a separate account. She used it for her clothes, her car, gifts that she bought for him and others. And she dutifully saved the rest in a 401K. But Charles's money had paid for their house, their taxes, their vacations. Certainly, she knew they were well-to-do.

But not *rich* rich.

Why hadn't Charles told her?

Why hadn't she asked?

Every year, she dutifully signed their joint tax return at the X. She'd never studied the numbers it contained. She remembered their first joint tax return. She'd been thrilled to finally have enough money to have to pay taxes. Looking over the numbers on the paperwork would have been presumptuous—Charles had earned almost all of the money. And somehow the pattern established in that first year had continued throughout their marriage.

And not just in the matter of taxes.

"Now, Charles left you this money with very few restrictions, knowing that you're a sensible person. But if you should marry again—"

"I'm not getting remarried." The sentence came out of her mouth with force that surprised her. She hadn't meant to be sharp to Alton; he was kind and gentlemanly.

Alton flexed his hands at the wrist, a gesture that denoted "calm down" in his understated lexicon. "Of course, you're not thinking of it at the moment, but given the difference in your ages, Charles always knew it was likely that he would predecease you. Consequently—"

Lydia leaned forward. "Wait. Charles discussed this with you?" Her husband had evaluated his younger wife's possible remarriage with his law partner but had never mentioned it to her.

"Charles wanted to protect you. An attractive woman with substantial assets can be a target for unscrupulous men."

Lydia felt her jaw dropping as if it weren't controlled by her own facial muscles. "Charles thought that once he was gone I'd rush out to start dating creepy Facebook stalkers and slimy gigolos on Tinder?"

Alton pursed his lips. "Of course not, Lydia. Charles respected your intelligence and good judgment. Nevertheless..." The lawyer took a deep breath.

"Nevertheless, what?"

"He felt it prudent to build in certain safeguards to your inheritance."

Lydia stared at her husband's partner until he continued.

"Charles had been using Mitchell Felson as his investment advisor, and he wished for you to continue to keep your assets under Mitchell's management. As a high net worth individual, you'll be inundated by opportunities to invest. But Charles has stipulated that you run all those past Mitchell before you make any decisions."

She had no idea what she'd do with the money she already had. Why would she want to make even more? "Fine. I have no desire to invest in Mars space missions and cures for obscure diseases."

"Of course. Charles dabbled in some high risk/high yield investments. But he was very careful to perform his due diligence. I don't recommend that you continue on that path unless you're willing to undertake the same level of research."

Charles had made risky investments? That seemed totally out of character for the cautious man she'd loved. But he couldn't have accrued nearly twenty million dollars by simply salting away his paycheck in a conservative mutual fund.

"I won't be doing any investing, Alton. What other *safeguards* should I know about?"

Alton noted her sarcasm on the word "safeguards" and shifted in his seat. "Yes...well..." he coughed. "If you were to decide to remarry, the terms of your pre-nuptial agreement would come into play."

"The pre-nup applied if I divorced him," Lydia objected. She had been a debt-laden grad student when she married a lawyer with assets. She hadn't objected to the pre-nuptial agreement even though it had dulled the gloss of their whirlwind courtship.

"There was a clause relating to what would happen in the event of Charles's sudden death."

Lydia's brow furrowed. There was? She didn't remember that.

"If you remarry, you would receive an annual annuity of two hundred thousand dollars. But the principal of Charles's estate would revert to a charitable trust. You would keep the house, of course."

"Of course." Lydia was too stunned to say more. It was not the money itself that mattered to her, but that Charles and Alton and presumably Mitchell Felson had been discussing this—*planning* this—for years and she had never known anything about it. Her future determined by these men.

Alton misinterpreted her silence. "You would still have an adequate income to support your lifestyle. Travel...clothes...entertaining. Charles would want you to enjoy your life to the fullest. He simply wanted to make you a less attractive target to, er, gold-diggers, if you will."

Lydia stood up. "So he's okay with my marrying a small-scale scammer who'd be satisfied with two hundred grand, just not with any big-time scammers. Like maybe men claiming to be long-lost princes in the Russian royal family."

Alton drew back as if he'd been slapped. "I believe Charles hoped that if you remarried, you would marry a man of means, a man who wouldn't need your money because he had plenty of his own. That's why he set up his will in this way. To protect you, Lydia. Charles always wished to protect you."

Chapter 4

L ydia stumbled out of the offices of Eastlee, von Maur, Finn and Morrone without seeing the oriental carpeted halls or responding to the greetings of the partners she passed. She succeeded in her goal of escaping the building without crying, collapsing behind the wheel of her navy BMW before the tears came.

Charles always wished to protect you.

Alton's words reverberated in her brain.

Protection.

Their relationship had been based on that word.

When she'd first met Charles, Lydia had sorely needed his protection. Left reeling by the death of her parents in quick succession, she had needed protection from a world of adult responsibilities she hadn't been ready to assume.

Lydia's father had been the quintessential middle American dad—mowing the grass and putting up the Christmas decorations, fixing leaky pipes and flat tires. He was quiet and low-key, and it wasn't until after he'd died that Lydia realized her father had been her emotional rock. Sure, she had talked more with her mom about boys, and clothes, and parties, but when she really needed advice about something big—where to go to college, what to major in—she had turned to her father. Her father always had a plan.

Her mother's death had broken her heart; her father's death, in her senior year of college, had left her totally unmoored. So she stuck with the last plan her dad had made for her: finish school. Then she enrolled in grad school to extend that plan for a few more years.

Then Charles had come along and made a new plan for her.

Then

Lydia had just seated elderly Mr. and Mrs. Buckworthy, shouting the daily special into the old man's better ear, when she saw a tall, thin man standing before her podium. As she hurried back to her post, she recognized Charles Eastlee. But she'd just reviewed the reservation list and knew his name wasn't on it.

"Hello, Lydia," he said before she could greet him.

How did he know her name?

She slid into her spot and picked up a pen. "Did you need to make a reservation?"

He smiled and placed his elbow near the tiny light illuminating her reservation book, close enough for her to smell his subtle aroma of mints and an expensive soap. "After a fashion. I stopped by to see if you were free for dinner on Thursday."

Thursday was her day off. Did he know that?

If he'd asked the manager or one of the waiters about her, they'd have told Charles Eastlee she had a boyfriend. Joel frequently came in after closing to finagle a free drink from the bartender as he waited for Lydia.

"Oh, I can't. I—"

He interrupted her by placing his index finger on the back of her hand. A pleasant frisson passed through her body.

Charles smiled only enough to show the edges of his perfect teeth. His eyes, yesterday so commanding when he had helped her get rid of the boorish drunk, today seemed yearning. "Say yes. It's only one dinner."

She knew Joel was planning on going to an open mic night at a bar in Brooklyn on Thursday, an endless journey she'd already begged off on the true claim she had a paper to write.

What would it be like to spend the evening with someone so confident yet so considerate?

So totally unlike needy, unhappy, unfocused Joel?

Why not find out?

"Yes. Dinner would be lovely."

Like Lydia's dad, Charles made their physical lives run smoothly and safely.

Unlike her dad, Charles had needed something in return.

Lydia had protected Charles as well. Protected him from the bitter disappointments of love. She learned soon after their first date that, in his twenties, Charles had been in love with a fellow student at Harvard Law. But when she got a clerkship with a Federal judge and then an offer from a prestigious DC law firm, she'd left Charles Eastlee without a backward glance. More than a decade passed before he recovered from that rejection.

It hadn't taken Lydia long to understand that Charles had fallen for her as much for who she wasn't as for who she was.

Wasn't a lawyer.

Wasn't competitive.

Wasn't demanding.

Charles had been exquisitely sensitive to criticism. Her role had been to reassure him when clients or colleagues proved difficult, to jolly him out of his moods and provide ample praise for his successes. She appeared at his side, gracious and smiling, oiling the wheels of their social life.

As with every marriage, they had established the parameters of what they needed from each other. The pattern had been set early, and it hadn't varied.

Wherever Charles was now, he was beyond the scope of her protection.

But apparently, she wasn't beyond the scope of his.

Chapter 5

When Lydia returned from her visit with Alton, a little Ford station wagon sat in the driveway. That meant Marta and her helper were cleaning the house. Marta had cleaned for them for over ten years, coming every Tuesday and Friday. But Lydia usually saw her only for a few moments before she left for the office.

Briefly, Lydia considered driving around for another hour so she wouldn't have to make small talk. But then she pulled her car into the garage.

Why should she avoid Marta? She hadn't seen another soul apart from Alton and his secretary in the past two days. And the petite, dark-haired woman was infinitely nicer than either of them. She walked into the kitchen, where Marta was vigorously polishing the already clean cabinets.

"You having lunch now? I can work somewhere else."

"No, stay and work here. You're not bothering me."

Marta studied her, twisting a dust rag in her hands. "Mrs. Lydia, I am so sorry about Mr. Charles. He was a good man. I never will forget what he did for me and my family."

Lydia accepted the condolences with a bowed head. Marta considered Charles her hero after his intervention had stopped the bank from foreclosing on her mortgage. Charles had come home early one day to change for a golf outing and found Marta in tears. A few questions...a few phone calls...a few letters on official law firm letterhead, and the bank had backed off. Marta and her husband's financial ship had been righted.

To Marta, what Charles had done was nothing short of a miracle.

To Charles, it had been a satisfying victory in a legal career that didn't always give him the chance to work for justice. After the Marta incident, Charles had sought out other pro bono cases, occasionally going off in his custom-tailored suit to stand beside some hapless soul and help him escape the gears of the legal system. Charles always returned home charged up by his victory. "I got his license restored," he would tell Lydia with a gleam in his eye. "I bargained the DA down to a misdemeanor....I kept her from getting evicted."

Lydia loved Charles best in those moments when he was tilting at windmills.

"I lit a candle for Mr. Charles in church on Sunday," Marta continued. "I am praying for you."

"Thank you, Marta." Lydia's eyes welled with tears. The cleaning lady's sympathy seemed the most heartfelt of all the condolences she'd received.

Marta polished the vast expanse of stainless steel on the front of the Sub Zero fridge. "You gonna stay in this big house all by yourself, Mrs. Lydia?"

"I don't know. I haven't thought about it yet." The house had been ridiculously large for two of them, so was it any more ridiculous for one?

Lydia glanced around her gleaming kitchen. How would she go about leaving? What would she do with all this stuff? How had two people managed to acquire so many chairs and sofas and beds and televisions? Her possessions felt like concrete blocks tied to her feet, dragging her to the bottom of the ocean like a character in a Mafia movie.

Rich people problems. You wouldn't catch Marta complaining about having too many belongings.

"How are your kids, Marta?" Lydia asked to distract herself from her thoughts.

"Oh, they are very good, thank you. Here is a picture from Felipe's graduation." She pulled a phone from her back pocket and showed a picture to Lydia. Six people, from a preschooler to a young adult in a cap and gown, faced the camera with broad grins and the same shiny black hair that Marta had. A short, brown skinned man stood behind them with his hands on the youngest's shoulders.

Marta scrolled to the next picture. "And this is our new dog, Pepito. You should get a dog, Mrs. Lydia."

"Charles is allergic." The words came from Lydia's mouth automatically. She pressed her fingers to her lips and shook her head.

Marta patted her shoulder. "I understand. I was the same when my papa died. Still always thinking what he would like or not like."

Lydia reached for Marta's phone and studied the picture. A funny, furry face stared back at her, head cocked, pointy ears raised. "What kind of dog is he?"

"No one knows. Little bitta chihuahua, little bitta poodle, little bitta terrier. Pepito, he's funny. He makes us laugh all day."

A dog. Lydia hadn't had a dog since she was a child. Honey, the family golden retriever, had died of old age when

Lydia and her sister were in high school. They'd both been too caught up in activities and preparations for college to beg for a replacement. And when she was single, Lydia had had a hard enough time taking care of herself.

In the early days of her marriage, the possibility of a dog had crossed her mind, but Charles's sneezing and red, weepy eyes whenever he was in the presence of a friend's pet had banished the idea before she spoke it aloud. Then the era of hypoallergenic labradoodles dawned, and Lydia had floated the possibility.

But Charles had countered with lawyerly logic. A dog would tie them down. A dog required constant walking, which he would not participate in. A dog peed on the rug and scratched at the woodwork.

Lydia realized she didn't want a dog as badly as Charles didn't want one.

But now..... Now Charles's logic, as well as his allergies, were a thing of the past. A dog might well tie her down, but what did she have to be tied down to? No job, no commitments, no schedule whatsoever.

A dog's leash could tether her to the real world.

Marta seemed to sense her consideration. "A dog is good company, Mrs. Lydia. A dog will listen to all your problems. A dog never tells you that you're wrong."

Who wouldn't appreciate that quality? "Where did you get Pepito?"

"Paws for People, on Larchmont down near the railroad tracks. You go over there, Mrs. Lydia—they got so many nice dogs who need a home. You find the one who's right for you."

Then Marta switched on the vacuum and swept her way out of the kitchen.

After Marta left for the day, Lydia walked through the gleaming, unoccupied rooms of her home and tried to imagine a dog curled on the off-white sofa or bounding across the marble-tiled foyer. She remembered the first time she and Charles had set foot in this house.

Then

After their honeymoon, Lydia had moved into Charles's bachelor townhouse. The place seemed plenty big to her after her years in student housing, but she could see Charles felt cramped by her arrival.

They immediately began house-hunting.

Charles had recently been promoted to managing partner and wanted a home befitting his position, a home in which they could entertain the other partners and new associates they were recruiting.

Lydia had enthusiastically seconded the real estate agent when she had suggested a stately Victorian in Palmyrton's historic district.

Charles had allowed himself to be shown a gracious Queen Anne with a wrap-around front porch and a curving staircase.

"Wow, this is gorgeous!" Lydia did a pirouette in the foyer, elated by the possibility of moving to such a house. She pictured herself as the heroine of an Edith Wharton novel.

But the fantasy hadn't lasted long.

Charles wrinkled his nose at the ancient cast iron radiators. "These would have to be replaced with forced air heat. And these windows!"

Lydia linked her arm through his. "Aren't they fabulous? They really bring the garden right inside."

Charles attempted to lift the sash of a huge window overlooking the perennial border. "They've got so many layers of paint, they can't even slide in their tracks."

The clincher had been a large stain on the parquet floor just visible at the edge of an area rug in an upstairs bedroom.

Charles hated the idea of other people's dirt. No amount of renovation would ever eliminate the traces of the many other people who'd lived in these historic homes.

To Lydia, that was their charm; to Charles, a horror.

So the Realtor had brought them to Palmer Ridge, at the time, the finest development of new luxury homes in Palmyrton. Lydia was awed into silence as the Realtor pointed out every amenity: the three car attached garage, the pantry, the walk-in his and her closets.

Charles beamed. This was his dream home, a house no one else had ever lived in. A house that would show the world who he'd become.

How could Lydia object? Certainly the place was far grander than any home she'd ever occupied. She poked her head into every empty room on the second floor. "Surely, we don't need five bedrooms?" she quizzed Charles.

They'd already agreed they wouldn't be having children: Charles because cystic fibrosis ran in his family; Lydia because the horror of losing her own parents made her unwilling to subject unborn children to the same possibility of pain.

Charles smiled and shrugged. "Plenty of guest rooms."

Lydia walked to the far end of the second floor hall and poked her head into the smallest guest bedroom, a room that no one had ever slept in.

Perhaps a dog would like it.

Chapter 6

The cacophony of barking reached her ears as soon as Lydia pulled into the Paws for People parking lot the next day. High pitched and frantic, low and growly, midtone and relentless—the dogs inside of the low-slung concrete shelter building made one thing clear: they wanted out. Now.

Lydia walked toward the front door with a mixture of anxiety and elation churning in her gut. For the first time since her husband's death, she felt she was doing something just for herself.

But was this something what she really wanted?

Everyone counseled her not to make any big life decisions while she was still grieving.

Did adopting a dog fall into that category?

Did she want to adopt a companion animal who desperately needed a home?

Or did she want to defy her husband with a peeing, pooping, shedding tornado?

Her dead husband.

Who'd left a will with restrictions.

The young woman at the desk had purple hair and multiple piercings in her lip, eye brow, and nose.

"I came to look at your dogs. I'm considering adopting," Lydia told her.

The girl scrutinized her up and down. Lydia fingered her pearl earrings—perhaps she was over-dressed.

"Have you filled out an application on our website?" the girl demanded.

"Uh, no—can I just do it on pen and paper here?"

The girl shook her head. "Our system is automated. You can use your phone to fill it out now. Here's our wi-fi password."

She slid a slip of paper at Lydia and nodded toward the battered vinyl chairs in the corner.

Sheesh! No wonder so many dogs here needed adopting if this was how they treated customers. Rule number one of customer service—the employee with the best social skills should sit at the reception desk.

Lydia plowed through the questions:

Can you afford to feed a dog and meet its veterinary expenses?

Yes.

I can afford to give him filet mignon daily and take him to the Mayo Clinic.

Where will your dog sleep?

Lydia pictured herself curled in one corner of the king-size bed she'd shared with Charles. When she woke this morning, she saw she'd barely disturbed the covers.

With me.

Do you have a fenced yard? Or an electric fence?

Was that a trick question? There were no fences in her development, yet plenty of people had dogs. Was an electric fence good or bad?

After she'd been plowing through the application for fifteen minutes, a middle-aged man with a graying pony-tail walked in with three exuberant dogs on leashes.

The sullen girl at the desk lit up like a Christmas tree. "There you are! How was your walk, Bingo? Wuz ooo a good boy? Wuz ooo?"

The dogs leapt on her, licking her face and practically knocking her off her desk chair.

She laughed and hugged each one in turn.

Clearly better with dogs than people.

Finally, Lydia pressed send on the application and returned to the desk.

"Okay—I submitted the application. Now, can I see the dogs?"

The girl at the desk looked at Lydia like she was a pedophile seeking admission to Chuck E. Cheese. "Your application will be forwarded to one of our screeners. We'll let you know if you've been approved in three to five days."

Tables turned: Lydia felt like the dowdy couple being turned away at Hennessey's. "Can't I even look at the dogs?"

The man who'd been walking dogs took pity on Lydia. "I'll take her back, Elise."

Elise frowned but allowed the older dog-walker to have his way.

"Thanks," Lydia said once they were out of earshot. "Is she always so strict?"

"Don't take it personally. She's passionately committed to the animals." The man smiled. "We don't let people back here unaccompanied. Sometimes they tease the dogs or stick their fingers into the cages, and it doesn't end well. But you seem like a good citizen. What kind of dog are you looking for?"

"I'm not sure. I'm open to all possibilities."

Lydia approached the cage of a cute little fluffy dog. Immediately, he began to hurl himself against the bars, barking frantically.

"Roscoe's a little neurotic." The man guided her further down the aisle. "I'm Jim, by the way."

"Hi, Jim. I'm Lydia." But she offered no additional information. "How long have you worked here?"

"I'm a volunteer. But I also do freelance dog training."

"This one's cute." Lydia crouched down to look into the pen of a medium-sized brown and white dog. "Alfie" his name tag proclaimed.

"Yeah—he just came in from down south."

"South Jersey?"

"South Carolina. Many people don't spay or neuter their dogs there, so there are a lot of strays. We pick them up and bring them here where there's a demand for young dogs," Jim explained.

He unlocked the cage. "I don't know Alfie that well yet. Let's take him out."

The dog hung back when Jim opened the door. He extended his hand for Alfie to sniff and spoke to him gently. "C'mere, fella. Come meet Lydia. Maybe you'd like to go home with her someday."

Alfie crept out cautiously. "He's a little shy. Still getting used to his surroundings. Do you have young kids?"

"No, no kids."

"Are you away at work all day?"

"No, I'm...I'm not working right now."

Jim scratched behind the dog's ears, and Alfie's tail began a slow wag. But when Lydia extended her hand to pet him, Alfie backed away.

"He doesn't like me."

"Nah, he's just checking you out. Here, offer him a treat." Jim slipped some small bone-shaped biscuits into her hand.

When Lydia offered Alfie the treat and spoke to him softly, he inched forward and grabbed the bone. Then he backed away to chew it.

"Your husband will have to come in and meet the dog, too," Jim said. "Every member of the family has to be in agreement."

Lydia's left hand froze holding another dog treat. Then she realized Jim had noticed her large diamond engagement ring and wide gold wedding band. "Actually, I'm a widow."

A widow. The first time she'd spoken those words. Her throat tightened, and she turned her head. She couldn't cry here.

"I'm sorry," Jim said. "I only asked because it's important to find the right dog for the right family. We try to avoid situations where people have to return a dog they adopted because it didn't work out."

"Really? People take a dog home without discussing it with the rest of the family?"

"Yep. One person really wants the dog, and she figures the others will come around. Or people have unrealistic expectations about dog ownership."

Lydia gazed at Alfie's sweet face. She'd seen those "I was rescued by my dog" bumper stickers. Did she have unrealistic expectations of salvation?

"It's hard to see their true personalities here in the shelter." Jim stood with his hands buried in the pockets of his sacky khakis. "Once they go home, the crazy ones settle down, and the shy ones come out of their shells."

Lydia looked up at him. "But then how can I be sure I'm choosing the right dog?'

"I know it sounds sentimental, but I always say, 'step back and let the dog choose you.'"

Alfie came forward and sat at Lydia's feet. Then he rolled over and waved his paws in the air.

"See that. He trusts you. He wants you to rub his belly."

Lydia scratched the dog's belly, and he went limp with bliss.

"Jim," a voice yelled. "I need you to take these adopters to see Benjy."

"Duty calls." Jim put Alfie back in his cage.

Lydia felt tears of disappointment prick her eyes. "What if someone else adopts him before the shelter approves my application?"

Jim patted her shoulder. "Then he wasn't the right dog for you. It's possible to get the wrong dog, but there's more than one right dog. Take your time. We're always getting new dogs in. Come back when you're approved, and I'll show you all the possibilities."

Chapter 7

L ydia lay in bed with the covers over her head.

In books, sounds the house made always frightened the lonely heroine. But Lydia didn't have that distraction.

Charles had maintained the house so well that no stairs squeaked, no furnace rumbled, no tripled-glazed window rattled even when assaulted by a gale-force wind.

Utter silence.

Lydia hung suspended in a sensory deprivation chamber.

While she nestled in her plush duvet, she imagined Alfie curled in the corner of his cold cage, huddled against the cacophony of yelping, whining, desperate dogs.

A tide of resentment rose within her against Elise, the rigid bureaucrat who kept her and Alfie apart.

At least last week she'd had decisions to make: lilies or gardenias at the memorial service, mahogany or rosewood for the casket, granite or marble for the tombstone.

People had come over with food, and the doorbell rang with deliveries of flowers and fruit baskets.

This week, nothing.

Her brother-in-law and sister-in-law had gone back to Chicago. Her sister had stopped calling every night. Kathleen had reverted to occasional texting. Lydia accepted that people had to get back to their lives.

What did she have to get back to?

The day stretched ahead of her, an endless expanse with no responsibility whatsoever.

Bitterly, she recalled weeks at work when all she'd wished for was a day with no decisions to make, no one clamoring—Red type or blue? Funny headline or informative? Google ads or Facebook?

Careful what you wish for.

Instinctively, she reached for her phone on the bedside table to check her email.

In her working days, her in-box filled overnight.

Now, nothing but an exhortation from Nordstrom to buy shoes.

But as she stared at the screen, a new message popped into her box. Subject line: lunch today? From Madalyn Schilling.

Noon or one, Madalyn wanted to know.

Lydia tried to restrain herself to wait until after breakfast to reply. She didn't want to look desperate.

But god forbid Madalyn got another offer.

Thank you. Noon at Casa Bella will be lovely.

———— ◆ ————

AT THE RESTAURANT, they went through the "ladies who lunch" ritual: hugging and complimenting each other's outfits. They studied the menu and ordered calorie-less, tasteless salads and glasses of white wine.

Finally, the waiter left them alone.

"So, how are you?" Madalyn asked.

"Fine." The answer to that question was always fine. No one wanted to hear "depressed," "lonely," "adrift."

Madalyn made a face. "I shouldn't have asked such a stupid question. Tell me the worst thing that's happened this week."

Lydia made a sound half-way between a laugh and a sob. Where to start? The terms of Charles's will? The rejection by a dog shelter? "The days are so empty," she finally whispered.

Mercifully, Madalyn didn't insist that free time was a blessing. "You'll have to work on developing a new routine."

"Don't tell me to do volunteer work. I'm not spending my days arguing with catty bitches about fundraiser decorations."

Madalyn smiled slyly. "Yes, Betsey von Maur and her crew are to be avoided at all costs. How about taking a class?"

"What kind of classes are offered during the day? Flower arranging at the senior center? I need a job."

Madalyn peered at Lydia over the rim of her wineglass. "Surely not, dear? You're...comfortable."

Comfortable was the word rich people used to make themselves seem like regular guys. Probably Melinda Gates insisted she was merely comfortable. "I suppose I've always been *comfortable*. But I wasn't ready to retire."

"So why did you?"

"Because Charles wanted to travel with me before he got too old. It would have been selfish to deny him that pleasure after all he's given me." Lydia bit her lip to stop the trembling. "But then he went and died the day I quit." She cradled her head in her hands. "Oh, God—I'm such a horrible person. How can I be angry with him? He's the one who's dead. I'm just unemployed."

Madalyn stroked her arm. "It's not uncommon to be angry with loved ones for dying. I was furious at my grandfather for allowing himself to be hit by a drunk driver and leaving me to cope with my crazy family."

Lydia lifted her head and wiped her eyes. The last thing she wanted to be doing was making a scene at Casa Bella. "Thank you for understanding, Madalyn. I'm okay now."

Madalyn waited until she'd taken a sip of water and straightened her blouse before resuming. "Can't you go back to Imago as a freelancer?"

"I don't want to sit at home and write ad copy all alone and submit it electronically. It's the watercooler I miss. I want to be in on the action—planning, meeting, deciding. And they don't need me for that anymore. I've been replaced. By a 28-year-old." Lydia took a gulp of wine to numb the vision of Bryce Salazar sitting at her desk eating soy nuts and drinking kombucha.

"So get a job at a different ad agency."

Lydia shook her head. "Even though I told the owner of Imago I was leaving to travel with my husband, he still made me sign a non-compete agreement to prevent me from joining a rival agency and luring Imago's clients there."

She squinted at Madalyn. "What do you do all day?" Lydia knew the question sounded rude, but she had to know. What did women who didn't have to work do with themselves?

"Our Ginny still needs a lot of my attention."

Of course—Lydia knew that. Tom and Madalyn's youngest daughter had autism, and although she lived in her own apartment nearby, she wasn't totally independent. "I'm sorry. I didn't mean to imply—"

Madalyn waved off her apology. "I do a lot of volunteering at the special school Ginny attended. Maybe you could tutor there. It's very rewarding."

"I don't think I'd have the patience. Neither Charles nor I wanted children. I don't have regrets about that. Little kids make me nervous." Lydia gazed through the window at the shops across the street. "Maybe they'd hire me at the bookstore. I could put my English degree to use and talk to people about novels all day. That would be nice."

Madalyn wrinkled her nose. "Retail is never nice. Customers are rude, and you have to work holidays. Besides, the woman who owns that store is a real dragon." She cocked her head to study Lydia. "Don't you have a master's degree in English?"

"Yes, that's what I was doing when I met Charles. I was stuck. I knew I didn't want to keep going for a PhD, but I didn't know what I could do with a half-finished master's. Charles encouraged me to finish the master's and then he recommended me for the job at Imago. And I've been there ever since. Until two weeks ago."

Madalyn's face lit up. "What about teaching college English?"

Lydia shook her head. "I'm too old to go back to get my PhD now."

"All you need is a Master's to teach at Palmer Community College. One of the teachers at Ginny's school used to be an adjunct there. She said they're always looking for adjuncts to teach freshman writing. You'd be perfect! The pay is dreadful, but that doesn't matter. And you wouldn't have to work nights and weekends like you would at a store." She pulled out her phone. "Let's see what it says on their website."

Lydia grabbed her friend's hand. "Wait! I don't know how to teach a class of college students. The only teaching I ever did was as a TA in grad school. I helped tutor the struggling undergrads."

"Isn't that exactly what teaching at a community college would be? They're not going to want you to lecture on James Joyce. You're a professional writer. You have a master's degree. I say, Palmer Community College would be lucky to get you."

"Thanks for your vote of confidence, Madalyn. But I've been away from academia for twenty years. I don't know if I—"

Madalyn raised her hand for silence. "You can't go back to advertising. Your options are retail and teaching. I'm simply encouraging you to explore the better option."

Lydia took a shaky breath. "You're right. I'll look into it when I get home."

"Good." Madalyn waved at the waiter. "Let's splurge on dessert."

Chapter 8

With no need to rush home, Lydia strolled around Palmyrton. She'd lived here for over twenty years, and the town's leafy parks and bustling streets were more familiar to her than the small Ohio town where she'd grown up.

On the corner of Elm and South Main she saw a sign stuck to a lamp post: *Estate Sale Friday and Saturday, 43 Lilac Court, Another Man's Treasure Estate Sales.* She'd noticed that company's sales fliers around town before. Lydia had never been to an estate sale because Charles was no fan of antiques. Although he'd never admit it, he considered an eighteenth century Duncan Phyfe armoire every bit as unsavory as a beat-up chest of drawers from Goodwill. Other people's fingers had pulled the handles; other people's clothes had filled the drawers. Colonial germs and modern germs were all the same to him.

Lydia kept strolling. In two more blocks, another estate sale sign popped up in the lawn of the library. This time it had an arrow pointing the general direction of Lilac Court. Lydia put the address into Google Maps and saw the house was a quarter mile stroll through the leafy streets abutting South Main.

She turned toward Lilac Court. Certainly, she didn't need to buy anything for her house, but it might be fun to poke around at the sale.

It was a reason to be out and about.

The first turn on the map took her along Phifer Avenue, the main drag of Palmyrton's historic district. Lydia gazed at a glorious cream and blue Victorian with a wrap-around porch that their real estate agent had shown them all those years ago. Would she be happier alone in that house now, or would it be just as forlorn as the house in Palmer Ridge?

As she walked the next few blocks, the houses got smaller and the architecture less dramatic. Still, the homes were elegant and tasteful. Finally, she turned a corner and found herself on a street she'd never been on before. Ahead was a little traffic island with a carved wooden sign: *Welcome to Historic Burleith, Palmyrton's Friendliest Neighborhood.*

She smiled at the bold claim. She didn't know who could verify that assertion, but she was pretty sure her own neighborhood wouldn't challenge Burleith for the title. Another estate sale sign with an arrow showed her she was close to her destination.

Now the houses were much closer together, with handkerchief front yards. Some of the houses were a little shabby, with saggy shutters and peeling paint, but most had square front porches with swings or rockers. At the corner of the first block, a fenced empty lot had been planted as a huge vegetable garden. Two ladies in floppy sunhats discussed some baseball bat-sized zucchini. They waved to Lydia. "Can we interest you in a squash?"

"Not today, thanks."

"Well, we'll have lots of vegetables to distribute at the block party. Come get some then." She pointed to a vinyl banner hung on the garden fence:

Annual Burleith Block Party
Games • Food Trucks •Beer •Bouncy House

"Thanks. I will."

A block party! How quaint—she hadn't been to one since she was a kid in Ohio.

Lydia kept walking, wondering if she had somehow overshot Lilac Court. She let out a little squeal when she stumbled on the uneven sidewalk where the roots of a giant oak had pushed up the pavement.

"Are you okay?" A man digging weeds in his front yard called out to her. "I've been calling the town to come out and fix that."

"No worries." Lydia leaned over his picket fence. "What are those pretty blue flowers?"

Some unruly cerulean stalks bobbed over his head. "These are delphinium." He touched their petals gently with his dirty gardening glove. "And those big pink and white ones trying to jump over the fence are hollyhocks. I'm making room to plant some phlox over here. You a gardener?"

"No. But I like the relaxed, English cottage garden look you've got going here."

"Thank you for recognizing my vision," he laughed. "My wife calls it the weed pit."

Lydia tugged on her collar. The silk blouse she'd chosen for lunch with Madalyn wasn't the best garb for a long walk. "I'm looking for the estate sale on Lilac Court. Is it close to here?"

"Cut through my alley and you'll be right there," the man directed.

So far, Burleith was proving to be as friendly as the sign promised. Her encounter with the flower man and the vegetable ladies was more conversation than she'd had with her own neighbors in years. Lydia did as he directed, staring with curiosity at the back of his house, where a jumble of kids' trikes and dump trucks leaned up against a pink plastic play house. A big orange tabby stalked through the shaggy grass and finally stretched out on a brick patio with a round umbrella table and a rather rusty gas grill.

In Palmer Ridge, her next door neighbors' yards looked exactly like her own: trimmed, tame, unoccupied. She liked this bohemian jumble.

At the end of the alley, she found herself at the back of what had to be the estate sale house. A crowd of people milled around the detached garage where a tall young African American man took money and answered questions. "Lots more inside," he said. "Furniture, collectibles, china."

Lydia slipped through the back gate. The young man looked her up and down, from her low pumps to her Ralph Lauren sunglasses, and issued advice. "Nuthin' but tools out here. Go on in the back door."

Lydia tread carefully along a stone path, crossed a brick patio over-run with weeds, and hauled herself up the rotting back steps with the help of a rickety railing. Maybe Charles was right about bedbugs and roaches in old houses. But she'd come this far; no point in turning back now. Cautiously, she pushed open the back door.

And stepped into a wonderland.

The kitchen, an astonishing shade of persimmon, held a collection of blown-glass orbs suspended before the large window on translucent fishing lines so they seemed to float in the air like little planets in a secret solar system.

A little boy stood under them, gazing up in wonder. "Are they candy?" he asked.

"They do look good enough to eat, don't they?" The woman sitting behind the sales desk smiled at him although Lydia noticed her keeping one eye on the kid's reaching little hands.

Open shelves on one wall held all sorts of pottery: the bowls and pitchers and plates in fanciful colors and designs emitted a forcefield drawing Lydia toward them. She examined a plate with droll little fish swimming around its rim. When she flipped it over, it was signed "Cat" with a pair of whiskers and a nose. A pretty sea green pitcher had the same signature. "Are these pieces all made by the same potter?"

"Yes, the owner's daughter. She claims she gave her mother her seconds, but I think they're all great. They've been selling well."

Lydia felt an overwhelming urge to possess one of these pieces that radiated such good cheer. Her gaze fell on a smaller bowl with a winking frog painted on the inside. How perfect to eat her cereal every morning until that smiling face appeared!

As she reached for it, Charles's voice whispered in her ear. "The glaze might be poisonous. Who knows how many people have handled that."

How he'd habituated her to caution!

"I'll take this one," she placed the bowl emphatically before the woman at the table. "Do I pay now?"

"You just got here." The woman smiled. "Don't you want to look at all the rooms?"

"Yes....I...I didn't know how things worked. I've never been to an estate sale before."

"A first-timer! Here, I'll keep the bowl for you behind the desk until you're ready to check out."

Lydia wandered further into the house. The dining room held a big oak table, dinged in places and marked with what appeared to be traces of paint or crayon. Probably generations of kids had done homework or art projects here. The bay window held a jungle of potted plants, and even these were for sale. Another customer made eye contact. "Five dollars for such a healthy African violet in a nice pot is a pretty good deal, right?"

Maybe the woman had a husband who suspected potted plants as sources of parasites. "Absolutely," Lydia encouraged. "Buy it before someone else snatches it up."

Lydia didn't need the old-fashioned cut-crystal wine glasses or the flower- speckled dinner plates. But she wished she could wrap up and buy the cozy vibe of the room. She could practically hear the echoes of big family dinners and the laughter of birthday parties and baby showers.

She crossed into the small entrance hall, dominated by a doleful stuffed moose-head wearing a jaunty deerstalker cap. The floral wall-paper would have overwhelmed most art collections, but the bold oil paintings lining the walls held their own. Lydia felt cheered by the house's utter disregard for neutrals.

Then she stepped into the living room and the world stopped. Floor-to-ceiling bookshelves filled one wall, interrupted only by a fireplace lined with beautiful Craftsman tiles. Two slouchy, over-stuffed loveseats faced each other before the fire. The cushions looked like the same heads and the same butts had burrowed into them for decades.

Customers browsed in front of the shelves as if they were in a bookstore. A group of twenty-somethings with tattoos and ripped jeans showed one another copies of *Lord of the Rings* and *Infinite Jest*. Lydia elbowed her way in beside a giraffe-like man with an armful of nonfiction. She was after different prey.

A collection of orange-spined Penguin Classic paperbacks filled two shelves. The books unlocked a memory she'd almost forgotten—her first argument with Charles.

Then

When they moved into the house in Palmer Ridge, Lydia started putting her books onto the shelves in their library.

She loved saying that. "Our library."

Charles came home from work one day and found her bent and frayed Penguin Classics taking up residence on his pristine new shelves.

"Lydia." He frowned down at her where she sat next to a half-unpacked box. "These ratty paperbacks can't stay in here."

"Don't act like these are cheesy romance novels and airport thrillers." She held up her well-thumbed copy of Bleak House. *"This is a masterpiece of British literature."*

Charles offered a reassuring smile. "So let's replace these with nice leather-bound editions. Make a list of all the titles you want, and I'll order them."

But for the first time in their short, impetuous relationship, Lydia resisted. "I don't want perfect, unread copies of Pride and

Prejudice *and* Tess of the D'Urbervilles*. I want the books I've actually read." She held up a high-lighted, margin-scribbled copy of* Jane Eyre*. "These books are my friends. You can't replace them with shiny, Stepford Wives imposters."*

Charles scowled. "Don't be melodramatic, Lydia. Just a few months ago, you cared so little for English Literature you were ready to drop out of your master's program."

That remark infuriated her. She'd never lost her love for literature, only for the nit-picking pedantics required by academia.

Lydia jumped to her feet and set Middlemarch *on the shelf. Charles swept it off.*

She called him pretentious.

He called her truculent.

Lydia stormed out of the library, giving the door a slam that knocked one of Charles's horse-racing prints off the wall in a spray of shattered glass.

She slept in a guest room that night, choosing the one furthest from the master bedroom so Charles wouldn't hear her strangled sobs.

In the morning, he slipped into the guest bed while she slept, waking her with gentle kisses.

It had been their first fight. Neither one of them uttered the words, "I'm sorry."

In the end, all her books had migrated upstairs to a wall of custom bookcases Charles had installed in one of their four spare bedrooms. It was to be her retreat. A room of one's own, as Virginia Woolf would say. After she started at Imago, Lydia would use the room as a home office. But one day, years later, she had a yen to re-read Middlemarch. *And when she went to look for it, her old friend wasn't there.*

Now, Lydia squinted at the titles on the shelf in the house on Lilac Court, fortunately arranged alphabetically by author: Austen, Bronte, Dickens, Eliot. Her hand shot out and plucked *Middlemarch* from the shelf before anyone else could get it.

Chapter 9

"So that's it—the bowl and the book?" the pretty woman with the tousled hair asked as she accepted Lydia's ten dollar bill.

Lydia offered a rueful smile. "I'm afraid I don't need much."

The woman raised her hands in defense. "I wasn't complaining. I'll sell it all by tomorrow. You just seemed very intrigued by everything here."

Was she that transparent? "Yes, it's a charming little house, isn't it? Did the owner, er....?"

"Die? No, she's a great old gal. She's moving out to Seattle to be near her grandkids. They're all clamoring for her. Nice to see people who actually like their elderly relatives." She wrapped the bowl in an extra plastic bag. "That's not the way it usually goes in my business."

"So, you're the owner of Another Man's Treasure?"

"Yep, Audrey Nealon." She shook Lydia's hand after Lydia introduced herself, then fished a slightly dented business card from the back pocket of her jeans.

Lydia studied it. *Estate Sales, Moving Sales, Downsizing*

Maybe she could hire Audrey to sell all the stuff in Palmer Ridge. The thought popped into her mind like a pornographic fantasy, too shocking to acknowledge. Charles would be horrified by hordes of people tramping through their home, examining the objects that had populated their life together.

Lydia tucked the card into her purse. "And this house—is it already sold?"

"No, I think the real estate agent feels it has a little too much personality. She wants the owner's children to paint everything white and stage it with contemporary furniture."

"No!" the word flew from Lydia's mouth as if she were protesting the drowning of innocent kittens. Filling this cozy cottage with hard-edged chrome and leather from Ikea would be a sacrilege.

"Yeah, I like the funkiness, too," Audrey agreed. "But my friend Isabelle Trent says the key to selling a house is helping people imagine themselves living in it. And that moose in the hallway might mess up the vision."

Lydia wasn't wild about the moose, but she could certainly imagine herself curled up in front of that fireplace with a good book.

"You know Isabelle Trent? So do I," Lydia said. "Is she selling this house?"

"This is kinda small potatoes for Isabelle. But her associate told me the house should sell quickly. There's not a lot available at the lower end of the market."

The group of twenty-somethings that Lydia had last seen upstairs in the master bedroom appeared behind her with arms full of felt fedoras and rhinestone brooches to reinforce their hipster reputations. The leggy woman in the group elbowed her male companion. "Hear that? Wouldn't this be an awesome house for Jared? He's been looking for, like, months." She called over Lydia's head to Audrey. "Excuse me? Do you know how much this house will be listed for?"

Audrey gave an exaggerated "beats me" shrug. The girl turned back to her companion. "Text Jared and tell him to meet us here. He should see this."

The friend's fingers flew over his phone's screen. "Yeah, he should make an offer."

Lydia felt a surge of protectiveness. She imagined Jared as a Bryce Salazar clone, buying the house so he could white-wash it.

Lydia stepped aside so the crew with the hats and jewelry could pay, and Audrey returned to work. "Nice meeting you, Lydia. Keep me in mind if you or your parents are planning a move."

Lydia looked back at the house once she was on the side-walk. A bird's nest protruded from the rain gutter over the porch. Moss grew on the shingles. But the potter in the family had made a custom address sign hand-painted with sprays of purple flowers: 43 Lilac Court. While Lydia stared at the house, a red Prius pulled up to the curb and a young man loped up the front walk.

Jared?

Lydia felt as she did at the semi-annual Nordstrom shoe sale. Nothing made a pair of sandals more desirable than someone else reaching for them.

⚬

THE WALK BACK TO HER car seemed longer than the walk to Lilac Court. Lydia's right shoe rubbed her heel and a trickle of sweat slipped between her breasts. Despite the discomfort, the heavy stone that filled her gut since Charles's death had lightened. With every step she took, Lydia thought about the house on Lilac Court.

In one ear, an upbeat voice chattered that it made sense to live in a smaller house in a friendlier neighborhood.

In the other ear, the voice of reason, which sounded an awful lot like Charles, objected that the house was falling apart. At minimum, it needed a new back porch, a new kitchen, and two new bathrooms.

The upbeat voice said that overseeing some repair projects would keep her occupied. And she could afford to hire the best contractors.

The voice of reason warned that she knew nothing about construction and could easily be taken for a ride.

The upbeat voice reminded her, indignantly, that she wasn't stupid.

Why was she so drawn to this house? She could downsize without taking on the risk and aggravation of remodeling. Palmyrton had plenty of moderate-sized houses in move-in condition.

A car gave her a short warning beep. She'd stepped off the curb without looking, that's how lost in thought she was. Lydia waved her apology and kept walking.

But a house in move-in condition was one that reflected someone else's judgement. Probably bland judgement—tasteful neutrals, inoffensive styles.

Lydia wanted to impose her own will on a house. Start from scratch on a house with good bones. She'd never done that before.

She stopped in the middle of the sidewalk. That was it. She wanted a starter house. She'd gone directly from her shared grad school apartment to a "finisher" house—the kind of house young people aspire to, not the kind they get the month after their wedding.

If she bought a starter house, would it come with a starter life?

Her safety net was gone.

It was time to walk the high wire.

Chapter 10

When Lydia got home, she kicked off her shoes, poured herself a glass of wine, and made a phone call.

"Hello, Isabelle? It's Lydia Eastlee. I want to sell my house." There. The words were out—no turning back now. Once Isabelle got her teeth into a listing, she was no more likely to let go than an alligator with his jaws clamped on an unwary Florida golfer.

A sharp intake of breath came over the line.

"Darling, I'll be right over."

Twenty minutes later, Isabelle clicked across the marble floor of Lydia's foyer. "Impeccably maintained. Neutral décor. But I have to warn you dear—these big, traditional houses are getting tough to move. Today's bond traders and Google executives are after an open floorplan. Less formality, you know."

"You think it will be hard to sell?" This possibility had never occurred to her.

Isabelle placed her perfectly manicured hand on her chest. "Not for me. With the right pricing strategy, every home finds a buyer." She tapped a pen on her leather portfolio. "It just might take a while. I don't want you to have unreasonable expectations."

In dogs...in houses... Just once, Lydia wished someone would tell her to expect the moon and the stars.

Lydia processed Isabelle's remarks as meaning the house wouldn't sell for as much as Charles would have expected. She knew better than to say she didn't care what it brought. "I'm confident you'll do your best, Isabelle."

"Let's fill out the paperwork for the listing, and you can tell me what you're looking for in your next home." Isabelle spread out the contracts on the dining room table. "Townhouse or condo?"

"Neither. Today, I saw the house I want to buy. 43 Lilac Court. I went to the estate sale there."

A shadow passed over Isabelle's face—shock, alarm?—but she banished it quickly. "Ah, yes—isn't that a precious house? Good location, flat lot. Needs a little TLC, as I recall."

"The estate sale organizer told me that an associate of yours is handling the listing. What do I have to do to make an offer?"

"Let's not be hasty, Lydia." Isabelle flipped open her computer to the latest multiple listings. "There are many lovely homes I can show you."

A prickle of irritation made Lydia clench her jaw. Isabelle sounded like Jim at the animal shelter. What was it with people trying to talk her out of what she wanted?

"I know what I want. I'm ready to make an offer on 43 Lilac Court." Lydia paused for dramatic effect. "All cash."

Isabelle's eyes darted to her computer screen displaying a luxury townhome and back to Lydia.

"Of course, if you'd prefer me to work with another Realtor...."

"Darling, no one is better equipped to take care of your needs than I am. But hear me out. Anyone can make a fast deal. I've built my business by making certain I've found the very best house for each buyer. Sometimes buyers have a strong emotional reaction to a house—either good or bad—and they don't know where it's coming from. For example, last month I found a house that was perfect for young couple with a baby on the way. There was no time to lose—she's seven months along. It had everything they wanted, yet the man refused to consider it. The wife was beside herself with frustration. I asked a few questions, and it turned out the house had a lingering smell of cigarette smoke, and the man's mother was a smoker who'd died of lung cancer. He was still angry that she hadn't been able to quit. I had the wall-to-wall carpeting ripped out and the drapes taken down. The smell went away, and they bought the house. They're happy as clams there. Thank me every time they see me."

"And your point is...?"

"I'm trying to understand why you've formed such a strong attachment to this house when you haven't even begun to look around at what's on the market." Isabelle cocked her head. "Why is it calling to you?"

Lydia didn't answer.

"Does it remind you of the home you grew up in?"

"Ha! I grew up in a split level outside of Cincinnati. Nothing like Lilac Court." Lydia had had a happy childhood, but her parents, a school secretary and an insurance salesman, hadn't had a funky bone in their bodies. But now that Isabelle had put the idea in her head, Lydia realized there was something about the house on Lilac Court that took her back to another place, another time.

And then it dawned on her. Gwen's house in Montclair.

Gwen had been her freshman year roommate, and they'd formed a fast friendship. After graduation, Gwen had gotten a job and moved to Montclair, twenty minutes away, while Lydia had stayed on campus for grad school. But they had stayed friends. Gwen threw impromptu parties at her house, which was furnished with thrift-store finds and decorated with Museum of Modern Art posters and silk-screened prints. People showed up with cheap jug wine and six packs of Coors Light. They grazed on bowls of chips and the occasional pan of pot brownies. They danced to the Red Hot Chili Peppers and had passionate discussions about politics.

Until....

Until Lydia had married.

Gwen and her boyfriend had come to the small wedding. A few weeks later, Gwen invited them to a party at the house in Montclair.

Then

Lydia took her time getting dressed, knowing the party wouldn't kick into high gear until ten o'clock at the earliest. After pulling on her tightest jeans and trying and rejecting various combinations of low-cut tops and sparkly necklaces, she came downstairs to find Charles pacing in the foyer.

He was wearing pressed khakis and Cole Hahn loafers, but Lydia wasn't about to suggest that he change after he'd been waiting for her for half an hour.

By the time they arrived at Gwen's street in Montclair, the party was in full swing, and Charles had to park three blocks away. The sound of a booming U2 song put a spring in Lydia's step. She grabbed her husband's hand and pulled him through the crowd in the living-room back to the even more packed kitchen.

"Lydia!" Gwen squealed, as she hugged her friend. "I'm so glad you guys made it. Have a beer." She thrust bottles of Bud from a cooler into their hands.

"May I have a glass, please?" Charles asked.

Gwen blinked for a second. "Oh...uhm...sure." She nudged aside some other guests, so she could partly open a cabinet door and handed Charles a tumbler.

Lydia and Gwen shouted news to each other over the music. When Lydia turned around, Charles was gone. She found him pressed against the wall in the living room.

"Let's dance!" Lydia grabbed his hand and pulled him toward the surging crowd.

Charles shook his head. "Not my kind of dancing. But you go ahead."

Lydia could tell from the resolute expression in his eyes that trying to cajole him onto the dancefloor would be fruitless. She danced to one song with her friends, and returned to find Charles giving legal advice to a guy who'd recently been arrested on a DUI.

"Wow, thanks, man—that's good to know." He took a hit from a joint that was being passed around and offered it to Charles.

Charles took a step backwards. "No thanks." He turned to Lydia and raised his eyebrows. "Perhaps we should be heading out."

"But we just got here," Lydia objected.

Charles inclined his head toward the small sunroom, which was quieter. When they could hear each other, Charles took both her hands in his. "Look, I'm sorry sweetheart. It's not like I've never smoked weed at a party in my twenties. But now I'm a partner in a law firm. I can't afford to be here if the neighbors complain, and the cops show up."

Lydia nodded.

They left without saying good-bye to their dancing hosts.

They were home asleep by eleven.

After that, Gwen and Lydia had drifted apart. There had never been an argument, or even a discussion about the party. Just a mutual acknowledgement that further socializing as couples wouldn't work out. They'd met a few times for drinks, just the two of them, but then Gwen got a new job and she and her boyfriend moved to California. When Gwen eventually married her boyfriend, she sent Lydia an invitation, but the ceremony had been too far away and at a bad time of the year to be away from work.

Lydia could barely remember Gwen now—did she have blue eyes or brown?—but she remembered that house. Not the precise location, but the general atmosphere. Gwen had been so proud of it, so eager to show everyone her little improvements. She and her boyfriend hadn't owned the house in Montclair, but it had been their first home together, the first place they could welcome their friends.

It had a bathroom door that didn't close tight.

It had a fireplace that smoked.

It had heart.

Isabelle studied Lydia waiting for an answer. Could Lydia tell her all that? "The house on Lilac Court does remind me of a house that brings back happy memories. A funny little starter house my friend had." Lydia jumped up and paced around the dining room. "I don't want a sterile, safe townhouse, Isabelle. I want a house with a little history. I want a house I can...can add my own history to."

Lydia stared at the Realtor, so perfectly coiffed, so efficient. She'd never make Isabelle Trent understand the attraction of Lilac Court.

But Isabelle surprised her. "Ah, I see. You *have* given this some thought. That's all I wanted to know." She pulled out another form. "We'll bid low. The place needs a lot of work."

———◉———

AFTER ISABELLE LEFT, Lydia experienced a surge of optimism that she hadn't felt since before she'd handed in her resignation at Imago. The house decision made her feel like she had regained control of a spiraling airplane. She was out of the nosedive; now she had to regain altitude.

Lydia flipped open her laptop and went to the Palmer Community College website. Under the "employment" tab she found a listing for instructors needed in the English department to teach a basic skills course. Grammar and essay structure.

Madalyn was right—she could do that.

The website said to submit a resume and cover letter online, so Lydia spent two hours revising her resume to emphasize her experience as a graduate teaching assistant and crafting a compelling cover letter.

She knew how to write sales copy. This time, the product was herself.

She took a deep breath and pressed SEND.

Chapter 11

Lydia drifted into consciousness as the sun brightened her bedroom. She extended her right arm, reaching for Charles.

The sheets beside her were smooth and cold.

The now familiar dread returned.

Another day of emptiness.

She reached for her phone and checked her email, more from habit than expectation that anything important had arrived.

But amid the spam, one subject line stood out: "Your adoption application has been approved."

She leaped out of bed.

Suddenly, she had a schedule.

She could go straight to Paws for People when they opened at nine and pick up Alfie. And what time did the pet supplies store open? Should she go there before or after the shelter?

She trotted down to the kitchen and made breakfast, truly hungry for the first time since Charles had died. As she waited for her toast to pop, she heard an email ping into her inbox.

Louise Cummings, Re: your application.

Lydia's stomach clenched. It was only eight-thirty. Palmer Community College wasn't wasting any time flushing her.

But when she opened the email, she got a surprise.

Dear Ms. Eastlee,

I have reviewed your application with interest. Although you lack extensive teaching experience, you do have other skills that make you a suitable candidate. I would be interested in meeting with you today. Can you come in at 1:00?

Dr. Louise Cummings

Chair, English Department

Wow! Imagine that! She fired off an acceptance to Louise Cummings as she gulped down her breakfast.

This felt like her old life. Busy. Full of commitments. Requiring a plan.

———◉———

WHEN LYDIA ARRIVED at Paws for People, a different woman sat behind the reception desk, but Jim stood before her. "I heard you were coming in today. I'm here to help you find the perfect dog. A new shipment of dogs arrived since you were here last."

Lydia's heart sank. "Why? Has Alfie been adopted already?"

"N-n-o-o. But I think it's important you consider all the options."

Options? She already knew she wanted Alfie. But to humor Jim, she agreed to look at some other dogs. First came Bentley, who exited his cage like a heat-seeking missile, knocking Lydia against the wall as he slobbered on her face.

"I think he's a little too exuberant." Lydia ducked out from under his paws. She appreciated Alfie's more aloof nature. Bentley was like a loud drunk dancing with a lamp-shade on his head.

Jim didn't argue, and guided her toward Pansy. She was cute—fluffy white with patches of black around her eyes that made her look soulful and world-weary.

A door slammed behind them, and Pansy leaped straight off the ground, all four paws scrabbling in mid-air. Then she put her tail between her legs and trembled, a stream of urine puddling around her paws.

"Too high-strung," Lydia said. Alfie wouldn't fall apart every time the doorbell rang.

Jim took her elbow. "Let's look at Squiggles."

"Squiggles?" Lydia made a face.

"You can change his name. He's very mellow."

Mellow was code for obese. Squiggles sat like a canine buddha, his belly dwarfing his legs. "He's too fat to get up," Lydia complained.

"You'd have to put him on a diet," Jim admitted. "His energy will improve when he loses some weight."

All these dogs needed work. Alfie was perfect as is.

By this time, they'd circled the entire kennel and were back near Alfie's cage. The dog jumped to attention when he spotted Lydia, running to the door and placing one paw plaintively on the bars.

"Let him out again, Jim. Please."

Jim unlocked the cage and Alfie performed a yoga stretch in front of Lydia.

"I know you have your heart set on him, but you need to know this." Jim crouched so he could look Lydia in the eye as she petted the dog. "Alfie was adopted before, but the family returned him. He nipped one of their kids."

Alfie turned his head like he was disappointed in Jim for gossiping.

"Well, the child probably pulled his tail. It wasn't your fault, was it?" Lydia stroked his back.

Alfie's eyebrows arched; he laid his head between his front paws and sighed.

"I'm not saying he's vicious. Just that he might work out better for an experienced dog owner. Alfie needs a firm hand."

What was she? A chump? She'd managed belligerent advertisers; she could handle a thirty-five pound dog. Lydia stood up to assert her authority. "I appreciate your guidance, Jim, I really do. But Alfie is the dog for me."

Alfie rose too and rubbed against Lydia's leg, trying to get his head under her hand. "See, he's chosen me."

Jim nodded. "Okay, Alfie has spoken. Let's fill out the paperwork."

Chapter 12

Alfie exited the shelter proudly sporting his complimentary Paws For People collar and leash. When they got to her BMW, it dawned on Lydia she should have brought an old towel to place on the cream leather upholstery. Or better yet, to have brought their third car, a Subaru Charles used on snowy days when driving his Jaguar was inadvisable. She'd been so excited to come and get Alfie that she'd charged out of the house without thinking. She looked back at the brick building. The shelter probably had a towel, but she didn't want to look like a priss. Real pet owners let their dogs ride shotgun with their ears blowing in the breeze. Besides, she didn't want Alfie to think he was going back inside.

She opened the passenger door, but Alfie didn't hop in.

"C'mon, Alfie." She patted the seat. "You're going to your new home."

Alfie backed away from the car.

Lydia tugged his leash. Alfie dug in with his hind paws.

An arriving shelter worker saw the struggle and came over to help. "He's just not used to riding in a car yet. Better put him in the back seat." She slipped her hands under Alfie and popped him in the car.

Lydia slid into the driver's seat and waved her thanks. "Okay, buddy. Say good-bye to that place. Today is the first day of the rest of your life."

Alfie declined to look out the window. He stretched out on the back seat and Lydia could hear him panting. She cranked up the air. Maybe the car was too hot for him.

A guy shot out of the supermarket parking lot, and Lydia swerved to avoid him. Behind her she heard an odd noise. Glancing in the rearview mirror, she saw Alfie standing with his mouth open, making a motion like a gobbling turkey. Then he lowered his head, and the smell of fermented dog food filled the car.

They were only a block from the pet supply store. Lydia drove there to assess the damage.

"Don't leave your friend in a hot car," a sign in the parking lot admonished. "Well-behaved pets are welcome in our store."

Lydia opened the rear car door and grabbed Alfie's leash. The mound of brown vomit had landed mostly on the floor mat. "Do you feel better now?"

Alfie wagged his tail and jumped out of the car, full of good cheer now that his ordeal was over.

"Let's go pick out some toys and a nice bed, okay?"

Alfie lunged at another car pulling into the lot, but Lydia managed to get him directed into the store. Inside, everyone who met him made a fuss over him.

"What a cutie!"

"Paws 4 People—way to go!"

"Look at those eyes!"

Alfie accepted the praise graciously, allowing himself to be petted. Lydia kept tight control of the leash, but Alfie showed no signs of nipping. With each admiring glance Alfie received, Lydia felt more and more sure she'd hit the canine jackpot with Alfie.

In the toy aisle, she selected an adorable stuffed racoon that made Alfie's eyes light up.

"My dog would have that torn apart in five minutes," a fellow customer advised. "I like these toys made from fire hose material. They're indestructible."

Lydia thought the fire hose toy was ugly, but tossed both into her cart. In the food aisle, she Googled all the brands, making sure she got the most nutritious. In the treat aisle, she got advice from a salesman, who then led her to the leash aisle when he noticed Alfie pulling. The clerk recommended an entire harness system designed to encourage safe walking.

"Do you have a crate?" he asked.

Lydia looked at the large cages on display. Alfie had just spent weeks of his life in a cage. She couldn't bear to put him back in captivity.

"I don't need one."

Feeding dishes...a bed...a doggy toothbrush—after forty minutes of shopping, Lydia pushed her loaded cart to the checkout.

A woman ahead of her had a little Pomeranian on a slack leash. The dog ambled over to Alfie and they sniffed each other, tails wagging.

"There's a little friend for you, Alfie." Lydia and the other woman beamed at their pets.

The Pomeranian made a funny, throaty sound.

In a flash, Alfie bared his teeth and flipped the smaller dog on its back.

The Pomeranian's owner screamed.

Lydia tugged Alfie away, but he strained at his leash, barking ferociously.

The clerk who had helped Lydia with the harness came to her rescue, getting Alfie and Lydia into another checkout lane far from the Pomeranian.

"Alfie, what got into you? That little fluff ball wasn't hurting anyone." Alfie sniffed a bag of rawhide chews, utterly unmoved by her reproach.

"It happens," the clerk said as he checked out Lydia's purchases. "We have scuffles in here all the time." He took her credit card and ran it through the machine for her since Lydia was still flustered by her experience. "Sometimes even mellow dogs meet a dog that just ticks them off. Like people, right?"

"I guess." Lydia looked down at Alfie. Bryce Salazar ticked her off for no good reason, but she'd never flipped him on his back and threatened to bite him.

⊱━━●━━⊰

ONCE SHE GOT ALFIE home, Lydia began to relax. She cleaned the mess in the car as best she could, figuring tomorrow she'd drop off the BMW to the detailer Charles used. Then she took Alfie for a walk around the block, excited by her new status as a pet owner.

Alfie kept his nose to the ground, sniffing everything in his new environment. He lifted his leg to pee against both a fire hydrant and a street sign. "That's right, baby—let those other neighborhood dogs know that you've arrived."

A UPS truck rumbled past. Without warning, Alfie lunged at it, nearly ripping the leash from Lydia's grasp. She hauled him back from the street, grateful she now had the harness. "No, no, no."

Alfie glanced back at her and resumed sniffing.

When they'd proceeded almost all the way around the block, Alfie marched into her neighbor's lawn and assumed a squat. Lydia's eyes widened. She'd forgotten to bring a bag to clean up after him. She glanced around for something to use, but of course Palmer Ridge wasn't the kind of neighborhood where plastic bags blew down the street. In the opposite driveway, she spotted a newspaper in the bright blue bag the New York Times used for home delivery. That neighbor must not be home if he hadn't taken in his paper by now. She left the poop in the yard and crossed the street with Alfie. Lydia slipped the newspaper out of the bag and prepared to go back for the clean-up.

"Hey! Leave my newspaper alone!"

A man in sweatpants came charging down the driveway. In all the years she'd lived in Palmer Ridge, she'd never met this guy.

"Hi, I'm Lydia Eastlee—your neighbor." She pointed to her house. "I was just borrowing your plastic bag for my dog."

He snatched up his newspaper. "You clearly can't *borrow* a bag for that purpose," he scowled. "You stole it. And left my paper unprotected."

Lydia looked up. "There's not a cloud in the sky. I wouldn't have taken it if it were raining."

"You're trespassing," he snarled. "Don't ever touch my paper again, or I'll call the police."

Armed with the bag, Lydia tugged Alfie back across the street. "People in this neighborhood are lunatics," she muttered. But now, in the wide smooth expanse of the other neighbor's lawn, she couldn't find Alfie's poop. "Damn, where is it?" She walked back and forth scanning the grass.

"Ex-kyooo-ze me," a voice trilled.

Lydia glanced up from her search. The owner of this house stood in her front doorway. "Can you please keep your dog off my lawn?"

Lydia waved and tugged Alfie back to her house.

"I hate this freakin' neighborhood," she told him.

Alfie walked home with his tail held high.

Back in the house, the dog followed her from room to room, never letting her out of his sight. They had a snack—yogurt for her, turkey jerky for him—and then Lydia broke the bad news.

"I have to leave you for two hours, Alfie. I have a job interview. But I'll be back as soon as I can, okay?"

Alfie lay down at the foot of her bed and watched her get dressed. Lydia rejected several outfits as too formal—she remembered her own college professors as terrible dressers—but finally settled on a rather nondescript taupe pantsuit livened up with a print scarf.

"Do I look suitably intellectual?" she asked the dog.

Alfie rubbed his paws over his snout and yawned.

Lydia grabbed her purse and went downstairs, Alfie right at her heels. But when she got to the laundry room door, which led into the garage, she back-tracked again. "This is the wrong purse for this outfit," she told the dog. She took her keys, wallet, and hairbrush out of the green designer purse Charles had given her and switched them to her work tote bag, which had been hanging on a hook near the back-door since her last day at Imago. Slinging the purse on the hook, she turned to the dog, "I'm leaving you in here, Alfie. Here are your new toys and some treats, and your bed. Jim says you can't have the run of the house until we're sure you're really housebroken." She held up two fingers. "I'll be back in two hours."

Chapter 13

The closer she drove to Palmer Community College, the more nervous Lydia got. She couldn't explain the tightening knot in her stomach. After all, she didn't need this job to feed her eight children or keep her electricity on.

She needed it to retain her sanity.

So, okay—tension accepted.

Lydia hadn't been on a job interview in eighteen years, and now she was presenting herself for a position she felt largely unqualified to fill. Of course, she'd been unqualified for the copywriter position at Imago, too, but Charles had opened that door for her. Here, she was on her own. Her interviewer didn't owe any favors.

Last night, Lydia had quite glibly sold herself as a feature-packed product. She sounded great on paper. What would she do if Louise challenged her? There was no denying her lack of teaching experience. How could she overcome that objection?

She tried to calm herself by playing the "what's the worst that could happen?" game. The worst that could happen was that Louise would say, "I'm sorry—you're not what we're looking for."

Lydia herself had spoken those words to job candidates. She'd seen the lip tremble, the Adam's apple jigger. Rejection sucked, no way around it.

Lydia vowed she wouldn't react with any visible emotion. She'd hold her head high all the way to her car before she let herself collapse.

She parked in the visitor's lot and followed the cracked sidewalk to the building that housed the English Department. Unlike her alma mater, PCC had no lush lawns or stately stone buildings with white columns. The low-slung brick halls were utilitarian, the grass a little beaten down. Parking lots occupied more space than research labs.

Her modest surroundings gave Lydia the boost of confidence she needed. She might be an academic imposter, but she wasn't applying for a tenure track position at Princeton.

Once she reached the English Department, she felt even more comfortable. It wasn't so different from her grad school days at Drew—a warren of book and paper-strewn offices filled with earnest professors and scruffy students.

When the secretary announced Lydia to Louise Cummings, the department chair glared at her over a pair of reading glasses as if Lydia were a street hustler offering to play three card monte. "You say you have an appointment?"

"You emailed me this morning," Lydia reminded her. "You asked me to come in for an interview for the job opening."

Instantly, Louise's face transformed. She swept some papers off a chair and urged Lydia to sit down. "Forgive me—I thought you were a textbook salesperson. Scourge of the earth!"

Louise had printed out Lydia's resume and now pulled it out of a haphazard pile on her desk. Her dark eyes scanned the words Lydia had spent hours crafting and proofreading.

Louise set the resume down and scrutinized Lydia.

"Why do you want this job?"

"I need a change. I'd like to get back into academia. This seems like a good opportunity to redirect my career."

Louise arched her eyebrows. "You understand you'll be teaching the least adept students at the school. You're not here to turn them onto Faulkner. You're here to teach them how to write a sentence that expresses a complete thought."

"I understand."

Louise took a deep breath.

Lydia gripped one hand in the other on her lap. Here it came.

"Can you start on Thursday? I have an instructor who quit in the middle of the semester. Very inconsiderate."

Lydia's hands uncurled. Her fear of rejection gave way to horror at her success. "Well, yes, but, but—shouldn't I have some training first?"

Louise swiveled, sending a towering stack of exam blue books fluttering to the floor. She grabbed a textbook from the bookshelf behind her desk and thrust it into Lydia's hands. "This is all you need." She peered through her open office door and yelled, "Roz! Come here!"

A zaftig woman with a mop of curly black hair paused in the hallway and back-tracked into Louise's office.

"This is Lydia Eastlee. She's taking over those three basic skills courses that Genevieve abandoned. Show her the ropes, would you?"

Louise's phone buzzed. She swiveled around and barked into the receiver before Roz could answer one way or the other.

"Dismissed," Roz muttered as she directed Lydia out the door in front of her.

"Look, I'm sorry to inconvenience you," Lydia said as she followed Roz down the hall. "If you don't have time to talk to me, I'll muddle through."

"No, come with me. I'm about to teach my afternoon basic skills class. You can observe."

Observing an entire class would take another hour and a half. Would Alfie be okay that long? Well, what was the worst that could happen? If he peed on the tile floor of the laundry room, she could wipe it up, no problem. "That would be great. Thank you."

Roz marched down the hall, her ample hips swaying. "Louise knows I'd kill to be hired full time here, so she always pawns off jobs on me that none of the full professors will touch."

Lydia remained silent. Was she an untouchable?

"Why did this Genevieve quit?" Lydia asked, as they headed down a flight of stairs to a corridor of classrooms.

"Let the students walk all over her and left in tears one day." Roz faced her outside the classroom door. "Don't do that, please. Louise will freak."

Roz strode into a half-full classroom and waved at the chairs. "Have a seat and watch the magic happen."

Lydia sat in the far corner of the first row, remembering from her own college days that the back row was bound to be the most in-demand seating. Roz bustled around the lectern, arranging her notes and getting the projector set up. The moment the clock struck two, she began taking roll.

In the middle of the process, a young man—still in his twenties but older than the others in the class—strolled in. He nodded to Roz then scrutinized Lydia. Unaccountably, she felt herself flush under his gaze. He was extraordinarily good-looking, with wavy brown hair, straight, dark brows, and brilliant blue eyes.

Perhaps she was sitting in his usual seat. He sat one row behind her and one seat to her right. From the corner of her eye she could see him extend his long legs and shrug off a hoodie, revealing strong, tanned arms.

Roz began her lesson. "Who can tell me what we learned last class?"

Immediately, a girl sitting in the center of the front row shot up her hand. Roz let her start the recap, but called on a kid in the back row to finish.

Lydia made a note: start each class with a review. Don't let the know-it-all do all the talking.

Roz started into her lecture. The first slide in her Power-Point showed a tattoo with a typo: To Cool 4 School

For a moment, the room was silent. Then the handsome guy behind her let out a guffaw. Other kids tittered. The girl in the front row whined, "I don't get it."

Lydia made another note: be funny.

Now that Roz had the class's attention, she dove into the meat of her lecture on improving essay structure.

At 2:15, a tall, rangy kid slouched into the classroom, tripping over the backpack of the girl sitting on the aisle.

Roz paused in her explanation of paragraph unity. "Mr. Fuller. So nice of you to join us." She gestured to the wall clock. "The class started fifteen minutes ago."

"My bad."

Roz drew herself up to her full height, which was only about five-two. "My bad? *My bad?* I believe the words you were searching for are, 'I'm sorry for disrupting the learning of the dedicated students in this class, Professor Schmidt. It won't happen again.'"

The other kids shifted and squirmed.

"Yeah, that," Fuller muttered.

The lecture continued, and Roz dimmed the lights again for another PowerPoint presentation. Soon, a kid a few seats away from Lydia lay his head down on the desk. His breathing slowed.

Lydia could remember her own eyelids drooping when the lights dimmed during a Beowulf lecture, but she'd certainly made every effort to remain upright, even if not alert. To have someone openly sleeping right in front of you as you taught seemed totally demoralizing. If a student put his head down in her class, how would she handle it?

Roz answered her silent question. "Brandon!" She rapped her heavy textbook on the edge of his desk.

Groggily, Brandon lifted his head. "Huh?"

"If everyone in this room, including me, put his or her head down and slept, would we have a successful class?"

Brandon shifted uneasily but remained hunched.

"Would we?"

"No," he muttered, pulling himself vertical.

"Okay—if it doesn't work for all of us to do it, it doesn't work for you to do it."

Brandon nodded and remained vertical.

Lydia jotted Roz's words in her notebook. They sounded like they might come in handy.

When the wall clock reached three, the kids began to gather their backpacks and water bottles. Roz raised her voice to keep their attention. "For Thursday, read the essay on page 153 and answer the questions that follow."

A girl flipped her long hair over her shoulder and waved her hand.

"Yes, Cassidy?"

"Do I have to have it done on Thursday? Cuz I have to work tonight? And then my aunt is coming to visit tomorrow, and I haven't seen her in, like, months? So could I have, like, an extension? Cuz I don't have time to do all that?" Both her questions and her statements ended on the same plaintive up-note.

Roz stared at her for a long moment. "My day has twenty-four hours. Your day has twenty-four hours. You choose how you want to spend them."

The girl looked puzzled.

"If you want to pass, get your assignments in on time," Roz clarified.

The class ended, and Roz called out to the fleeing crowd. "Seth, could I have a word?"

The handsome guy paused, grimaced, and returned to Roz's desk.

"I'm still waiting on that paper."

Lydia hung back. She had planned to talk to Roz after class, but she didn't want to appear to be eavesdropping on this conversation. She felt trapped in her seat.

"Yeah, well—my weekend got a little... complicated... so it didn't get done."

Lydia kept her gaze focused on the desk. She could only imagine the complications this guy's weekend must hold!

"Complicated?"

Seth's chin jutted out. "Look, I don't owe you an explanation, okay? You told us on the first day of class you didn't want to hear lame excuses. So I'm not going to stand here spinning you some weepy story like Cassidy does."

Roz conceded the point with a nod. "You're a smart guy. It doesn't take that long to write a 500 word essay. Just do the work so you pass."

"Back off me, wouldja? I hate this class. Writing these essays is pointless."

Seth slung his backpack over his shoulder and stormed out.

Roz watched him go and pursed her lips. She turned to Lydia. "Another one who's going to fail for no good reason. It doesn't bother me when the dumb ones fail. But he's actually quite smart."

"He always knew the answers to the questions you asked. Why did he say he hates the class? He seemed pretty engaged."

"He's older than the others. Works as a carpenter to support himself. Wants to study architecture. Seems to think the basic undergraduate required courses are a needless barrier between him and his goal."

"He told you all that?"

"Wrote about it. Quite eloquently, in fact, except for the comma splices. He liked that assignment. But if I ask him to write about a topic that hasn't caught his imagination, he can't be bothered." Roz headed toward the classroom door. "Too cool for school, I guess."

Chapter 14

Lydia drove home engulfed by alternating bouts of fear and elation.

She had a new job! Louise had hired her. True, the chairman was desperate to replace a person who'd quit without notice. And true, the job paid a fraction of her salary as creative director, but still.

She'd gotten the job totally on her own.

When she stopped to think about it, Lydia realized that she had never before gotten a job without some prior connection. Her first job, as a lifeguard at the town pool, was a position handed along by graduating seniors on the high school swim team to younger kids coming up in the ranks. Next, she had been referred to her position as greeter at Hennessey's by a fellow grad student.

And, of course, her first job at Imago had come to her through Charles.

There was nothing wrong with this, of course. It was the way the world worked—referrals, connections, networking.

But she had just gotten a job the hard way: by sending in a resume and a cover letter in response to an ad.

When she was done patting herself on the back, the fear set in. Lydia knew she had the knowledge to teach her students what they needed to learn. But did she have the management skills? In an office, subordinates listened to their boss even if they might complain behind her back. If she gave an order at Imago, her staff complied.

The mood in a community college classroom was clearly different. How could she coax the reluctant students. How would she handle outright defiance? Roz pulled it off with a mixture of sternness and humor.

Lydia gripped the steering wheel. She'd just have to figure out what worked for her.

Once she reached home and pulled into the garage, Lydia could hear Alfie whimpering.

Even as she felt a stab of guilt for leaving him, she also nursed a thrill that a living creature in the house missed her enough to cry.

"Here I come, baby!" Lydia opened the door from the garage into the laundry room.

Tumbleweeds of stuffing drifted across the floor. It took Lydia a moment to realize that Alfie had eviscerated his new stuffed racoon. The brown and black striped tail lay in front of the washer; the paws and squeaker were across the room. Clearly, the customer who'd advised against the raccoon knew her dog toys.

"That's okay. You were bored and lonesome, right?"

Alfie sat at her feet and bobbed his head. That face! Who could be mad at him? But why was the fur on his muzzle green? She peered at the floor. What were those green shreds mixed in with the stuffing?

Lydia spun around. The purse she'd left hanging on the hook by the door was gone.

The Federico Lomonte purse Charles had bought her for her birthday.

The purse so expensive she had been nervous to use it. The purse Charles took such pleasure in seeing her wear.

Six thousand dollars of affection now lay on the floor in a tangle of tooth-marked straps and golden buckles.

Anxiety twisted Lydia's stomach. How could she explain the purse's absence?

Then her emotions realigned—a surge of relief followed immediately by a wave of horror.

She didn't have to worry about her husband's reaction.

Charles was dead.

The stark reality sent a flash of pain through her as unexpected as when she'd cracked her head against the sharp corner of an open cabinet.

Charles was dead.

He'd never again pay her a compliment. Squeeze her hand in a private signal. Light up with pleasure when he saw her walk into a room.

Charles was dead.

Lydia leaned against the washing machine, her knees suddenly weak. Nearly three weeks had passed since Charles collapsed in Hennessey's. She'd relayed the news of his death countless times. Why had the finality of it hit her so hard right here, right now?

Was it the destruction of this last gift Charles had given her?

Alfie gazed up at her expectantly, seeking praise for a job well done. As Lydia stroked his silky ears and his silly green-bearded mouth, she realized she didn't care about the purse. She'd never wanted it in the first place. True, it was beautiful, but how beautiful did a receptacle for carrying keys and wallet and lipstick need to be? Her parents had raised her to be thrifty: shop the clearance rack, clip coupons. It had taken her several years of marriage to accept she didn't need to wait for asparagus to go on sale to buy it.

But larger extravagances had always made her uncomfortable.

Sitting on the laundry room floor amidst the chaos Alfie had created, Lydia flashed back to her last birthday with Charles.

Then

I've made a reservation at La Coqatrice," Charles told her when she got home from work.

"That new place in Summit with the celebrity chef?"

Charles smiled. "I thought it would be a refreshing change of pace from Hennessey's. A forty-fifth birthday deserves special attention."

Lydia kissed him and ran to change into a dress and heels.

On the drive to the restaurant, Lydia felt as keyed-up as a child on the road to Disneyworld. She'd seen the gorgeously beribboned box Charles had stowed in the back seat. What did it contain? It was too big for jewelry, unless he'd hidden a smaller box inside. Too square for a cashmere sweater or pashmina shawl.

Charles had excellent taste. What had he picked out for her?

Then an idea struck her. Perhaps the box contained tickets to that new Broadway show that was sold out for months. Perhaps Charles found a way to get them—he never accepted no for an answer—and had planned a getaway weekend in Manhattan. Maybe the custom-wrapped box was just a ruse.

Charles loved surprises!

Lydia gasped as they entered the restaurant. Striking murals decorated the walls and pin-point lights illuminated the tables. The maitre'd led them to a corner table where they could sit side-by-side on a plush banquette. Lydia squeezed her husband's hand. "This is so romantic. It reminds me of the restaurant in Paris where you proposed."

"Very romantic to be here with the love of my life," Charles murmured in her ear.

Dinner was delicious. They traded bites of each other's selections, and drank most of a bottle of a fine French burgundy. As Lydia grew a little tipsy, the gift seemed to wink at her from its spot on the banquette next to Charles.

Charles didn't care for singing waiters who drew the attention of the entire restaurant, but he did arrange for her favorite dessert—crème brulee—to be served with one sparkling candle. "Make a wish," he urged her.

Lydia closed her eyes and wished for a getaway weekend as romantic as this dinner.

At last, Charles placed the gift in front of her. Her heart quickened as she pulled the beautiful gold ribbon and lifted the lid of the sturdy box. She pulled out a layer of tissue paper, and there it was.

A Federico Lomonte purse in buttery green leather. Its big gold FL buckle glimmered in the restaurant's spot lighting.

Lydia was stunned into silence.

Charles beamed. "Surprised, eh?"

She certainly was! What had possessed him to buy such a thing? Why had he thought this status symbol would please her? Lydia prided herself on dressing with discreet elegance. She appreciated quality, but she had no desire to follow the herd and acquire whatever hot item was trending at the moment. In fact, she'd often made wisecracks about how many different designer labels Betsey von Maur could manage to wear at one time.

But Charles was looking at her eagerly, the way she used to look at her dad on Christmas morning when he unwrapped whatever garish tie or polka-dotted socks she had picked out for him. She summoned up the appropriate response.

"I love it! It's gorgeous! I never expected this."

No one wants to know their gift has fallen flat.

In the car on the way home, Lydia reproached herself. What kind of woman is ungrateful for a lovely, expensive gift? Charles had bought it to let her know just how cherished she was. She had created her own disappointment by fantasizing about a romantic theater weekend. It wasn't Charles's fault that he had failed to read her mind.

At home, they slipped into bed and Lydia willingly accepted Charles's embrace. They made love, and she drifted off to sleep contented.

But the next week, when they were getting ready to go to Alton Finn's annual brunch, Charles had unsettled her.

"Aren't you going to wear your new purse?" he asked as they were about to leave their house.

Lydia frowned. Her husband never commented on her wardrobe choices other than to compliment her. "I wasn't going to take a purse at all. We'll only be there for two hours."

"Won't you need lipstick or a brush? Go on—get your new purse."

So Lydia had carried the Federico Lomonte purse to the brunch. And predictably, Betsey von Maur had made a huge fuss over it. As the other partners' wives gathered around clucking that this was the very newest model in the hardest to find color, Lydia caught Charles observing the scene with satisfaction.

And then she realized the only reason to give your wife a six thousand dollar purse is to show the world that you can.

Now Alfie trotted across the laundry room, picked up the gold FL buckle, and dropped it in Lydia's lap. His teeth had scratched the shiny finish and she could see the dull metal beneath the surface.

These past three weeks had been one long tribute to her husband. The obituary, the eulogy, the many condolence notes—all had extolled Charles's virtues: his legal acumen, his thoughtfulness, his generosity.

And Lydia had agreed. All of that praise was true.

But as she turned the purse buckle over and over in her hands, she wondered how it could be that Charles had known her so little after eighteen years of marriage.

And how had she let herself be so misunderstood?

That night, after Lydia washed her face, she slid the two-carat diamond engagement ring and matching wedding band from her finger and set them in her jewelry box.

Chapter 15

Lydia had spent the day between her interview and her first day of teaching poring over the textbook and the syllabus for the class. Alfie interrupted her periodically, demanding play time. She took him to the dog park to wear him out, and from the other dog owners, learned about a doggy day care center that would watch Alfie while she worked.

"Eventually, you'll be able to leave him home alone," the woman at the park said. "But given how active he is, Happy Tails is your best bet."

So Lydia enrolled Alfie in day care, setting up a schedule for the week that would probably eat up most of the money she earned teaching. Alfie gazed up at her, eyes full of trust. "It's okay, Alfie. As long as you're content, Happy Tails is money well spent."

Once they were back home, Alfie collapsed on his bed, and Lydia went back to lesson planning. Roz had generously shared some of her own PowerPoint presentations and grammar exercises. By the time Lydia climbed into bed at ten, she felt she'd laid out an excellent lecture on using transitional words, which is where her predecessor had left off, according to the syllabus.

Lydia showed up an hour before her four o'clock class and went to the office all the adjunct professors shared in the basement of Founders Hall. Roz Schmidt was there, and she introduced Lydia to some of the others: Marty in sociology, who, like Roz, juggled adjunct teaching gigs at several schools to make a living; Celine in French who wanted to work part-time while her kids were young; and Harry, who had retired from teaching high school calculus but needed extra money to help support his grandkids.

Lydia couldn't let on to the others that she didn't need money but needed this job as desperately as any of them did. Needed it so she had a reason to wake up in the morning. A place to go. People to talk to. Something to call herself. Other than "used to be." Used to be Mrs. Charles Eastlee. Used to be Creative Director at Imago.

Lydia gave herself a little shake. She couldn't afford to go to that dark place now. She had a class to teach in half an hour.

A girl with a backpack slung across her tattooed shoulder slouched in the doorway, half-in, half out of the room. "Uhm, is Professor Miller here?"

Not a head turned. The girl shifted her weight to her other leg. Finally, Marty spoke without moving his gaze from his computer screen, "You don't see her, she's not here."

The girl didn't move. "I need her to sign this? Today?" She pleaded to their backs.

"What department is she in?" Celine asked. When the girl said history, Celine directed her to the History Department office. Now, was that so hard?

"Enabler," Roz said. "She'll be back in fifteen saying she couldn't find History or nobody up there ever heard of Miller. I keep telling you—solving all their problems for them is like feeding feral cats. Just encourages them to come back for more."

"Oh, this from the woman who once drove a kid to campus twice a week for half a semester to keep him from dropping out," Harry said from the back corner.

"He was right on my way in. Besides, that was years ago. I'm tougher now."

Roz was tough, no doubt about that. But Lydia suspected that underneath the Teflon exterior beat a heart of pure gold.

"Do you just have the one class to teach today, Lydia?" Celine asked.

"Tomorrow I have two in the morning, but today just the one from 4:00 to 5:15."

"Eeew—that sucks," Marty and Celine said in unison.

Roz had warned her late afternoon wasn't a good time to teach Basic Skills, the English class full of resentful slackers and kids who, as Roz said, couldn't punctuate their way out of a paper bag. They would be tired, restless, eager to get home or get to their after-school jobs. But Lydia had been grateful to get that section. She wanted to stay on campus as late as possible. Anything to postpone her inevitable entry into the huge, dark, echoing house that she now lived in alone.

She glanced at the clock on the office wall. "Is that the right time?"

"No, that one's always slow," Harry said.

"And the ones in your classrooms are always fast." Celine added.

"Is there a clock anywhere on campus that tells the right time?" Lydia asked.

"Only the stopped one in Blair 202. It's right twice a day."

The adjuncts laughed.

Lydia gathered up her folders and books and prepared to meet her class.

When she walked into the windowless room, no one looked up. Every head hunched over a phone screen. Even unhappy advertising clients made the effort to look up before a meeting started.

Lydia took a deep breath and cleared her throat. "Hello, everyone, I'm Ly- uh, Professor Eastlee. I'm taking over this class from Professor Connolly."

One head came up. An Indian woman in her thirties sitting in the first row with a textbook, notebook and five pens and pencils arrayed before her. "What has happened to Professor Connolly?" She seemed genuinely concerned.

"She was unable to finish the semester, but she's okay."

"Does this mean none of the tests we took with her count?" a kid in the back row asked hopefully.

"Afraid not—they still count."

He slumped back down and resumed staring at his phone.

Lydia called the roll, trying to associate each name with an identifying feature. Surindra Patel: five pens; Jake Felton, sullen anxiety.

Lydia began with a review, as she'd seen Roz do. "I believe last class Professor Connolly taught you about independent and dependent clauses," Lydia said.

"No, she didn't," Cole contradicted.

Surindra shook her head in mournful agreement with Cole. The others looked baffled or indifferent in equal measures. Lydia had no choice but to abandon her lesson plan and backtrack to an improvised lecture on clauses and sentence structure. She struggled through, noticing anxiously that half the students took notes while the other half gazed into space.

"Now, I'd like you to write a paragraph on the ideal way to spend a summer day and vary your sentence structure. Use both compound and complex sentences."

The students stared at her blankly.

"What we just talked about," Lydia prodded. "Sentences with two independent clauses. Or one independent clause and one dependent clause. Remember?"

Surindra nodded.

Cole shrugged.

The others shifted anxiously in their seats.

Lydia sat down and watched. Immediately, Surindra picked up her pen and began covering a notebook page with perfect, rounded script. The tip of her tongue peeped out between pursed lips. Jake Felton picked up his pencil and stared at the blank page. Cole Geraci fidgeted and squirmed until the girl next to him tore out a sheet of paper and handed it to him. Jose Mendoza's face was frozen, his eyes fixed on a point far, far away.

"You collectin' this?" someone from the back row called out.

Lydia gave the kid her yoga smile. "Why do you ask?"

He scowled and scratched out a few sentences.

Five minutes passed. Surindra had started in on her second page. Jose hunkered over his paper, but the words seemed to be coming. The others wrote steadily. Only Jake had nothing on his paper.

Lydia approached. "Are you having trouble?"

He dodged her gaze and said nothing.

"If you have trouble getting started, it can help to write down exactly what's going through your head." Lydia paused and lowered her voice. "Like, 'I wish the teacher would go away' or 'I wish this class were over,' and then see what flows after that."

He picked up his pencil and Lydia smiled and continued her stroll around the class.

In the quiet room, she heard the snap. When she turned to look, Jake was halfway to the door. His open notebook lay on his desk. His pencil, tip broken, lay on top of it.

"Jake?" But he was gone, the door slammed behind him.

The other students stared at her, expecting something from her.

Lydia offered what she hoped was a reassuring smile. "Guess some people really hate in-class writing."

They returned to their work, but Lydia felt the class had gotten off to a bad start. What had she said to upset him? What would Roz have done? Chase after the kid?

A wave of restlessness passed over the class. Lydia glanced at the wall clock. 5:17. Who knew if that was correct, but clearly they'd all had enough.

"Hand in your papers. I'll see you next Tuesday."

The papers fluttered onto her desk as the students raced out the door. Only Surindra lingered. "I am very sorry my essay is containing many errors," Surindra said. "I am hoping I will learn to write good, so I can apply for a more better job at nursing home where I work."

Lydia smiled. "There's no need to apologize. I know your writing will improve."

Lydia looked at the empty classroom. One desk still held a notebook. She went to collect it. Maybe Jake would come back on Tuesday.

She picked it up. The pencil point had dug deeply into the paper, leaving a hole. Two words were written on the first line.

I hate.

———◦———

LYDIA WALKED SLOWLY back to the faculty parking lot. She felt as shaky as she did after a client presentation that had run off the rails. Not winning a new client was bad, but losing a student was worse. What if she let these students down? What if Surindra failed the class? Would she lose her shot at the promotion she wanted? What was wrong with Jake? Was he troubled or just unhappy at school? Could she turn him around?

"Well, how was your first day of teaching?"

Lydia spun around. "Hi, Roz. I feel a little shaky. That was a lot harder for me than it looked when you did it."

Roz seemed pleased by the compliment. "These kids are lions. Never let them see you as a lame antelope." She looked Lydia up and down. "They were probably intimidated by having a professor who's such a snappy dresser." She tugged at her own saggy stretch pants. "I can't rely on that tactic, so I have to use my wits."

"How was your class? Did Brandon stay awake?"

"He's been bright-eyed and bushy-tailed. Must be the cocaine."

Lydia's eyes widened. Then she realized Roz was joking. "Did that other kid ever hand in his paper?"

Roz's face fell. "He didn't show up for class. I suppose this is the end. A waste."

Lydia felt their conversation winding down. Now or never—do it! She spit the words out quickly before she lost her nerve. "Say, I'd love to thank you for helping me out. Your advice was invaluable. Can I take you out for a quick meal and a glass of wine?"

Roz seemed startled by the invitation.

"My treat. And I have to pick up my dog by seven." Lydia took a step backward. "But if you're busy, I totally understand."

"No, I'd love to go out. That's really nice of you."

"The Brass Rail Pub, right on Route 10?"

Roz grinned. "See you there in ten."

Lydia realized her heart was beating faster than normal. The effort of reaching out to make a new friend was an aerobic activity. She watched Roz load her bulging tote bag into a dilapidated Hyundai with a rusted bumper that clung to the car with the help of a walking fish Darwin magnet. Lydia waited until Roz pulled out before getting into her own BMW. Her nose twitched. Richie at Elite Detailing had done a good job of banishing the dog vomit stain, but a faint smell persisted.

Once she'd given Roz a head start, she set off for the Brass Rail.

Chapter 16

The Brass Rail was an innocuous place, marginally better than Applebee's and spacious enough that there was never a wait for a table. They sat in a large booth, ordered burgers and cheap cabernet, and fell into easy conversation about teaching. Roz was full of a veteran's war stories.

"So I have certain tried-and-true writing prompts," Roz said waving a French fry, "but these kids still manage to surprise me. I tell them to write about a time when things didn't turn out as planned, and ninety-five percent of them write about the prom. Thought it would be wonderful, turned out to be a bust. But then I get the kid who wrote about cooking meth. Thought it would be easy. Turned out he blew up the kitchen."

Lydia's wine sprayed from her mouth.

"And don't get me started on the girl who wrote about losing her virginity."

"No! She didn't!"

"Oh, yes—in glorious detail. I told them to use all five senses. She was excellent at following instructions." Roz crunched into her pickle. "I guess I should have seen that one coming. I mean, what girl ever pops the cherry according to her romantic script? After all, a teenage boy is the other actor."

"Oh, my god, Roz—I haven't laughed this hard in years." Lydia wiped a tear from her eye and swallowed some water to wash down the bread she'd choked on during Roz's last story.

Roz's shrewd brown eyes studied her. "Why is that, Lydia? You seem....somber."

"Oh, I don't want to bring you down with my troubles."

"You're not bringing me down. I'm a student of human nature. I'm dying to know the real reason why you took this job teaching English."

"Real?" Lydia dropped her gaze. "I mean, why does anyone work?"

"What did you do before?"

"I worked in advertising. But I needed a change." With two glasses of wine under her belt, Lydia let her story tumble out. The forced retirement...the planned cruises...the sudden death...her loneliness.

Lydia left out the sixteen million. She wasn't that tipsy.

"You didn't want to go to Greece?" Roz chased the last French fry on her plate.

"Not for a month trapped on a boat full of Harvard Law alumni."

"True. That could be gruesome. How much older was your husband than you?"

"Eighteen years."

Roz leaned on her elbows. "So why'd you marry him?"

Lydia flinched at the bluntness of Roz's question. No one had ever asked her that. How many people had wondered but kept their mouths shut? But there was something mesmerizing about Roz's brutal honesty. It made Lydia want to talk.

"When I was twenty-five and he was forty-three, the difference didn't seem so great. I was in a difficult spot in my life."

Lydia hesitated.

Roz poured more wine in Lydia's glass and rolled her fingers for further explanation.

"During my senior year in college, both my parents died. First, my mom got diagnosed with cancer, then my dad had a fatal heart attack, then my mom died."

Roz winced. "That's awful. Are you an only child?"

"No, I have an older sister. But she met a guy on her junior year abroad and she ended up marrying him and moving to Australia."

"Geez. So you were all alone."

"It felt like it. I hadn't planned on going to grad school right away, but campus was the only home I had. After the medical bills and the funeral expenses, there wasn't much money left. I enrolled in the graduate English program on a fellowship, so I wouldn't have to leave Drew."

"Makes sense. But how did you meet Charles? Was he the university lawyer?"

"No, I was the greeter at Hennessey's. He came in with a group of clients. I was struggling with an obnoxious customer, and Charles scared him off. The next night, he came back and asked me out."

"You didn't feel like he was robbing the cradle?"

"He was handsome. I was flattered by his attention. He took me to nice places. Held the door. Helped me on with my coat. Took my hand when we crossed a busy street. I know it sounds silly now, but it felt so nice to be cared for."

Roz's face looked as it had when her student Cassidy was offering lame excuses. Like she was evaluating the plausibility of this explanation and coming up short.

Lydia forged on. "I had been involved with this perpetually unemployed, terminally depressed poet who feared commitment."

Roz snorted. "Only one? I've dated some version of that guy five or six times."

Lydia smiled.

Roz could joke about deadbeat boyfriends, but her situation with Joel had been more dire. He'd been using heroin. Stealing from her. She worried he might be HIV positive, yet she kept having sex with him without a condom.

She wouldn't tell her new friend the depth of her self-destructiveness in those days. But she wanted to keep talking. "I hated grad school. I couldn't stay a greeter at Hennessey's forever. Charles came along and he had a career. He was everything Joel wasn't: confident, considerate, well-groomed. And ready to get married."

"And were you ready to get married?"

Then

"Pack a bag. We're going away for a long weekend." Charles spun her around in a whirl of excitement.

"Where?"

"It's a surprise. Just pack some underwear, your sneakers, and a pair of high heels. Everything else we'll buy when we get there." He paused. "Oh, and your passport."

Lydia trailed Charles through Newark airport, looking at each gate they passed: Cozumel, Rio, London.

Paris.

Charles stopped and waved her into the boarding line.

"We're going to Paris?" Lydia clapped her hands in delight. She'd never been to Europe, only had a passport because she'd visited her sister in Australia.

The weekend held one joy after another—meals in sidewalk cafes, the view from the tower of Notre Dame, the Louvre, the shopping spree in which Charles bought her a fabulous dress unlike anything available in Palmyrton.

And then, in a restaurant overlooking the illuminated Eiffel Tower, Charles had pulled a small box from his pocket.

"I love you, Lydia. Will you be my wife?"

He popped the box open, and the huge diamond glittered in the Eiffel Tower's reflected light.

"Yes."

What other answer could there be?

Lydia raked her fingers through her hair. "None of my friends were married. I hadn't even thought about it. But Charles was ready. He was tired of dating. He was the only single partner in his firm. He had a list of pros for marriage, and I couldn't come up with any cons."

"Did you love him?"

A prickle of sweat broke out on Lydia's chest. How many times had she chased this question to the far corners of her consciousness like a cat pursuing a mouse and then letting it go? Was love the heart-pounding cyclone described in romance novels? Or was it the steady encouragement of a reliable partner?

But she couldn't admit doubts to Roz. She'd just met the woman. "Of course! I needed him. I couldn't bear to lose him. He took me to Paris and presented me with a ring. It was the most romantic proposal ever. Six months later, we were married."

Roz narrowed her eyes. "Sounds like he didn't sweep you off your feet, he knocked your feet out from under you when you were already on shaky ground."

"No!" Lydia protested. "Charles actually set me back on my feet again. He encouraged me to settle down and finish the master's since I was nearly done. Then he got me the interview at the ad agency. But I did the rest myself."

Lydia realized she wanted Roz to think well of her. Charles might have opened that door, but Lydia had made her own career.

"So, do you regret it?"

"Man, Roz—you really know how to ask the tough questions!"

"Yeah, Homeland Security called to offer me a job after they found out I could get teenage boys to talk about their emotions. Figured they could use me to interrogate the Taliban. But I turned it down because I couldn't imagine not living hand-to-mouth as an underpaid adjunct with no health insurance."

Lydia saw an opportunity to turn the conversation. She'd reached the limit of baring her soul. Time for Roz to bare hers. "You really have no health insurance?"

"I pay through the nose for a policy that doesn't cover anything I need, so yeah. But I hang in at Palmer Community because Louise keeps dangling that full-time position with benefits just out of my reach. I finished my PhD in Eighteenth Century British poetry just so I'd be qualified to teach those kids how to write five paragraphs with no dangling participles."

"You've applied for a full-time position more than once?"

"Three times. The first time I was rejected in favor of Sondra Retherford, who had a PhD. So I went back and finished my PhD. The second time, I was rejected in favor of the diversity candidate, Thant Yaw. He's Burmese, and you know our huge community of Burmese students really relates to him. Not. And the third time, I was rejected because I'm fat."

"What? You're not fat, and even if you were, isn't that discriminatory?"

"Louise told me I was her top pick, but that I hadn't impressed the Academic Dean." Roz put bitter emphasis on "impressed." "Since I answered every question he had about Blake's use of animal imagery and the intersection of insanity and faith in the poetry of Cowper, I have to assume that meant he wasn't bowled over by my too tight blue pantsuit on which I discovered an egg stain while I was waiting to be called into his office."

Roz leaned back from the table. "So now I'm on a diet. I've lost fifteen pounds although you'd never believe it from the way I ate tonight. And there's a new Academic Dean, and a full-time position is opening up this fall."

"You'll get the job this time." Lydia said the words to be supportive.

But she could see that Roz knew her career and her finances were a crap-shoot beyond her control.

Chapter 17

The next morning, Lydia awoke to Alfie tugging on the sleeve of her nightshirt. "Okay, okay—can I wash my face and brush my teeth before we go outside?"

The dog considered this an outrageous concession. He paced and whined outside the bathroom door as Lydia studied herself in the mirror. She was a wreck! Her bangs were practically to the bridge of her nose, and she could see gray roots at her temples. She'd chewed her cuticles and her pedicure was chipped.

She would never have let Charles see her like this.

Yet here she was, a month after his death, looking like the "before" picture in a magazine make-over article.

"Get a grip, woman!" she scolded herself. "Are you going to let yourself turn into one of those sad creatures who goes to the supermarket in bedroom slippers? Just because the standard of fashion is a lot lower at Palmer Community than it was at Imago doesn't mean you have to sink to that level."

She vowed to make an appointment at the salon as soon as it opened this morning.

Alfie scratched at the door.

All right, higher standards begin tomorrow! Lydia pulled on a pair of yoga pants and yanked her uncombed hair back with a clip. She opened the bathroom door just as Alfie raised his leg.

"No!"

She ran with the dog down to the back door and clipped on his leash. As usual, Alfie pulled her down the street, hell-bent on pursuing every squirrel he saw. When a landscaper's truck rumbled by, he switched directions and lunged at it.

"Alfie, no!" Lydia yanked him back with inches to spare.

After an exhausting trip around the block, Lydia fed Alfie his kibble, then took eggs and cheese from the fridge to make herself an omelet. Between the fridge and the counter, one of the eggs slipped from her fingers and splatted on the tile floor. Alfie skidded to her side and began lapping up the egg, shell and all.

"No, Alfie." Lydia grabbed a damp paper towel, nudged the dog aside, and began to wipe up the mess.

Alfie lunged at her moving hand and bit.

"Augh!" Lydia leaped up and backed away from the dog. Her hand throbbed, and a spot of blood appeared where Alfie's sharp incisor had broken her skin. She trembled.

Meanwhile, Alfie systematically licked the floor in a five foot radius of the egg until he was sure he'd found every drop. Then he casually strolled over to his bed and lay down.

"You bit me! You hurt me!" Lydia stared at her pet from across the room.

Alfie rolled on his side and shut his eyes.

"Bad dog! That was very, very bad."

Alfie's only response was a slight twitch of the tail.

Lydia sank shakily onto a kitchen chair. This dog was getting the best of her. Jim had warned her Alfie needed a firm hand, but she had been so sure all the dog needed was love and a safe and comfortable home. She didn't want to admit she'd been wrong, but she needed help.

Lydia searched through her bag until she found Jim's card. She hesitated before punching in the numbers, not sure what she would say. Finally, she took the coward's way out and texted.

Alfie's doing great, but I think he could benefit from some obedience training. Do you have any availability?

He responded immediately. *What kind of problems?*

He pulls on his leash. He chews when he's left alone. She hesitated with her fingers on the screen. But it was like going to the doctor and not mentioning a lump. *And he bit me.*

I can be there by noon.

———————◈———————

LYDIA KEPT HER DISTANCE from Alfie until Jim rolled up in a mud-spattered Jeep SUV. She opened the front door before he could ring, so he wouldn't hear Alfie losing his mind at the sound of the doorbell. Jim stood on the front porch in his usual drooping khakis, worn-out Birkenstocks, and a faded Talking Heads t-shirt. A beautiful brown and white dog with blue eyes sat beside him.

"Hi, Lydia. This is my dog, Harley. She helps me in my work."

Lydia let them in. Jim looked around the foyer with open curiosity. Harley sat politely while Alfie ran excited laps, skidding across the marble.

"I'm moving soon to something smaller," Lydia explained, sensing judgment in Jim's stare.

Alfie charged into the living room, careening from the sofa to the loveseat and nearly knocking over a lamp in the process.

Jim frowned and stood in the doorway of the large room. Lydia suspected he didn't approve of the perfectly matched furniture all in shades of cream and sandstone.

"You have a Steinway," he commented on her baby grand. "You don't want Alfie jumping up on that."

"Yes, my husband got it for me as an anniversary gift." Lydia wasn't sure why she'd mentioned that, but having come that far, felt she needed to continue lest Jim ask about her playing. "I haven't played much lately. I should get back to it."

"And where is Alfie's crate?" Jim asked as Alfie tore past them again.

"Uhm, I don't have a crate. I can't bear to put him in a cage. Not after all he's been through."

Jim put his hand on Lydia's arm. "A crate is not a prison cell, Lydia. The crate will give Alfie a place to calm down when he's over-excited like this. He'll associate it with security, not captivity. Please get one for him."

"Okay, right." Lydia wasn't going to argue with Jim before their training session even began. But she knew Alfie didn't want to be locked in a cage.

Jim nodded. "Let's go to the room where you spend the most time with Alfie."

"That would be the kitchen." Lydia led the way to the rear of the house.

Jim made Lydia hold Alfie on a leash while he put Harley through a series of commands: sit, stay, come, and leave it. She performed each one perfectly, even sitting patiently staring at a piece of chicken on the floor until Jim told her she could have it. Meanwhile, Alfie nearly tore Lydia's arm from her socket trying to get to the food.

"Wow. How long did it take you to get her to do that?"

"A year."

Lydia's heart sank.

Jim noticed the change in her expression. "Training a dog requires time, patience, and consistency. There are no short cuts. But if you keep it up, you'll both be happier." Jim pushed at a strand of hair that had slipped from his pony tail. "That's what's important to remember. Alfie is looking to you for leadership. He'll be happier when he gets it."

Alfie chose that moment to break away from Lydia. He tore around the kitchen, sniffing at Harley and leaping up on Jim to get at the treats in his pocket.

"Alfie, no! Don't jump up like that."

Jim turned his shoulder until Alfie stopped jumping. He held his cupped hand above the dog's head, made eye contact, and spoke firmly. "Sit."

Alfie sat.

"Good sit." He gave Alfie a treat.

"He never does that for me," Lydia complained.

"You have to use the same words and the same hand signals every single time," Jim explained. "Dogs don't understand long paragraphs with multi-part instructions."

Neither do remedial English students.

"And when he jumps up, don't give him attention. That only rewards bad behavior. Turn away from him until he stops."

Lydia hunched her shoulders. She felt like she had in third grade when the art teacher had scolded her for drawing a robin with a purple chest. "But I like talking to him. I don't want to issue commands like a brigadier general."

"You can keep talking to him. He likes the sound of your voice. But if you want Alfie to understand you, you have to use a few consistent words." Jim coached her as she gave Alfie commands and rewarded him for following them.

Sometimes Alfie got distracted and meandered away.

"Speak firmly. Get right up close to him, so he knows you mean business."

Lydia shot Jim a doubtful glance. She didn't like this authoritarian stuff. She wanted a pet, a companion, not a robotic slave.

"Show leadership," Jim insisted. "When I was in the Army, I always felt safer under a commander who gave orders with confidence."

"You were in the Army?" Lydia lost focus on Alfie and studied Jim with greater interest. She wouldn't have pegged him as a veteran—he seemed more the tree-hugging, peacenik type.

"For a couple years out of high school. I didn't want to make a career of it, but it was the right choice at the time."

Lydia would have asked him more questions, but Jim returned immediately to the obedience lesson. "Now, we have to work on the food aggression." Jim pulled a thick leather glove from his backpack. He put Alfie's dish on the kitchen counter and filled it with kibble sprinkled with some chopped hot dog. Alfie watched the proceedings with keen interest.

Jim set the bowl on the floor, and Alfie tucked in. Before the dog had eaten more than a few bites, Jim used his gloved hand to pull the dish away.

Alfie growled and snapped.

Lydia cringed. "He scares me when he does that. He seems so, so...feral. This is why that other family returned him, isn't it?"

"You're right—Alfie is reverting to his pack instinct, where the most aggressive dog gets the most food. We don't know about his earlier life. He may have had to fight to get his fair share as a puppy. He's got a scarcity mindset. We have to reassure him that he's now in the land of plenty. That if you take away something you don't want him to have, he'll still get plenty of other food." Jim placed his hands on Lydia's shoulders and looked into her eyes. "You're an adult, the only person in Alfie's universe, and you can learn how to handle this. I can't teach a small child how to do this, but I can teach you. Let's practice."

Lydia took a deep breath and nodded. Jim was right. She couldn't allow the dog to intimidate her. She had to get control of the situation.

Jim took her through the steps several times. By the last try, Alfie followed the command to sit and allowed Lydia to remove the bowl although he followed its journey with a riveting stare.

"Now, let's try it without the leather glove."

Lydia gulped. "Do we have to?"

"Yes. Move with confidence. Animals sense weakness and will always use it to their advantage."

So do remedial English students.

Hoping that Jim wouldn't notice her hand trembling, Lydia removed the leather glove and went through the routine.

Alfie sat while she took the dish away.

Lydia gave it back, and Alfie finished the last of his kibble. Then he went to his bed in the corner and curled up for a nap. Jim smiled. "He's worn out. Learning new commands is tiring."

"And nerve-rattling." Lydia glanced at the clock. "Is it too early for a cocktail?"

Jim hopped on a stool at her island. "Somewhere in the world, it's happy hour."

She'd just been joking—she hadn't sunk to day-drinking yet—but she seemed to have invited him for a drink. Well, it was the least she could do, given that he'd dropped everything to come to her aid. "Beer? Wine?"

"I don't suppose you have any Irish whiskey?" Jim's eyes were as hopeful as Alfie's at the sight of a rotisserie chicken.

"I'm sure there probably is, in my husband's bar." Lydia slipped down the back hall to Charles's study and returned with two nearly full bottles. "Are either of these any good?"

One was Glenfiddich—she'd heard people order that. But Jim bypassed it and went for the other. "Red Breast 12 year. Nice!"

He poured himself a glass and spent what seemed like an eternity swirling it before he took a sip. He wasn't a person who felt compelled to chat, for sure.

"I'm selling this house," Lydia volunteered when the silence grew too long for her. "I'm in the process of buying a smaller place in Burleith. It needs some work, but it has a small fenced yard for Alfie, and it's near the dog park."

Jim studied her for a long moment. "You're making lots of changes. New dog. New house."

"I have a new job, too." She told him about her classes at Palmer Community, and ended with a wink. "I think I can apply some of my new dog training skills there. Show leadership. Don't back down."

"Yes, if only people were as reliable as dogs."

A rather mournful remark, Lydia thought. She couldn't guess his age. Fifty? Maybe younger, maybe older. The stringy ponytail was shot with gray, but his hands had no age spots. "Were you ever married?"

"Briefly, a long time ago. I have a son. He's grown now."

Jim didn't volunteer more, and the topic seemed to sadden him. Maybe his wife had dumped him for a man with a better job.

He stared into his glass. "What do you need to be happy, Lydia?"

Geez, what happened to cocktail chatter? "I...I don't know. I'm trying to figure it out. I mean, I'm fortunate to not have financial worries. But I need meaningful work. And a wider circle of friends. Married couples travel in matched sets like—" her gaze roved the kitchen—"like salt and pepper shakers. When there's only one of you, people just don't know how to react."

"Only connect," Jim said, and knocked back the last of his whiskey.

Only connect? What did that mean?

Jim didn't elaborate. He stood and Harley immediately jumped to attention. "I've kept you long enough. Thanks for the drink. Don't hesitate to call if you have more problems with Alfie."

He headed toward the front door.

"Wait." Lydia grabbed her purse from the counter. "What do I owe you for the obedience lesson?"

He paused. "Oh. Forty will be fine."

She handed him two twenties. "Surely, that's not enough. You were here for over an hour."

He shrugged. "Most of my clients don't offer me such fine refreshments."

And with that, he left.

Lydia stood at the sidelight next to the front door and watched him and his dog get into the dirty SUV. How did he manage to hold body and soul together with such haphazard business practices?

Alfie pressed his nose against the glass and wagged his tail in farewell.

Only connect.

What had he meant?

Chapter 18

I n the days she had worked eight to six, Monday through Friday, Lydia had a standing appointment at La Belle Femme on Thursday evening for a mani/pedi and on the first Monday of the month for a cut and color. She had cancelled all her appointments in the numb days after Charles's death. Now, she had to start over to find a spot.

Her hairdresser managed to squeeze her in the next day, but there were no openings in the manicurist's schedule until later in the week. Lydia looked at her uneven nails and ragged cuticles and decided she'd go to one of the many walk-in Korean-owned nail salons in downtown Palmyrton.

She couldn't bring herself to enter the unfortunately named House of Nail, but she seemed to recall someone she knew sing the praises of Ruby's.

"Pick a color," the woman at the desk commanded as soon as Lydia entered.

At the shelf displaying hundreds of bottles, her hand went to the sedate beige-y pink she usually favored. Then it stopped as if it had a will of its own and dropped down to the row of brilliant corals and reds. Lydia picked up a bottle and squinted at the name on the bottom.

Persimmon Playdate.

Why not? She'd match the walls in the kitchen of her new home.

"Chair four!" the owner barked, and Lydia took her place in the line-up of women having pedicures. As her feet soaked, she scanned a magazine full of gossip about actresses and pop stars she'd never heard of.

"Lydia! How great to see you!"

Lydia looked up to see Eleanor, the head copywriter from Imago, settling into the chair beside hers. She felt the desire to be sucked down the drain of the footbath, but Eleanor seemed genuinely happy to see her.

They went through the usual "how are yous?" before Eleanor leaned across the armrest between them and whispered, "There's a lot of shit going down at the office since you left."

"Oh?" Lydia didn't want to appear overeager, but she was dying to know the office gossip.

"We lost the Pantry Pride account, and Bruce Hartigan from Fitness Unlimited is acting up again. You were the only one who could ever manage him. He rejected every headline I wrote for his ad and insisted on using one he wrote himself. Fit U Up. Isn't that awful?"

Lydia laughed, and the lump of misery that seemed wedged under her ribcage crumbled a bit. Who wouldn't be cheered by the news that the office was falling apart in her absence? "Didn't Bryce try to talk him out of it?" Eleanor had given her a good opening to enquire about her successor.

Eleanor gave a dismissive wave. "He can't be bothered managing the details. He's always off-site at meetings." Then she switched directions. "And guess who's sleeping with Cassie in Accounting?"

Eleanor kept Lydia entertained until both their pedicures were done. As Lydia sat under the drying lamp, Eleanor came by one last time. "We're all going out for drinks on Friday at Tito's Taqueria. Why don't you meet us there?"

"Oh, I...I—" Lydia had been a part of all official Imago celebrations, but as the Creative Director, she hadn't been included in her staff's weekly TGIF drink-a-thons. After all, the point of those was to complain about the boss.

"Oh, come on," Eleanor insisted. "Everyone will love to see you."

Was that true? She wasn't their boss anymore, but did that make her one of the guys?

Eleanor sensed her hesitation and squeezed Lydia's shoulder. "Get out a little." She spoke in a softer voice. "It'll be fun."

Eleanor was right. She couldn't spend every evening of the rest of her life watching Netflix with the dog. "Okay. Thank you for including me."

"See you there at six-thirty."

<hr />

ON THE WAY HOME FROM the nail salon, Lydia felt a magnetic force pulling the car in a different direction.

Go to Lilac Court.

Ever since telling Isabelle to put in a bid on the house, Lydia had been second-guessing her own decision. Maybe she had been too hasty. Maybe she should look around more.

But she couldn't imagine calling Isabelle to say she'd changed her mind. She'd look crazy, indecisive.

All she needed to do was see the house again and remind herself why she loved it. Lydia made a U-turn in a bank parking lot and headed toward Burleith.

Her confidence grew as she passed the sign welcoming her to Palmyrton's friendliest neighborhood. Someone she didn't know waved to her as she turned onto Lilac Court.

Lydia waved back.

Yes, this was the place for her.

Then she pulled up in front of Number 43.

A crack spanned one pane of the bay window. The chain of the porch swing had leaked rust onto the wood. The shutters on the second floor had given up their struggle with the forces of gravity. A tree next to the driveway stood naked of foliage, ready to crush the house in the next summer thunderstorm.

Lydia's hands clenched the steering wheel. Had the house looked like this on the day she had first seen it? It must have.

Lydia closed her eyes and took a cleansing breath. The inside, she reminded herself. The inside had captivated her. She could easily have these exterior flaws fixed.

Isabelle's For Sale sign had an "under contract" addendum slapped over it. But Isabelle said Lydia could still get out of the deal if the walk-through revealed extensive problems. In the meantime, they would continue to show the house to other buyers.

Lydia got out of the car and walked onto the front porch. The closed curtains were still on the windows, so she couldn't see inside the house. But she could sit on the swing.

It creaked under her weight, but it had a nice, gentle sway. Lydia looked out at the view. The neighbors on either side had bright pots of flowers and cheery borders. She would plant some, too. In the distance, the volunteers at the community garden moved among the rows of vegetables.

Lydia's tension ebbed away with each back-and-forth of the swing.

It would be okay. She could fix the problems. The house was right for her.

On her way back to the car, Lydia smiled at the For Sale sign. Contract pending, baby; remember that.

Chapter 19

On her second day of teaching, as Lydia strolled down the hall toward the adjunct office, the sound of a piano stopped her in her tracks.

She followed the sound to a half-open door marked Rehearsal Studio One. A man at the piano threw himself into the last notes of Gershwin's "Rhapsody in Blue," oblivious to her presence. When he finished, she couldn't help but clap.

He looked up, surprised. "Was I pounding away with the door open? I hope I didn't disturb a class you were teaching."

"Not at all. I stopped to listen because I used to play that piece years ago, but now I'm too out of shape to even attempt it."

"Take some classes." He rested his hands on the keys and smiled at her. "I'm Conrad McPartland. I teach keyboard and percussion here. And you are?"

Lydia introduced herself. "I'm just an adjunct. This is my first semester teaching here."

"Never say 'just', Lydia. The college would be lost without adjuncts like you."

Since Conrad seemed so friendly, Lydia stepped further into the practice room. Piano lessons. That was a good thought. She had taken lessons for twelve years as a kid, but had fallen away from playing in college and grad school. "Can you recommend someone who's good at teaching rusty adults?"

Conrad patted the bench beside himself. "Let's see what you've got."

With trembling fingers, Lydia began to play "One Fine Day" the only piece she could recall from memory. Her fingers felt stiff and clumsy on the keys. She played a few measures and stopped. Hung her head.

"Oh, God—I sound like a Clydesdale clomping on the keyboard."

Conrad patted her shoulder. "Don't be nervous. It's the students who are Liberace in their own minds that are impossible to teach."

Lydia took a deep breath, flexed her fingers, and began again. This time, she played fairly well until she got to the refrain. "Oh, I forget how the next part goes."

Conrad began to sing in a rich baritone. The song came back to her, and Lydia began to play and to sing along. She played the second verse and they sang together, harmonizing on the refrain. At the end, Conrad pounded out a finale at the bass end of the keyboard.

Lydia leaned back and laughed. "Oh, my gosh—that was fun!"

"As music should be. Next semester, you must audit one of my classes." Conrad beamed at her. "I'd put you in advanced intermediate. And you should take a voice class, too. You've got a lovely soprano."

For the second time in two days, Lydia felt the stone in her gut shift. "Thank you, Conrad. I'm going to do that."

Lydia entered her classroom feeling more confident than she had on her first day. The combination of Conrad's encouragement and Jim's dog training tips made a difference in her bearing, and the students seemed to sense it. They paid closer attention, participated more. She left campus feeling like she'd actually done some good.

At home, the encounter with Conrad inspired Lydia to practice the piano. After feeding Alfie—setting down and taking away his dish twice without incident—she headed into the living room.

The Steinway awaited her like Queen Elizabeth's royal carriage. She remembered the first day she saw it.

Then

"I'm home!" Lydia called out to Charles as she entered the house through the kitchen on a Thursday night. It was their first anniversary and they were supposed to be going out to dinner. "Sorry I'm late—my boss pulled me into a last minute-meeting that wasn't even important. I couldn't get him to stop talking."

"No worries." Charles kissed her. "Come here," he pulled her toward the front of the house. "A package was just delivered for you, and I'm not sure what to do with it."

"A package? I don't remember ordering anything."

She followed him into the foyer, which was empty. "I put it in here." Charles pointed toward the living room.

They hardly ever used the living room. Why would he put a package in there?

Lydia walked into the room and stopped short at the sight of a Steinway baby grand piano, its gleaming black surface reflecting the soft glow of the room's lamps. Her eyes widened as if a space ship had landed in their home.

She whirled to see Charles beaming with delight.

"Where—?...How—?"

"Happy anniversary," Charles said. *"You told me you missed playing the piano. I thought you might like this."*

"Like it! It's magnificent!" Lydia didn't know what to do first—kiss Charles or play the piano. She flung her arms around him, and he laughed and urged her to play.

She sat down and played a few hesitant chords. The instrument's astonishing tone rang through the room. Charles watched her as she played. *"Is it in tune? The tuner just left, but he said he'd come back if you weren't satisfied."*

Lydia looked up. *"You planned this. You had my boss keep me after work so the piano could be delivered."*

Charles rocked back on his heels, delighted with how well his subterfuge had worked. *"I wanted you to be totally surprised."*

Her eyes welled with tears. *"This is the best present I've ever gotten."*

Lydia played the Steinway every day to make sure her husband knew how much she appreciated this thoughtful and generous gift. She practiced for an hour after work, soon realizing that her teachers had been correct to make her play those dreaded scales and warm-up exercises before launching into sonatas. Naturally, she made mistakes and went back over certain passages in Mozart and Chopin, playing them over and over again. The magnificent tone of the Steinway reverberated through the house.

Until the day Charles had closed the living room door sharply as she worked out the trills in a Chopin Nocturne.

She ran upstairs to check on him. *"Are you okay? Am I disturbing you?"*

Charles massaged his temples. "I just have a headache. And that piece is so frenetic. Maybe you could play something more soothing....that you know a little better."

Lydia learned early in their courtship that Charles wasn't a classical music fan. And, of course, listening to the same five measures of Chopin played over and over wasn't likely to win converts. So after that, she saved Mozart and Chopin for summer Sunday mornings when Charles played golf. And when Charles was home, she limited herself to Billy Joel and Elton John tunes.

Now, Lydia lifted the seat of her piano bench and searched through the selection of sheet music stored there, finding the Chopin buried beneath "Candle in the Wind" and "Piano Man." Twenty minutes of warm-ups helped the flexibility in her fingers. Then she plowed through the Chopin, measure by mistake-filled measure.

And when she was done, she started again at the beginning.

Just as she set a Mozart piece on the rack, her phone rang.

Mitchell Felson. What could he want? She had a missed call from him earlier in the day when she had been teaching, but he hadn't left a message. Whatever it was, it could wait. She was in the mood to play piano, not discuss the allocation of her investments between stocks and bonds.

Lydia started in on the Overture to the *Magic Flute*. Her fingers felt stiff and clumsy on this more challenging piece, like she was striking each key with a rubbery sausage. But the longer she played, the easier it became. She hit fewer wrong notes; she began to feel the rhythm.

Alfie sat quietly beside the piano, watching her.

"You like classical music, don't you?"

Alfie stretched out and laid his head on his paws.

Lydia finished the overture and moved back to Chopin.

Alfie lifted his head and pricked his ears.

Lydia concentrated on hitting all the sixteenth notes in a tricky passage.

Alfie leapt up and barked.

Lydia paused, but could still hear music.

The doorbell's Westminster chimes. Alfie tore to the front door, barking madly. Lydia followed the dog, expecting to find the box of indestructible chew toys she'd ordered from Amazon. She remembered Jim's admonition to make Alfie work for all his rewards. She gave him the sit/stay command at the door.

Remarkably, Alfie complied.

Lydia opened the door a crack, not confident that Alfie wouldn't dash out.

Mitchell Felson stood on her doorstep.

Lydia made no move to welcome the financial advisor into her home. She couldn't believe he was making a house call just because she'd failed to return his two phone calls. "Mitchell. What a surprise." Alfie growled softly behind her.

Mitchell straightened his already straight tie, then pointed over his shoulder to the sign in the lawn. "I see you've got Isabelle Trent selling the house. Why didn't you discuss this with me?"

That's why he'd been calling her? What did selling the house have to do with investments? "There's nothing to discuss. This house is too big for me. Isabelle's the best Realtor in town."

"Yes, but this isn't the ideal time to sell. And what do you intend to buy? There's a lot to—"

Lydia felt the joy of her piano practice dribble away. "Are you telling me I need your *permission* to move?"

"Now, now—don't get so prickly. Of course, you're free to move. I just don't want you to make a hasty decision you'll later regret."

A power-walking neighbor stared at them with clear curiosity as they stood talking through the half-open door. Reluctantly, Lydia waved Mitchell into the house, holding Alfie by the collar.

He looked at the dog with surprised distaste. "You're still in a vulnerable emotional state. Charles has only been gone six weeks," Mitchell continued, heading for the living room as if the house belonged to him.

"I've never been more sure of a decision." The words sprang from her lips although she'd been agonizing over Lilac Court for days. Lydia followed Mitchell, releasing the dog, who bounded ahead and leaped onto the sofa. After Mitchell's arrival, Lydia was in no mood for continued enforcement of dog training rules.

Lydia sat beside Alfie and glared at her unwanted guest, who perched on the edge of the opposite love seat. "I'm rattling around in this pile like a marble in a refrigerator box. I've never liked this neighborhood. I've lived here seventeen years and only know two of the neighbors, and only one of them is nice."

"You've got lots of privacy." Mitchell nodded approvingly at the draped windows.

"Privacy for what? I don't do anything that couldn't be done in the middle of Palmyrton Square."

At the mention of the square, Mitchell's face lit up like a cartoon character with a bulb over his head. "The real estate market's a little sluggish now. You don't need to be in a rush to sell. Why not rent for a while—one of those new luxury apartments on the square?"

"The dog wouldn't be happy there. I promised the shelter he'd have a yard."

Mitchell glanced at Alfie and reflexively brushed imagined fur from his suit sleeve. "That's hardly legally binding."

"It's morally binding." Not that Mitchell would care about a moral commitment to a dog.

Mitchell paced around the room, Lydia presumed because he wanted to conceal his eye-roll. "All right—let's say you sold this house. Where do you want to move?"

Lydia braced herself for an explosion. "I've already made an offer on a house in Burleith. Three bedrooms with a small backyard for Alfie."

Mitchell spun around, his eyes wide, his shoulders hunched. If he had a tail, he could star in a YouTube cat video. "Burleith? Why in God's name would you want to live *there*?"

"It's not the South Bronx, Mitchell." Up until this moment, Lydia had been suffering recurring bouts of anxiety about her impulsive offer on the house on Lilac Court. But Mitchell's contempt for the neighborhood solidified her resolve. If this constipated number-cruncher hated it, she was sure to love it. Of course, she couldn't let on what had drawn her to the house—the promise of the block party and the Halloween parade, the hollyhocks leaning over the fence, the porch swing, the organic vegetable garden in the empty lot. He'd petition the courts to become her guardian if she told him that.

But Lydia had once advertised Segway tours to AARP members. She knew how to spin.

"The house is a manageable size in a neighborhood with good community cohesiveness close to shopping and restaurants. You know, Mitchell, these huge houses on the outskirts aren't in demand by Millennials." Lydia waved in the direction of her two-story foyer. "It's best for me to unload it now and move to a gentrifying neighborhood."

"Gentrifying!" Mitchell spluttered. "Those old houses are falling apart. They're money pits."

"One has to be ahead of the market to profit in real estate, Mitchell. Surely, you know that. I suppose you would've advised against buying in Jersey City ten years ago."

"Entirely different scenario." Mitchell put his hands on his scrawny hips. "Stop and think, Lydia. You can't be happy in a dinky little house in Burleith. You're used to the very best." He gestured to the luxuries of Lydia's living room. "There's no need to downsize *that* dramatically. I can get you out of the contract on the walk-through." Mitchell pulled out his phone, ready to call Isabelle. "A house that old is bound to have problems we can object to."

"I already had the walk-through," Lydia lied. "There were no big issues." To end this debate, she fell back on an old advertising technique. She'd learned if she gave a client unlimited options, he'd nit-pick and agonize endlessly. If she offered him only one choice, he'd automatically reject it. The winning approach was to offer two safe choices to give the impression the client was in control. "I made a cash offer. Would you prefer I take the money from the Vanguard account or the Fidelity account?"

But Mitchell wasn't as easily manipulated as a marketing manager for a soap brand. "I can't allow you to go through with a real estate transaction that I know will be disadvantageous to your financial position."

Lydia felt a wave of heat rise up from her core. How dare Mitchell Felson treat her like she was an irresponsible child star who couldn't be trusted not to squander all her money! "The cost of the Burleith house is a drop in the bucket compared to my net worth. Why do you care?"

"I made a commitment to Charles to protect your assets." Mitchell folded his hands primly.

"He intended to protect me from swindlers peddling dodgy investment opportunities. He didn't give you power to control where I live."

Alfie stood up on the couch and barked sharply, echoing Lydia's increasingly agitated tone.

"You need a few days to think this over." Mitchell spoke in the voice of a nanny well-versed in dealing with spoiled children. "We'll review your options next week."

An unfamiliar fury surged through Lydia's veins. Her life had unfolded so smoothly up to now, she hardly knew how to respond to Mitchell's smug finality in thwarting her wishes. Her eyes narrowed. She wouldn't beg, that's for sure.

She'd find a way to put Mitchell in his place now, or she'd be fighting him the rest of her life.

"You'd better leave now." Through sheer force of will, Lydia kept the tremble out of her voice.

As Mitchell headed for the front door, Alfie bounded after him and nipped at his heels. The financial advisor jumped and scampered. "You can't even fit your piano into a house in Burleith!" he called over his shoulder.

Lydia locked the door behind him and gave Alfie a treat.

Chapter 20

Lydia sat in the family room with a glass of wine, Alfie curled beside her.

Mitchell Felson was just like the dog, only not anywhere near as cute. If she didn't show leadership, she'd be cowering in his presence for the rest of her life. And she couldn't send Mitchell back to the pound the way Alfie's first owners had.

She reached out to stroke the sleeping dog's back, and Alfie instantly jolted awake with a little growl. "Sorry. Everything's okay."

Alfie rested his head on his paws and looked up at her through his doggy eyebrows.

"I bet you always had to watch your back when you were down in South Carolina. That's why you're so defensive." Lydia sipped some wine and kept talking aloud to the dog. "I wonder what's motivating Mitchell's behavior? Do you really think he's just looking after my investments?" Alfie groaned. "Or is there some other reason he's so determined to stop me from buying Lilac Court?"

Lydia felt her throat tighten. The bigger question was why Charles had felt it necessary to set up all these controls to take effect after his death. Why had they never even talked about what would happen when Charles died?

She knew why *she'd* avoided the subject. It seemed gruesome to bring it up when he was most likely closer to the finish line than she.

But Charles was a lawyer. It was in his blood to plan for every eventuality. If he hadn't discussed his will with her, that decision had to have been intentional, not procrastinating over an unpleasant task.

Charles never procrastinated.

But parents didn't discuss their will with small children. Dependents.

Lydia's breathing became heavier as the truth dawned on her. Charles had considered her his dependent.

Not an equal partner.

How could she fight this battle when Mitchell was just a proxy for her true opponent?

Charles.

But Mitchell was here on earth, so she needed an ally who was also in the here and now and understood where Mitchell was coming from.

Tom Schilling.

He knew Mitchell as well as Charles. He and Madalyn were closer to her than anyone else in their circle. Tom would know how to handle this.

She didn't have his cell phone number but called the Schillings' landline.

Tom answered immediately. "Hi, Lydia. What's wrong?"

His voice was low, and she realized how late it was. Madalyn must be asleep. She apologized, but she had no intention of hanging up. The story about Mitchell poured out of her.

"Hmmm." Tom said. "That's Mitchell being Mitchell. You know he's got a Napoleon complex—a short man always trying to assert his influence."

Tom's sarcasm surprised Lydia. She'd assumed Tom could persuade Mitchell as a friend. But he seemed to feel as antagonistic towards Mitchell as she did.

"Don't worry—there's a way around this," Tom reassured her. "Let me think about it tonight. Meet me for lunch tomorrow at Hennessy's."

Lydia agreed and hung up. The unaccustomed anger had exhausted her, and she fell asleep promptly without dwelling on what Tom had said.

She awoke the next morning immediately thinking about Tom and Mitchell and Charles. Lying in bed before Alfie realized she was awake, Lydia reviewed what she knew about the friendship of the three men.

Tom and Charles had been friends the longest—undergraduate roommates at Princeton. Even though they were very different in temperament—Tom an extroverted risk-taker, Charles a careful planner—that freshman year bond had survived through the decades.

After graduation, Tom went to work for his family's struggling manufacturing business, turned it around, and sold it for a big profit. Then he'd gone on to make a fortune doing the same thing with other floundering companies. Charles, of course, had gone to Harvard Law and joined the leading firm in Palmyrton.

When had Mitchell come along? He hadn't been a guest at their small wedding. But she couldn't remember a time when Mitchell hadn't been in their circle. However, he seemed to float at the perimeter.

Tom was such an affable man—he genuinely liked everyone he met. But he seemed not to like Mitchell. Did Tom know the terms of Charles's will or the extent of her inheritance? If Charles hadn't told her how much money they had, would he have told Tom?

As Lydia took the time to analyze the situation, she realized that although Tom and Mitchell were often at the same big social events, they were rarely together at small dinner parties or intimate gatherings. Lydia and Charles had occasionally gone out to dinner with Mitchell and his wife, a meek woman with endless ailments, but Charles and Mitchell had a standing weekly squash game. That had to be where the two of them had hatched this plan to control Lydia's finances until the end of her days.

Lydia threw back the covers, waking Alfie. "Get up, sleepyhead. Breakfast and a walk, then I'm going out to line up my allies in our fight for a new house."

⸻⬤⸻

THERE WAS NO NEED TO look at the Hennessy's menu. Tom and Lydia both had it memorized.

Once the waiter disappeared with their order, Lydia swallowed a gulp of water and plunged in. "Tell me, Tom—did Charles ever discuss with you his concerns about dying before me and how I would...er...manage?"

"Naturally, he worried because he was so much older than you." Tom made a waffling gesture with his hand. "Charles was a lawyer, Lydia. His entire professional life revolved around anticipating worst case scenarios and minimizing risk. A man can't just turn that off when he leaves the office at night."

Lydia's eyes widened. "So he *did* tell you he intended to give Mitchell Felson control over my finances? Why didn't Charles tell me?"

"No, certainly not. Look, Lydia, over the years, I turned Charles on to various investment opportunities. Charles was more cautious than I am, and he used Mitchell to help him vet those opportunities. Mitchell thought he had a lot more influence over Charles than he actually did. Charles respected Mitchell's opinion, but in the end, Charles made his own decisions."

That sounded like the Charles she had known and loved: cautious but decisive. "That makes sense. But what made Charles think I needed Mitchell to look after me? Why would my husband think I'd run off the rails if I wasn't supervised?"

Tom spread butter over a roll as if he were performing brain surgery. Finally, he spoke. "Maybe Mitchell planted the idea in Charles's head that a wealthy widow would be the target of scammers."

"Then he put himself forward as the remedy to the problem," Lydia added.

Tom looked up from his meticulous buttering. "He earns a percentage-based fee for managing your assets. The more he controls, the more he earns."

Tom leaned across the table and lowered his voice. "Look, Mitchell's always been a self-important prick. Now that Charles is gone, he sees an opportunity to really assert himself with you. Make you dependent upon him."

"And earn more for himself in the process." Lydia paused while the waiter set down their food. "What can I do to put Mitchell in his place? Have you thought of anything?"

Tom sliced into his steak. "Do you have any money in your own name?

"I have a 401(k) account from my time at Imago. I certainly won't be needing that for my retirement. But it's not enough cash to buy the house outright." Lydia pushed at her salad. She had no appetite.

"Yes, but you can use it as the down payment and get a mortgage for the rest."

Lydia set down her fork. "A mortgage in my own name? I can do that?"

"Sure. Madalyn told me you have a job now." Tom bit into an ice cube in his Manhattan. "Obviously, your credit is good. Mitchell can't prevent you from applying for a mortgage you're eminently qualified for."

She did have a job. And credit cards in her own name that she'd paid off every month for eighteen years. The mortgage on the Palmer Ridge house had been based solely on Charles's income and credit because she'd still been a grad student when they bought it. And Charles had paid it off in ten years. Lydia felt foolish for not thinking about the process most people used to buy a house. "I've never applied for a mortgage. What do I do?"

"Leave it to me." Tom grinned. He seemed delighted to be helping her while blocking Mitchell. "I've got a mortgage broker who will get you the best rate."

"It seems crazy to take out a loan when I have plenty of money."

Tom patted her hand. "No one loans money to the poor, my dear. People with plenty of money are the banks' best customers." Tom flagged the waiter. "Two glasses of champagne. We're celebrating a new house!"

Chapter 21

L ydia spent the afternoon in consultation with Tom's mortgage broker. By the time she finished with the paperwork, she was very glad that she could end the day having drinks with the crew from Imago. She approached Tito's Taqueria at six-forty-five—late enough, she hoped, that she wouldn't be waiting for the others to arrive, but not so late that she'd be crashing a party already in full swing. She'd chosen to wear slim black slacks and the kind of fitted blouse she'd always worn to work since this was an after-work gathering. Lydia heaved a sigh of relief when she spotted Eleanor and two of the newest graphic artists standing around a high-top table in the corner of the bar.

"Lydia!" Eleanor waved. "Bennie, get this woman a margarita."

A few other people from Imago showed up as Bennie put a frosty, salt-rimmed glass in her hand. Lydia told everyone about adopting Alfie and showed his picture around, grateful to have something upbeat to talk about. Everyone oo-ed and ah-ed, passing her phone with Alfie's lop-eared face from hand to hand.

But soon the conversation turned to the week's projects. How Stephanie had screwed up the Pfizer pitch. How Palmer Community Bank couldn't decide on their logo revision and now all the printed materials would be a rush order. Commentary whizzed back and forth, and Lydia didn't have a word to add to the debate. She stood surrounded by people she had known well just a month ago. Now she felt like a tourist in an African marketplace where people bartered in scores of tribal languages.

The bar got louder and hotter. The combination of sweet and salt in the margarita made her empty stomach roll. She glanced at her watch. She'd only been here forty minutes. It was still too early to leave without provoking objections and pleas to stay.

And then Bryce Salazar showed up.

Lydia spotted his beaky profile and ludicrous hair bobbing through the crowd as he wove his way towards them. Why did that bun irritate her so much?

"Yo, Bryce!" Tyler the graphic artist fist-bumped Bryce as he entered their circle. "Cool the flow."

"Cool the flow."

"Cool the flow." Everyone dissolved in laughter

Cool the flow? Clearly, some inside joke.

Lydia plastered a weak smile on her face.

The minute Bryce appeared, the vibe in the group changed. People seemed to be vying for his attention. Sucking up. Even sensible Eleanor looked inordinately pleased when Bryce laughed at one of her quips about a client.

Lydia felt herself melting into the background. She was becoming invisible, a ghost of her former self. Coming here had been a mistake. Could she simply slip away? Leave without saying goodbye? Tempting, but certainly cowardly, especially since Eleanor had been so gracious to invite her.

Lydia edged toward Eleanor, hoping to whisper a farewell in her ear and escape. Her movement caught Bryce's eye, the way a hawk spots a mouse's slightest ripple through the grass.

"Lydia! I didn't notice you there." Bryce thrust one scrawny shoulder toward her; his eyes scanned her up and down. "You look like you're ready to red-pencil some copy."

Lydia felt heat rising to her cheeks. With one sentence, he'd managed to insult both her conservative appearance and her reputation as a stickler for grammatically correct copy. Was that her legacy at Imago? Would she go down in corporate history as the woman in Eileen Fisher slacks who never let anyone use they as a singular pronoun?

A snappy comeback eluded her. No doubt she'd think of something in the middle of the night. "I'll leave that to you." Lydia raised her hand in farewell. "It was great seeing you all. Good luck with the new accounts."

Lydia pushed through the crowd in the bar. She hadn't felt such a hot mash of rage and shame since Wendy Friedland had driven her away from the cool kids' table in the junior high cafeteria for wearing a Miami Vice t-shirt to school.

Lydia reached the cool air of the sidewalk and took a steadying breath. Why was she letting Bryce Salazar bug her so much? Sure, he was a little snarky, but that wasn't a quality that usually bothered her.

It wasn't his fault that he'd been hired to replace her.

She had quit.

Because Charles had wanted her to.

And she hadn't resisted.

But she should have.

Was that Bryce's fault?

She should be mad at herself, not her millennial replacement.

Lydia walked toward her car, clutching her keys so tightly they dug into her hand. People surged past her—some laughing, some scowling, but all walking with purpose in their strides.

Imago was her past.

She had to find a way to build a new future.

Chapter 22

A few days later when the broker called to tell her she'd got the mortgage, Lydia was as thrilled as when a short story she'd written in college was accepted for publication in an obscure literary journal.

Someone in authority had bestowed validation of her worth.

Needing to share the news, she called Madalyn Schilling. "Guess what? I got my mortgage! Tell Tom I really appreciate his help."

Madalyn shouted the news to her husband, and Lydia could hear a loud, victorious whistle through the phone line.

"How's your new job?" Madalyn asked after they exhausted the mortgage topic.

"It's great. I like my students and my new colleagues." Lydia paused.

"....but?"

"No but. Well, it's just....I only teach two days a week. The job doesn't keep me as busy as my job at Imago did." Lydia paced around her bedroom as she talked. "Oh, but here's some news—I've started studying piano again."

"Wonderful." Madalyn sounded like the encouraging mom that she was. "Would you be interested in another opportunity?"

"Another job? You're like my personal Linked In!"

"Not a job, a volunteer opportunity," Madalyn said. "I know you don't want to do the society fundraiser stuff, but this is an organization that coaches low income kids in getting their college applications together. They have a volunteer training session in November, and I'm going. Do you want to join me?"

"Sure—that sounds interesting." Madalyn gave her the details and Lydia marked her calendar. Meanwhile, she could hear Tom saying something in the background.

"Tom says you'd better be prepared for a call from Mitchell, " Madalyn reported. "He might've gotten notifications on the requests for your credit rating."

Lydia scowled and thanked her friend for the warning. And no sooner had she hung up, than her phone rang again.

Mitchell's office.

Lydia answered suspiciously. A woman's voice replied—Mitchell's secretary. "Mr. Felson would like to see you. Is tomorrow at two convenient?"

What was this—a command performance? "No, I'm teaching then."

"Wednesday. Morning or afternoon?" The secretary was pleasant but persistent. Lydia realized that passive/aggressive resistance was pointless. She needed to confront Mitchell head on. "Three on Wednesday. Tell him I look forward to speaking with him."

<hr />

LYDIA SPENT THE NEXT two days in alternating cycles of confidence and anxiety. On one hand, Surindra and some of her other students were making slow but steady progress in their writing. But five students had totally bombed a grammar exam required by the English Department.

"I feel like I let them down," Lydia said to Roz. "Especially poor Jackie. She wants to be a nurse. She tries so hard I can practically see steam coming out of her ears when she's working on the grammar exercises. But she got a forty-five on the test. I was stunned."

Roz offered a sad half-smile. "You're a teacher, Lydia, not a magician. If Jackie can't pass a punctuation test, how can she possibly pass the organic chemistry class required for nursing? It's better that she learn now that her life plan is not realistic."

"She's only nineteen," Lydia objected. "That's too young to give up on her dreams."

"It's not giving up; it's just redirecting. We all have to do it eventually." Roz turned back to grading papers.

Redirecting.

Lydia supposed that's what she was doing. And Mitchell was her version of organic chemistry. Jackie might not be able to clear that hurdle, but Lydia was determined to clear hers.

When Lydia arrived at Mitchell's office on Wednesday, the financial advisor sat behind his large desk looking like a little kid playing office. Why should she be intimidated by such a twerp?

"I got a notice from the bank." He put on his fiercest face. "You have *incurred debt* to buy this house."

Mitchell said "incurred debt" with the same tone of shock and horror that a doctor might use to say "contracted Ebola."

"I used my own resources to buy the home I want."

Mitchell pounded his fist on a stack of spreadsheets. "Ridiculous! It makes no sense for you to borrow money."

"I agree. But what really makes no sense is that a forty-five year old woman should have to ask permission to get access to her inheritance like a ten-year-old asks for an advance on her allowance."

Mitchell pointed at her with his pen. "Tom Schilling put you up to this, didn't he?"

How would Mitchell know that Tom helped her get the mortgage? Just a lucky guess? "No one put me up to anything. I'm simply conducting my business like the adult that I am. I'm selling the house in Palmer Ridge and buying the house in Lilac Court. I'll be using some cash to pay for necessary home improvements...unless you want me to take out a home equity loan."

Mitchell's face turned purple. "Don't... of course not—"

Lydia cut him off in mid-sputter. "You and I will review my investment portfolio twice a year, Mitchell. I trust that you'll make solid, safe investments. I expect you to trust me not to send money to lonely Russian bachelors or make donations to creepy cults. I do not expect you to be monitoring my day-to-day expenditures. I know that's not what Charles intended your role to be."

Mitchell drew himself up to his full height. "Charles intended that I safeguard his assets."

"Protect them from me? His sole heir?" Lydia leaned across the desk and forced Mitchell to look her in the eye. "If you keep this up, I'll hire a lawyer to look into whether you pressured Charles into putting you in this role, so you could use it for your own gain."

Mitchell's eyes bulged. "That's outrageous! A totally groundless accusation."

"Maybe. Maybe not. You and I both know how lawsuits work, Mitchell. If I bring the suit, you'll have no choice but to defend yourself. It could drag on for years. Win or lose, your reputation will take a beating."

Lydia rose to leave. "We can cooperate. Or we can do battle, head to head. Think about it."

Mitchell shouted after her as she walked toward the door. "I know Tom Schilling is behind this. You watch out for him, Lydia. You don't realize what a shark he is."

Chapter 23

In the days after winning her battle with Mitchell, Lydia's elation gradually waned. She was still glad she'd put him in his place, but doubts about Tom and Mitchell's rivalry plagued her. Clearly, something was going on there that she didn't fully understand.

Her gut instinct inclined toward Tom—enthusiastic, affable, funny Tom.

But Charles himself had chosen Mitchell to rein in Tom's extremes.

What troubled her was the idea that Charles had apparently felt she was prone to extremes that needed reining in.

But she had never been extravagant. Indeed, Charles was the one who bought expensive gifts, who urged her to shop at upscale stores.

Yet Lydia knew Charles would not approve of Lilac Court.

Was she making a mistake buying this house? Was she moving forward simply because reneging on the deal would be a point in Mitchell's column?

The day of the walk-through, Lydia arrived at Lilac Court early and stared at the house as she waited for Isabelle. Again, her stomach churned at the shabbiness of the place. Today she noticed a woodpecker pounding a hole in one of the porch columns.

She squeezed her eyes shut. Once Isabelle arrived and they got inside, everything would be fine.

As if summoned by Lydia's worries, Isabelle rolled up in her sleek cream Mercedes. She strode toward Lydia waving cheerily until a loose brick in the sidewalk tripped her. Isabelle arrived at Lydia's side frowning at a scuff on her formerly flawless pumps. "Hello, dear. Here comes our inspector. Let's do this."

The flowered wallpaper assaulted Lydia as soon as they walked into the foyer. What were those vivid orange and royal rectangles interrupting the sweep of peach and sky blue? Oh, the outlines of the paintings that had once hung there. The wallpaper had once been even more garish than it was now.

Lydia sensed rather than saw Isabelle's disapproval. The inspector, on the other hand, made no effort to conceal his dismay. "Bathroom upstairs must be leaking," he said, pointing to a crack in the shape of the Rio Grande bisecting the hall ceiling. Eager to escape both of them, Lydia ducked into the dining room she had found so welcoming. Circular water stains on the woodwork of the bay window were all that remained of the festive jungle of potted plants that had once enlivened the space. Scratches on the hardwood floor illustrated the path into the kitchen. She kept walking.

Stripped of the arty pottery and glass, the persimmon kitchen looked like an exhausted old movie star wearing garish lipstick and not much else.

What had happened to the charming, festive little house she'd fallen in love with? It was as if she'd picked up a handsome stranger in a bar and awakened in the morning next to a snoring, farting old lecher.

Throughout Lydia's explorations, Isabelle and the home inspector kept up a steady litany of mechanical problems. Electrical service...hot water heater...sagging ceiling—Lydia tuned in to snippets of the conversation in the way of a plane passenger overhearing snatches of dialogue from the row behind.

Isabelle dabbed her forehead with a tissue. Lydia realized she too was sweating—not just dewy, but drenched. "Can't we turn on the AC while we do the walk-through?"

Isabelle and the inspector turned and stared at her. "The house doesn't have central air, Lydia. Surely you realized that?"

Lydia's head snapped from left to right, searching for cooling vents. "But it wasn't stifling in here the day of the sale."

"Window units," Isabelle snapped. "Audrey must have sold them all."

A wave of despair overtook Lydia. How had she allowed her romantic dream of a little house with character to overwhelm her fundamental common sense? Buying this house was the equivalent of cramming six friends into a Ft. Lauderdale Motel 6 during spring break—fun when you were twenty, a nightmare when you were forty.

A sharp rapping at the front door distracted them. Before anyone could move to answer it, the door opened and a mid-thirty-ish man popped his head in. He flushed when he saw them. "I'm sorry. I saw the cars outside, and I thought Mrs. Maguire might be here. I wanted to say good-bye."

"Doing a walk-through," the inspector said gruffly.

But Isabelle, always alert to the possibility of a new customer, ushered the man in. "Aren't you sweet! And do you live here in the neighborhood?"

"I grew up across the street in Number 38. This is such a great neighborhood that my wife and I recently moved back—bought a place over on Dogwood Terrace." He gazed around the entrance hall. "Lotta good times in this house. Graduation parties...Fourth of July picnics...and Tony Maguire and I had a rock band that practiced in the garage." He chuckled. "Mostly we just smoked weed and pounded on our drums, but Mrs. M never minded."

Lydia saw their visitor sizing the three of them up: the inspector with his clipboard, Isabelle with her stilettos. Ultimately, he focused on Lydia. "So, you're buying the house?"

"Well...."

"You're so lucky. I would have snapped this house up if it had been on the market when we were looking." He caressed the wood of the newel post. "Look at the Craftsman artistry. And of course you've seen the tiles around the living room fireplace. The house I bought doesn't have any of those architectural details. Not to mention, this house comes with all the great Maguire karma!" He grabbed Lydia's hand and pumped it. "Welcome to the neighborhood."

Her neighbor headed toward the door. "I'll see you at the block party."

Lydia waved good-bye. "Definitely. See you there."

Chapter 24

After the roller coaster ride of the walk-through, Lydia felt discombobulated back in the big house in Palmer Ridge. She tried to focus on making a to-do list of projects for Lilac Court, but found herself gazing into space like one of her students during a lesson on semicolons. When her phone rang, she pounced on it.

The screen flashed a name: Roz Schmidt.

Her heart gave a silly flutter as she answered.

"Hi, Roz—what's up?"

"Wanna go to Blue Monday tonight? It's open mic night. Always a hoot."

"What's Blue Monday?"

"You live in Palmyrton and you've never been to Blue Monday?" Roz sounded as incredulous as a student learning a paper would be due after a holiday weekend. "The place is a legend."

"Do you mean that bar near the railroad tracks that's painted Smurf blue? I've only ever seen it from the train window."

"Oh Lydia, Lydia—what am I going to do with you? You've lived such a sheltered life. Meet me there tonight at 9 o'clock. And take an Uber. You're going to have too much fun to drive home."

WHAT DID ONE WEAR TO open mic night at a bar that was literally on the wrong side of the tracks? Lydia stood in her closet agonizing over her wardrobe selection more than she did when choosing a dress for the annual partners dinner. Just as she had never wanted to embarrass Charles by her appearance, she didn't want to humiliate Roz by showing up overdressed. Of course, she owned jeans and boots. But the jeans weren't Levi's. And the boots had a heel. And her blouses had all been pressed at the dry cleaner. Lydia studied herself in the full-length mirror. She looked too dressed up, too pulled together. She'd spent her life striving for this polished look. How could she dial it back?

She got down on her knees and dug through shoe boxes at the back of the closet that she hadn't touched in months. There she found a pair of ankle boots with a leather fringe at the heel that had seemed cute at the store but over-the-top when she got them home. She'd written them off as a mistake, but now she was glad she'd never returned them.

They *were* cute.

She just had never had a place to wear them to before.

Lydia whipped through her tops until she found a soft, over-sized shirt that covered the designer logo on her ass. Replaced her gold necklace with the beads a girl in the Imago art department had given her in last year's Secret Santa. Took the clip out of her hair.

Lydia smiled.

The woman in the mirror smiled back. She looked relaxed and maybe even a little bit funky and ready to have some fun.

After she left the house, Lydia watched her Uber driver's GPS as it crawled closer to Blue Monday. The bar was on a dead-end street that she'd certainly never driven down in twenty years of living in Palmyrton.

She heard the place before she saw it. A loud bass beat made the car window vibrate. Then the car went around a bend in the road, and its headlights ignited a big blue explosion. The rambling, two story frame building looked like it had been assembled by kids with their first set of Legos .

Or a very stoned architect.

"Looks like a good night at the Monday," the Uber driver commented as he dropped her in the packed parking lot.

Lydia wondered how she'd find Roz. *I'm here*, she texted. *I'm at the bar. Right side. Under the Horny Toad craft beer sign*.

Lydia stood aside as two burly firemen exited the bar on a wave of music and laughter. *You're not at Hennessey's anymore.* She pushed through the crowd of drinkers, keeping her eye on the giant hanging toad. Roz had snared a bar stool and somehow managed to save the one next to her for Lydia.

Roz slid a cocktail down the bar. "It's a paloma. I ordered one for you, but if you don't like it, I'll drink it."

Lydia sipped the pale pink concoction of tequila and grapefruit juice. Sweet and tart and smooth. "Refreshing. I'll buy the next round." She looked around. Booths lined the walls, and a small stage with a lonely microphone illuminated by a single spotlight stood at the end of the bar. The crowd surged around her—a mix of kids in their twenties and old hippies and broad-shouldered men with very short hair.

The bartender set a basket of fresh popcorn down in front of them. "Extra salt, no butter, just for you, Roz."

"You know the bartender? How often do you come here?"

"I used to date a firefighter, back in the day. This place is a hangout for our brave men and women in blue. I consider myself a similarly heroic civil servant for my efforts to get the youth of Palmer County to use pronouns correctly."

That explained the heavy dose of men with necks as thick as her thigh.

Suddenly the juke-box went silent in the middle of "Bed Medicine," and the bartender banged on a soup pot with a big metal spoon. "Attention, all you patrons of the arts. Open mic night is about to begin. Give it up for Jeff Wing."

A kid with long stringy hair and an acoustic guitar came onto the tiny stage.

"Blue Monday doesn't allow amps and long equipment set ups. You gotta come ready to play so the acts keep moving along," Roz explained.

The kid strummed a few chords, turned a peg to tune, and glanced nervously into the crowd. "Uhm, this is a little tune I wrote, kinda inspired by Kurt."

"Who's Kurt?" Lydia whispered to Roz.

"Cobain. Nirvana, remember?"

"Right. Of course."

The kid on stage began to yowl a mournful, unintelligible song lacking any discernable melody. Lydia didn't think it sounded anything like "Heart-Shaped Box," the only Nirvana song she could pull from her memory.

She wasn't the only one. "The crowd is booing him? That's so mean!"

"He sucked." Roz popped a handful of popcorn in her mouth.

"Well, yeah. But he had the courage to get up there. People could at least be polite."

"That would only encourage him to believe he has talent, which he clearly does not." Roz turned away from Lydia and shouted at the stage. "Bring on the next victim. The crowd is hungry for blood."

"Next. Next. Next." The room erupted in a chant.

Someone handed the mournful guitarist a beer, and his buddies all clapped him on the back. He didn't seem any worse for his ordeal. Lydia began to enter into the spirit of Blue Monday.

The bartender passed by, and Lydia ordered another round of palomas before a very pretty young woman with a pitch pipe took the stage. She tossed her long blond hair, which earned her applause from the men in the room before she even began to sing.

Roz rolled her eyes. "Oh, brother."

The girl found middle C and began a passable imitation of Adele's "Chasing Pavements".

"Derivative!" a big, chesty red-head in a cop's uniform shouted at the end of the song, overwhelming the tepid applause offered by the drunk guys in the other corner.

The acts continued.

"Are they getting better, or am I just getting drunker?" Lydia asked.

"Both. Acts that have been popular in the past get to perform later in the line-up."

Next, a tall, handsome man walked out carrying a portable keyboard. The crowd erupted in cheers.

"So, they like him, eh?"

"Conrad McPartland. He's a professional. Only plays here 'cause he likes the vibe."

Lydia squinted at the stage. "Hey, I know him. He teaches—"

"Yep. At Palmer Community. When did you meet him?"

"I talked to him about auditing a piano class next semester. He was so nice and encouraging."

"You play piano?" Roz tilted her head in interest.

"I dabble. I've been practicing more lately."

Conrad chatted with the crowd as he continued to set up. "It's great to see so many friends here tonight."

Roz put two fingers in her mouth and let out a piercing whistle. Conrad laughed and waved, then raised his eyebrows and waved harder when he caught sight of Lydia next to Roz.

"He's cute," Lydia said. "Is he—"

"Creative, funny, nice, and knows how to match a tie to a shirt. Yeah, he's gay."

Lydia laughed. "That's okay—I'm not in the market."

"Well, you should be. Guys in here have been checking you out all night."

Lydia drew back. "They have not!"

"You're not tuned into it. There was a guy across the bar staring at you for the longest time." Roz craned her neck. "I don't see him now."

"You're hallucinating."

No sooner were the words out of her mouth than the bartender set two drinks in front of them. "We didn't order those," Lydia protested.

"Sent by the guy in the green shirt," the bartender explained as he moved on to his next customer.

"Green shirt." Roz arched her eyebrows. "That's the guy who was staring at you."

Lydia wasn't sure how to process this. She hadn't been stared at in a bar since grad school. Was it flattering or creepy? She looked around for a guy in a green shirt, but the lights over the bar dimmed, and a spotlight illuminated Conrad on stage.

He played a few loud chords, and the crowd began to cheer. Then he broke into a full-throated rendition of "I Don't Like Mondays." The crowd joined him shouting "down, down, down" the last word of the song.

"Now, I need a helper for this next number. Someone to sing soprano to my bass." He played a few familiar measures on the keyboard. "And I know just the lady to help me out. Lydia, come on up here."

Lydia's head spun left to right. There must be some other Lydia in the bar. But no one got up. All eyes were on her. Roz pushed her off her bar stool. "You go, girl!"

"Lyd-ee-a, Lyd-ee-a!" the crowd chanted as Conrad continued playing a long, vampy intro to the song. The notes registered in her subconscious brain. It was "One Fine Day," the song they'd sung together in the practice studio. They had just been fooling around. How could Conrad possibly think she'd want to sing that song in front of hundreds of people?

"Go ahead." Roz gave a little shove in the small of Lydia's back. "You don't know anyone here but me and Conrad."

Lydia made eye contact with him on the stage, wide-eyed as a fawn separated from its mother by eight lanes of speeding traffic. But Conrad just smiled and held out his hand.

"Lyd-ee-a, Lyd-ee-a!"

As if she were hypnotized, Lydia moved toward him. Her feet felt loosely connected to her body, either from fear or drink. When she reached the stage, Conrad helped her up the two steps and pulled her into a hug. "You'll be fine," he whispered in her ear. "Just sing it the way we did at school. I wouldn't have called you up if I didn't think you could do it."

Lydia flashed on her own classroom, when she'd insisted that Drew answer the question instead of letting him off the hook.

Because she knew he could do it.

Shakily, she sat down beside Conrad at the piano. She kept her eyes focused on the keyboard to avoid looking at the crowd. Conrad began to sing, and Lydia chimed in on the refrain in the first verse.

He grinned at her. "Now harmonize on verse two."

And she did. Just as in the rehearsal studio, she let the music carry her and lost all her self-consciousness.

The crowd fell away. There was just her and Conrad and the piano.

By verse three, they were really belting it out.

When they finished, the last note dissolved in a second of silence.

Then the crowd erupted.

Lydia snapped out of her performance trance. She heard the applause, the cheers, Roz's obnoxious whistle.

And she laughed.

She'd done something crazy, and it was fun.

Lydia made her way back to Roz. As she wove through the crowd, her gaze connected with a guy on the other side of the bar.

A guy who was staring at her.

A younger guy.

A guy with a man bun.

Bryce Salazar.

Admiring or incredulous?

Chapter 25

Lydia woke to Alfie's hot dog breath on her face. Her stomach heaved. Her head throbbed. Her tongue stuck to the roof of her mouth.

Pushing the dog away, she stumbled into the bathroom and drank two glasses of water before even looking in the mirror.

Sweet Jesus!

Black rings of mascara circled her eyes. She'd slept in her shirt, which was so wrinkled and stained she might just throw it away rather than face the clicking tongue of Mr. Lu at the cleaners.

People had bought her congratulatory drinks after her performance. What had possessed her to drink them?

What had possessed her to sing in a bar?

Roz said she knew no one there.

Except Bryce Salazar.

Of all the damn people! He had probably texted everyone at Imago the moment he saw her. What if he'd taken a picture—a video!—of her singing?

Lydia felt the bathroom floor tip and sway and grabbed the edge of the sink. She was more than hungover; she was still drunk.

Ripping off her smelly clothes, Lydia took a long, hot shower while Alfie pawed pathetically at the glass. She longed to dive back into bed, but just as Alfie had given her a reason to get up in the morning, he now delivered an ultimatum on sleeping in: he wanted breakfast and a walk *pronto*.

Stumbling down to the kitchen, she started a pot of coffee and poured out Alfie's kibble before allowing herself to think. What had she done last night? What came after the song? Clearly, she'd had a lot to drink. She vaguely remembered talking to a group of people Roz seemed to know. Then there had been dancing when the jukebox came back on. Had she danced? If there was a God, she hadn't. She didn't even remember the ride home, only that Roz had ordered her an Uber when Lydia couldn't make her fingers work the apps on her phone.

Alfie scratched at the back door to remind her what she was supposed to do next. Lydia clipped on his leash and stepped outside, where the whine of the landscapers' leaf blower pierced her skull. Why didn't he just come and pound nails into her head?

Following behind Alfie's fluffy tail, Lydia resumed her self-flagellation.

The bartender said the man who sent them drinks wore a green shirt. Lydia wracked her brains trying to remember the color of Bryce's shirt. Had it been green? She'd been so stunned to see that beaky nose and stupid bun, she didn't bother looking further down his body. Had he been watching her all night? Had he sent her drinks to try to get her drunk?

Now she was getting paranoid.

Lydia pulled out her phone. Ten-thirty—was it too early to call Roz?

Maybe. But Roz had gotten her into this mess, so she deserved no mercy.

"What the fuh-"

"Wake up. It's me."

"I know. Who else would be up this early on Sunday morning except you and the freakin' Mormon Tabernacle Choir."

"I need to know what happened last night."

"You drank. You sang. We drank some more. We laughed. We left."

"I made a fool of myself!"

"You did not. You sang really well. That's why people were buying us drinks. First time I ever came home from Blue Monday with cash still in my pocket."

Lydia hardly found that reassuring. "What if I get fired from my job?"

"Why should you get fired from teaching at Palmer Community for singing with a tenured professor at Palmer Community? If Conrad can do it, so can you."

True. One fear absolved.

"What about the guy you saw staring at me? Did he have a man bun?"

"I can't remember his hair. I can't even remember the ride home. You couldn't finish all the drinks people bought you, so I had to help."

"Think, Roz! It's important. Picture him. Was he younger than me?"

"Mmmm. Maybe. Nah—I don't know."

"Was he staring at me like he couldn't believe his eyes? Like he could hardly wait to go start a social media flame war against me?"

"Lydia, you're over-reacting. So what if a guy from your former office saw you singing in a bar? Why would he care? Why do you care? You don't work there anymore."

"Yes, but—" But what? Why did she care about Bryce Salazar? She hadn't spoken to anyone from Imago since she met them for drinks at La Taqueria. That encounter had clarified that her colleagues and her clients were things of the past. She no longer had a professional image to maintain.

So maybe it wasn't Bryce Salazar's opinion she feared. Maybe she had violated a more ingrained principle. Charles hated a scene. Charles never drank more than two glasses of wine. She could see the thin press of his lips when Shelly Perrone got tipsy at the Fourth of July picnic. The way he drew down his brows when someone in a restaurant or on a plane disrupted his peace by talking too loudly. The time he flatly refused to wear a costume to a Halloween party.

Decorum.

Maintaining decorum meant a lot to Charles. So it had meant a lot to her.

"I just feel uncomfortable that I let myself get out of control," Lydia whispered into the phone.

Roz roared with laughter. "Oh my God, Lydia—if that was out of control, you've got a lot to learn. We had fun. No one got hurt. No one got arrested. Let it go."

Chapter 26

The days that had dragged interminably after Charles's death now sped by at breakneck speed. Her students faced their final exams. The closing on 43 Lilac Court went off without a hitch.

Lydia now owned two houses. She threw herself into planning the renovations that would make the new house a home.

Charles swore by a Ukrainian handyman named Viktor Zyma. Only Viktor was painstaking enough to suit Charles's high standards. Only Viktor could fix anything and everything without calling in unreliable subcontractors. Lydia had met Viktor several times over the years. He was a man of few words, who focused all his energy on his work. Surely, Viktor could rise to the challenge of renovating 43 Lilac Court. Lydia didn't have to search very long through Charles's meticulous records to find the man's phone number.

Lydia had told the story of her husband's untimely passing many times, but it never got any easier. Viktor was so shocked by the news he lapsed into a long stream of Ukrainian, which was either cursing or praying, she couldn't be sure which. Eventually, Lydia managed to explain the project: she had bought a smaller house and needed his help with extensive repairs.

A long silence descended during which Lydia could hear only heavy breathing. Then Viktor responded. "What about house you live in now?"

"It's too big. I'm selling it."

Viktor clicked his disapproval. "Is good house. Get your family to move in with you."

"I don't have any family in New Jersey."

Viktor muttered something which clearly expressed incredulity even to a non-speaker of Ukrainian. "When you have good, solid house, you should keep. Maybe rent out."

Lydia became briefly giddy at the prospect of renting her house to a huge extended family of Ukrainians and creating a Little Kiev in Palmer Ridge complete with grandmas in babushkas and boiling pots of cabbage soup. She came to her senses and got back on track with Viktor. "That's not an option. So, regarding the new house—do you have time to work on it?"

"Yes, yes—for you, always time. You meet me there tomorrow, and we will talk."

———◉———

WHEN LYDIA PULLED INTO the driveway of 43 Lilac Court, Viktor's unoccupied truck was already parked at the curb. Leaving Alfie in the car with the windows cracked, she found the contractor in the back yard, gazing at the porch.

"Hi, Viktor!" She strode up to him with her hand outstretched, but Viktor ignored the gesture. His forehead creased with concern. His pale green eyes squinted. "Porch no good. Has to come off. I build new one."

Well, hello to you, too. "Let's go in through the front door. There are more urgent priorities inside."

Viktor followed her silently as they circled back to the front of the house. Lydia filled the dead air with chatter about her plans to repaint, refinish the floors and redo the kitchen. They entered the foyer and Lydia pointed up. "The home inspector says that crack in the ceiling is caused by an old leak from the bathroom above, so maybe that should be your first proj—"

Viktor gasped and pushed past her, trotting quickly up the stairs. Lydia followed, talking to his back. "We'll need to strip this wallpaper, of course, and pull up the old carpet. I plan to have the floors refinished once you're done with all the repairs."

Lydia's final words were addressed to Viktor's butt, which pointed straight up in the hall bathroom, while his head twisted under the claw foot tub.

"*Ty nechysta sylo!*" His words echoed against the cast iron.

Lydia didn't know what that meant, but she was pretty sure it wasn't Ukrainian for "What a pretty old tub."

"Will the whole floor need to be pulled up to fix the leak? Because I like the old black and white tile, and the tub has such graceful lines."

Viktor clambered to his knees. "No good! All gotta go. I give you new." He pulled a pen knife from his pocket and jammed it into a crack in the floor tiles like he was slaying a vampire. "Whole floor rotten! You take bath in here, you end up downstairs."

She hadn't realized the leak was so dire. Lydia backed out of the bath as Viktor sprang to his feet and charged down the hall. He entered every room, shaking his head, taking notes, and keeping up a steady conversation with himself in Ukrainian. Sometimes his voice went up in a question, and he'd shake his head woefully as he provided his own answer. Lydia trailed behind him, totally superfluous. After he toured the house top to bottom, he put his hands on his hips and delivered his verdict. "You sell this place."

"Sell it? I just bought it!"

"House no good. You stay in nice house your husband bought."

Viktor didn't realize he'd just waved a red cape at a bull. But two could play that game. "Look, Viktor—I called you to give me an estimate on the work in this house because Charles had great respect for your abilities. But if these projects are too difficult for you, I can easily find someone else who's better prepared."

"Prepared? Viktor is prepared for anything!" He threw back his shoulders and thrust out his chest. "Is nobody else like Viktor."

The handyman poked his heart with his thumb. "I will fix house. I start tomorrow."

Then he got in his truck and roared away.

Once she was alone, Lydia got Alfie from the car and went out to her new backyard to explore. Charles had employed Espinoza Brothers Elite Landscaping to keep the lawn and shrubbery at Palmer Ridge perfectly trimmed and weed free. But as Lydia contemplated her postage-stamp sized yard, she wondered if the Espinozas' huge riding mower would even fit back here. Surely that behemoth would chew up the patch of weeds that passed for a lawn in two turns.

Lydia toured the yard examining the fence for breaks before she let Alfie off his leash. Although the pickets needed painting, the fence seemed sturdy enough to contain her dog, so she set him loose. Elated, Alfie ran laps around the yard while Lydia pulled up some of the largest weeds. Then he put his paws up on the gate that faced the back alley and started barking.

A little boy had been riding his bike, but now he stopped and stared into the yard with open curiosity.

"Hi, I'm Lydia." She brushed the dirt off her hands and crossed over to the gate.

"Are you going to live in Mrs. Maguire's house?" the kid asked.

"Yes. I won't be moving in right away, though. I'm having some repairs done."

"Dad!" the boy shouted. "That lady's here!"

A man appeared in the backyard across the alley. It was the guy Lydia had asked directions from on the day of the estate sale. So much had happened since then—it seemed like a lifetime ago.

He crossed the alley and leaned on the fence. Alfie licked his hands. "Hi, welcome to the neighborhood. I'm Aaron Morrow and this is Timmy."

Timmy had lost interest in Lydia and tugged on his father's sleeve. "Da-a-ad, when are we going?"

"The block party starts at noon, and Timmy can hardly wait," Aaron explained. He looked up at the cloudless blue sky. "What a perfect day we have! You're coming, right? It's a great way to meet all the neighbors."

"Oh, today—I, uhm, I hadn't realized it was so soon. And I have the dog with me...." Lydia had been charmed by the idea of a block party, but the reality seemed more intimidating. She'd never been good at going to parties where she knew no one, and the vision of wandering around alone and forlorn surrounded by people having fun with friends squashed her enthusiasm.

"You can bring the dog—everyone does."

Timmy tugged on his father's shirt more insistently. "When are we leaving for the party, Dad?"

"As soon as your sister wakes up from her nap." Aaron turned to Lydia. "We'll see you there."

Chapter 27

Lydia retreated to the persimmon kitchen. Between the jousting with Viktor and the prospect of attending the block party solo, the day had lost some of its luster.

The block party was exactly the kind of weekend afternoon activity she would have done with her friend Kathleen while Charles was off golfing. It seemed ludicrous now that Kathleen had been her only single woman friend. But couples socialized with other couples. She and Charles had been plenty busy going out to dinner or the theater or wine tastings with the Schillings and the Finns and the Morrones. Now Kathleen was in Pittsburgh preoccupied with her pregnancy and her upcoming wedding, and Lydia had no one to fill the void her old friend had left.

Lydia toyed with her phone.

Unless....

Would it be weird to invite Roz to a neighborhood block party? To invite her at the last minute as if she thought Roz had nothing better to do?

Lydia took a deep breath. That was the beauty of texting. She could issue the invitation without having to hear Roz stammering for an excuse not to go.

Hey, there's a block party today in the neighborhood around my new house. They have food trucks and silly games—I thought it might be fun. Any interest?

She hit send.

Before Roz could possibly reply, Lydia texted again.

I know it's last-minute. No worries if you don't want to come.

The three dots appeared, indicating Roz was typing a reply.

Lydia watched the pulsing circles as if waiting for a jury foreman to stand and deliver her verdict.

What time? I need to finish grading some papers before I can go anywhere.

Lydia flushed with pleasure. *It runs until nine. Come whenever you're ready. 43 Lilac Court.*

Lydia and Alfie were sitting on the front porch when Roz rolled up at four.

Roz trotted up the uneven walkway, waving cheerfully. "So this is your new house? Cute!"

Gratitude surged in Lydia's heart. Naturally, Roz would appreciate this house!

"Come in and see it. It needs too much work for me to move in yet, but the contractor is starting on Monday."

Roz gushed in all the appropriate places: fireplace, bay window, breakfast nook. If she noticed the sagging ceiling in the hall, she didn't mention it. Then they set off for the block party.

They watched Timmy Morrow win a goldfish at the ping-pong ball toss, and waved to the old ladies working at the bake sale. They played horseshoes and ring toss, and Lydia won a purple stuffed bunny which she unloaded on the first little kid she saw. Roz struck up conversations with everyone they encountered, while Lydia followed up by explaining she had just bought the old Maguire house.

"Oh, the Maguire house! Lots of good memories there!"

After the fourth response along those lines, Roz muttered in her ear. "Are you sure you didn't buy a crack-house?"

Suddenly, Alfie began pulling ferociously on his leash. Lydia yanked him back. "Alfie—stop! What's wrong with you?"

Then Lydia saw what Alfie did. Jim the dog trainer stood in front of the ice cream truck eating a Creamsicle with another guy. "Relax—we'll go see him. But be on your best behavior, please."

Jim smiled and waved when he saw Alfie heading his way. The humans shook hands all around and performed introductions. "What brings you here?" Lydia asked.

"I grew up near here," Jim waved in an easterly direction. "The Burleith Block Party was always a good time." Just then a roving photographer for PalmyrtonNow.com strolled by and lined them up for a picture.

After they chatted and moved on, Roz looked back over her shoulder. "That guy looks familiar."

"Jim?"

"No, his friend, Pete." Roz shrugged. "Probably seen him around town or on campus."

They left the block party with burritos and empanadas from the food truck and headed back to Lydia's house to eat.

Sitting at the worn table surrounded by the sagging kitchen cabinets, Lydia basked in a peaceful glow. "Thank you for coming today, Roz."

Roz had just bitten into a burrito and couldn't reply.

"I got into a rut while I was married," Lydia continued while Roz chewed. "I'm an introvert, you know. Not shy, but content with just a small circle of friends. But I let the circle get too small, and now it's a struggle for me to expand again." She reached across the table and touched Roz's hand. "So thanks."

Roz took a swig of beer. "No need to thank me. I'm kind of getting back on the friendship bus myself. My mom died last year. Before that, I was her caregiver for five years after she had a stroke. That put a crimp in my social life. Not to mention my finances. I had to sell her house to pay for home health aides to watch her while I worked."

"I'm sorry. I didn't know."

"Yeah, well—I don't like to talk about it. No one wants to hear my kvetching."

Lydia pushed an empanada toward her friend. "You can kvetch to me. I don't mind."

Roz, usually so gruff, blinked her eyes rapidly. "It's just....people think I should be relieved that my mother finally passed. But I miss her. Her mind was still sharp even though her body was a wreck. She was only sixty-seven."

"No woman is ever ready for her mother to die," Lydia said. "I miss my mom all the time, and it's been twenty-three years since she died."

They sat in silence for a moment until Roz shook herself and tossed the last bite of her empanada to the dog. "Enough of this pity party. I'm focused on getting that full-time position at work. Chester Renault has said he's retiring at the end of the semester, and Louise has all but promised me the job. All I have to do is make it through the next two months without any catastrophes."

Roz drained her beer. "How hard can that be?"

Chapter 28

On Monday, Viktor insisted the first project had to be the renovation of the hall bathroom on the second floor. All the tile had to be ripped up. Reluctantly, Viktor agreed the tub, the focus of Lydia's bubble bath fantasies, could be reused. He scratched his bushy head. "Don't know how it got up here. Easier to keep." He glanced up at Lydia. "I order tile. You want white or beige?"

"Neither. I may use white subway tile on the walls, but I want glass accent tiles in sea foam or celadon." Lydia outlined the location three quarters of the way up the wall.

Viktor frowned.

"Green," Lydia clarified.

"Green no good." Viktor spoke with finality and exited the bathroom.

Lydia trotted after him. "What do you mean, green is no good. Green tile is just as easy to install as any other color."

"Bathroom should be white or beige. Call that neutral. Easier for to resell."

Good grief—a man who'd probably grown up in a Communist workers collective was giving her decorating advice! "I don't want neutrals for the resale value. What's the point of decorating my home to please the next person who will buy it? I want to please myself. I'm the one who lives here."

"Green too crazy. No one want," Viktor insisted.

"I'll order the tile in the colors I want. You just take the measurements and tell me how much I need."

"I like order from Top Tile. Good quality. Ukrainian owned."

"I have an imported Italian tile store in mind."

She and Viktor glowered at each other, both with their arms crossed across their chests. Finally, muttering Ukrainian curses that would probably call forth the hounds of hell, Viktor walked away.

The next day, after her classes ended, Lydia dropped by the fancy Italian tile store she had driven by many times without ever having a reason to enter. The place was like an art museum of gorgeous porcelain and glass.

Lydia wandered through the displays and finally settled on beautiful sea green tiles that reminded her of the ocean in Greece.

"We'll order it for you. It takes about four months to come in," the man behind the counter said.

"Four months?"

He narrowed his eyes over his reading glasses. "This is artisan-crafted tile, made to order in Milan. Then shipped here. On a boat."

Lydia looked longingly at the tile like a child being dragged away empty-handed from the American Girl doll display. She couldn't hold out for this tile when her bathroom floor was about to collapse.

But she was damned if she'd go to Home Depot and order plain white squares for her new bathroom. "Don't you have anything unusual in stock that I could have right away?"

A woman working behind the counter nudged the man helping Lydia. "What about that cancellation you were so mad about last week? That tile is gorgeous."

"It's nothing like this," the man objected.

Lydia made eye contact with the woman. "Let me see it, please."

The woman emerged from the back room with a box. This tile was more aquamarine than green, and it had fanciful impressionist sea creatures in four different patterns. "You'd use this as an accent tile," the woman explained. "Pair it with a plain white like this."

Lydia's eyes lit up. "I love it! It's even better than my original choice."

The grouchy salesman shook his head and turned the sale over to his colleague.

"Men," she whispered to Lydia with a wink. "They take everything so literally."

Chapter 29

"Darling, great news—we have a very serious offer on the house." Isabelle's breathless voice came through Lydia's phone three weeks later. "Executive relocation. The family is coming from Sweden—they're even interested in buying most of your furniture."

"Wow, fantastic. What's the next step?"

"We need to accelerate the attorney review, and I'm not anticipating any issues with the home inspection. I told Audrey Nealon to give you a call because you'll need to sell quite a few personal effects to make the move to Lilac Court. The buyers need to close by the end of the month, so they can get their kids enrolled in school. I told them it wouldn't be a problem since you already own the house you're moving to."

"What? I'm not ready to move in there! It's a construction zone. Viktor is nowhere near done."

The past three weeks had been an endless round of battle with Viktor. He'd grudgingly accepted the aquamarine accent tiles since the rest of the bathroom would be white, but he dug in his heels on the fancy pedestal sink claiming the existing pipes couldn't be moved even one inch. He hated the medicine cabinet she'd chosen (too wide), the light fixtures (too dim), the curtain rods (too heavy). Lydia had developed a rudimentary Ukrainian vocabulary of negativity: *ni, ne dobre, nemozhlyvo.*

No, no good, not possible.

Lydia could only imagine the response she'd get if she demanded he wrap it up by the end of the month.

"I can't move to Lilac Court right now," Lydia repeated.

"Well, move to a hotel. Or I can help you find a rental, I suppose."

"Not with the dog," Lydia reminded her.

"Right." Isabelle sounded relieved to have those options off the table. "So, as I said, get ready to move to your new house. People live through renovation projects all the time. If we let these buyers get away, who knows how long the house will be stuck on the market."

"But I need time to figure out what I'm keeping and what I'm getting rid of."

"Audrey will help with that. And there's nothing like a deadline to help you move forward with those decisions. You said you were eager to start a new stage of your life in a new neighborhood. There's no reason to delay."

Lydia had been treating the remodeling at Lilac Court as an exercise in project management. Her daily tangles with Viktor and his crew kept her engaged and mentally alert the way a 1000-piece jig-saw puzzle kept senior citizens from fading into senility. But now Isabelle had presented her with the actual reality of moving. Leaving behind the house she'd shared with Charles, the possessions she'd acquired with Charles.

Leaving behind her marriage.

And starting the second act of her life on a stage with a new set and new props.

She decided to transfer everything small she planned to take with her to Lilac Court into one room of this house, and to tag every large item. That would be a tangible sign of progress before her appointment with Audrey in the morning.

She began in the kitchen, a room that presented no emotional challenges: blender, coffee pot, sharp knives, a few pots and pans. The family room yielded a pottery vase, some baskets, and a small area rug.

The dining room upped the ante a bit. A huge breakfront contained their wedding china and glassware, used three or four times a year for catered dinner parties. At the moment, Lydia felt like she'd never entertain again. But if she did invite people to the cozy dining room at Lilac Court, she wouldn't feed them with seven-piece table settings. She planned to buy some hand-thrown pottery dishes, the kind where every plate was slightly different.

Only a pair of crystal candle sticks made the cut in this room.

The living room caused Lydia's eyes to prick with tears. The ceramic bowl she and Charles had bought in Italy, the seascape acquired in a gallery on the Pacific Coast highway, the small print they'd discovered in a tiny shop in Paris. These recalled happy times: walking hand-in-hand through ancient streets, people-watching in sidewalk cafes, laughing as they tried to make themselves understood in a foreign language. Charles had enjoyed showing her—a girl whose family vacations had always been a week in a cottage on Lake Erie—the world beyond her limited horizons. She carried these mementoes into the dining room, pausing to put a "move" sticker on her piano.

But the furniture all would go. When they'd moved into this house, Lydia had been intimidated by its size and overwhelmed at the prospect of filling every room. So when Charles had suggested they hire a decorator, Lydia had eagerly embraced the idea.

The decorator ordered every wall painted in neutral tones: sandstone bisque, Nantucket dune, English cream, tawny taupe. Lydia hadn't realized there were so many ways to say beige. The furniture and rugs were equally sedate. Whenever the decorator flipped open her sample swatches, the jewel tones drew Lydia's eye, but Charles and the decorator somehow whittled her colorful impulses down to subtle threads of navy and maroon in the throw pillows and accent rugs. At twenty five, she hadn't been confident enough to object. Besides, she didn't have an alternative vision to offer.

For eighteen years Lydia had lived in this muted, sedate cocoon. Now, even her new address came cloaked in vibrant color: Lilac Court. She planned to remodel the kitchen, but keep the rich persimmon tone on the walls. She'd use the tiles around the fireplace as her color palette for the living room: emerald, cerulean, ruby. She and Charles had once visited Monet's house in Giverny, where the room in which the artist hosted jolly dinners was painted a sunny yellow. She'd loved the room so much she'd bought a postcard of it—that would be the color for her bedroom.

No interior designer this time; the vision for this house would be hers and hers alone.

Heading into the rear of the house, Lydia stopped with her hand on the door knob to Charles's study. She hadn't been in this room since she dug through her husband's files to find Viktor's number. Now, the scent of Charles struck her like a March gust: the leather of his favorite chair, the mint of the candies he chewed, the faint traces of his very subtle cologne. He had smelled this way since the very first time she rested her head on his shoulder and inhaled. His scent permeated every object in the room, yet she knew even if she packed it all up and took it with her, the scent would be left behind.

She slipped into his desk chair where she could see the silver-framed picture of them on their wedding day. He hadn't chosen to display the formal portrait, but rather a candid shot where the photographer had caught grains of flying rice heading toward their smiling faces. She picked up the photo and held it against her chest.

"I'm sorry," she whispered. "I appreciate all you gave me, but I have to go."

⸺●⸺

AUDREY NEALON AND HER assistant, Ty Griggs, showed up the next morning at nine.

"I've marked the few things that I'm taking with me to my new house, and moved all the smaller items into the dining room," Lydia told Audrey. "Everything else, you can sell."

"Thanks for being so well organized," Audrey said. "You make our work easy." She began snapping pictures of Lydia's twin sofas and large coffee table, while her assistant disappeared into the kitchen.

"This furniture is way too big for Lilac Court," Lydia explained as she trailed behind the estate sale organizer.

"Absolutely."

Lydia liked the way Audrey spoke that word—agreeing with her without any hint of argument. "For the new house, I thought I'd get a love seat and two soft arm chairs for reading in front of the fireplace."

"That would work well." Audrey took pictures of the matching end table and made a note on her iPad.

"I'm not even sure where to go shopping for what I want," Lydia continued. "I don't want to use a decorator."

"You should stop by Vintage Visions. A customer of mine owns it. She buys old wrecks at my sales, cleans them up, and resells them at a profit. She's got a good eye." Audrey twisted her head to examine the underside of a floor lamp.

"Do you think I'm crazy for selling this house and moving to Lilac Court?" Lydia blurted out to Audrey's back.

Audrey lowered her iPad and patted one of the stiff Queen Anne chairs to encourage Lydia to sit down. Then she perched on the arm of the nearby sofa. "Moving is traumatic for everyone. It's normal to be nervous about a big change. Usually, my clients are older people having a hard time letting go of the family home even though they know they need to move to a condo or a one-level ranch. I think it's a good sign that you're willing to sell everything here. It means you're ready to start your new life."

Lydia ran her foot over the impeccably clean cream carpeting. "My...my husband's financial advisor thinks I'm too used to living in a big, fancy house to get adjusted to a small, older home."

"You don't need a lot of space, Lydia." Audrey leaned forward and spoke in a calm voice. "You can only sit in one room at a time. People get big houses so they can fill them up with stuff. If you're not attached to the stuff, you won't miss the house."

Lydia relaxed in the chair, letting Audrey's words sink in. "Thanks. I never thought of it that way."

Audrey eased away and aimed her iPad camera at another piece of furniture. "Free therapy included with every estate sale."

Upstairs, the guest bedrooms presented no challenges. But when she entered the master bedroom, Lydia hesitated. Letting Audrey and Ty into the room where she and Charles had spent their final night together felt like a violation.

The king-sized bed had always seemed wide as a football field to Lydia. She would have been happy with a cozier queen, but Charles required space to sleep soundly. Certainly, this behemoth wouldn't fit in her new bedroom. Did she even need a queen? She might as well have a nun's narrow cot to hold her sleeping body. The thought of having sex with a man who wasn't her husband terrified her. It's not like she'd never had an errant fantasy while watching a steamy movie or reading a trashy book. But letting a real man who wasn't Charles touch her?

Lydia shivered.

The master bedroom contained his and her walk-in closets, each as big as the smallest bedroom in Lilac Court. Lydia entered her closet and ran her fingers over the neatly hung rack of clothes: business suits for meetings she'd never attend again, cocktail dresses—a new one for each event—that she'd worn to the annual partners dinner and the charity fundraisers that had occupied half their weekends. She slid the dresses and suits together along the closet rod. "All this can go," she told Audrey.

She stopped ten feet from the other closet door. "My husband's clothes are in there."

Audrey and Ty exchanged a glance. Then Ty stepped forward and laid his hand on her shoulder. "Don't you worry about this, ma'am. We know it's hard. That's why we're here to take care of it for you."

"Go away for the weekend," Ty said. "When you come back, it'll all be gone."

Chapter 30

Lydia wished she could take Ty's advice, but she had no place to go away to and no one to go away with.

She had no choice but to camp out at Lilac Court during the sale that would empty her house in Palmer Ridge. And soon after that, the Swedish executive and his family would arrive, so she might as well stay at Lilac Court from now on. The things she intended to keep, in particular the piano, would stay in storage until the renovations were complete.

After packing a few necessities for herself and Alfie, Lydia made a Target shopping list of things she'd need to survive in the half-completed house: an inflatable airbed, some inexpensive curtains for the bedroom and kitchen, a mirror for the closet door. She folded the paper and stuck it in her purse. Then she pulled it out and added one more item: cushions for the porch swing.

"You stay here while I go shopping," she told Alfie. "When I come back, be ready to go to your new house."

Alfie grabbed his stuffed moose and settled down to wait.

HAVING CUT A SWATH through Target and collected Alfie from Palmer Ridge, Lydia headed toward Lilac Court. On the way, she passed a row of stores that she'd never paid much attention to before. Now, a swinging wooden sign caught her eye—Vintage Visions.

The store Audrey had recommended. It had a cute wrought iron café table and chairs out front.

Lydia slowed, backed up, and parallel parked. She cracked the windows and admonished Alfie to be good. "I'll be back in five minutes."

Approaching the entrance, she ran her fingertips over the café table out on the sidewalk. It had once been sky blue and then had been painted yellow. Now both colors showed in various spots. Lydia could picture it on her back patio once she got the weeds pulled out from between the bricks.

Lydia pulled open the door to the store and a bell tinkled above her head. Inside, the scent of potpourri overlaid a slight mustiness. Jam-packed thrift shops and antique stores always made her feel itchy and overwhelmed. But this store clearly reflected its owner's sensibility. She had arranged little tableaux throughout the space: a chair, a lamp, and a table with a tea cup; a small dining table set for dinner for two, complete with champagne flutes and a fresh flower arrangement; a 1930s style dresser with vintage perfume bottles and a lacy doily. Lydia pushed deeper into the store, and there she saw it: her chair.

Low slung, with soft velveteen upholstery in a rich, port wine shade—not too bright. A thick, squishy seat cushion. Curving, elegant armrests. And a back draped with a fringey, flowered shawl.

Lydia sank into the chair. It was every bit as comfortable as it looked. Snuggly! A little hassock had been placed in front of the chair, with a leather-bound edition of *Great*

Expectations resting on top. She wouldn't have thought to group the chair and hassock together, but it worked. She propped her feet up. Ah!

"Isn't that a great chair?" The voice materialized behind Lydia. "Make yourself at home."

Lydia twisted around to see who had spoken. The woman had dyed red hair, an armful of bracelets, and long, expressive fingers. She rearranged some ceramic candle holders while she talked. "I found that chair in the most marvelous little home library—absolutely stuffed with books. I'll only sell it to you if you promise me you'll read in it."

"Oh, I will!" Lydia flexed her feet on the hassock. "I'm going to put it in front of my fireplace."

Lydia realized she'd agreed to buy the chair without examining it for flaws or bargaining on the price. Weren't you supposed to haggle in stores like this? But what difference did it make? This was her chair! She'd been daydreaming about a chair and then this appeared like an illustration of her fantasy.

"I want that little café table and chairs outside, too." She followed the owner to the front desk and pulled out her credit card. "When can you deliver it?"

The owner laughed, but not in an unkind way. "No deliveries, dear. But my son will help you tie it onto your car."

Lydia had a vision of her café table bouncing down South Main Street. "Is that safe?"

"As long as you don't live far."

"Oh, I'm right nearby. I live in Burleith."

She felt good saying it.

Chapter 31

Lydia pulled her overloaded Subaru into the driveway of 43 Lilac Court looking like the Joads fleeing the Dust Bowl in *The Grapes of Wrath*. She stood beside the car contemplating her predicament: she and the guy from Vintage Visions had worked together to get the chair in the back of the car and the table and chairs on the roof rack. How was she going to unload it alone?

She looked around—no neighbors were out in their yards, and she wasn't about to bang on their doors to demand a favor as her first neighborly action.

While Alfie ran around the yard, Lydia carried Viktor's ladder into the driveway. She climbed up a couple steps so she could get a better grasp on the ropes tying the table and chairs to the roof. What knots! The kid helping her must've been an Eagle Scout. After a ten-minute nail polish-chipping struggle, the knot finally came undone.

Immediately, the two chairs made a suicidal leap off the car roof, one of them clipping Lydia as it fell.

"Ow!"

Taking a deep breath, she climbed back up and dragged the table to the edge of the roof, then gently tipped it over and attempted to grab it as it fell.

The table knocked her flat on her ass.

Lydia pulled herself out from under it. Who knew a table for two could be so heavy?

She lugged her purchases to the back of the house and set the café table and chairs on the patio, but the bricks were so uneven the furniture tilted like deck chairs on the Titanic. Lydia gnawed on her bottom lip as she contemplated the problem.

Add "reset the patio bricks" to Viktor's list.

She could hear the heavily accented response as clearly as if he were beside her. "*Ni*. I pour concrete. Nice and flat."

As fast as Viktor finished a project at the top of the list, she added another to the bottom. At this rate, the two of them would grow old together at 43 Lilac Court.

Lydia returned to the Subaru and pulled and shoved the arm chair out of the back. Half dragging, half carrying it, she managed to get it onto the back porch. There, in a bright beam of sunlight she noticed a stain on the arm that hadn't been apparent in the dimly lit store. No wonder the owner had that shawl draped so artfully.

Well, she'd have to keep her own lights low and buy a shawl, too.

Lydia wrangled the chair into the house, then returned to the car to get her Target purchases.

Alfie chose that moment to run across the yard and leap up on her, leaving two muddy pawprints above her breasts.

"Oh, Alfie! Look what you've done! I can't go around like this." Lydia headed into the house lugging her new air mattress, and Alfie followed. He stood in the kitchen with his head cocked and his ears pricked.

"Why are you looking at me like that? This is our new home. Go sniff around."

But Alfie seemed nervous in his new surroundings and stuck close to Lydia's side. "Okay, come help me set up the air mattress in my new bedroom. Then I have to do a load of laundry, thanks to you."

Alfie trotted behind her as she lugged the package up the steps, leaving footprints in the plaster dust Viktor and his crew created. Lydia knew he had finished painting her bedroom yesterday, after a long argument about why powder blue would be a better paint choice, and she was eager to see the results.

She dragged the air mattress over the threshold and stopped in her tracks.

Oh. My. God.

The walls pulsated.

The yellow was so bright, the whole room seemed to throb with color. The effect was nothing like Monet's kitchen. It was more like being trapped in a school bus garage.

Alfie lay down and rubbed his snout with his paws.

Lydia took a deep breath. Maybe the paint looked wrong because the room was totally empty. Once she got curtains on the windows and a rug on the floor, it wouldn't look so vivid.

"I hope," Lydia muttered. One thing was certain—she wouldn't give Viktor the satisfaction of knowing he was right. She'd tell him she loved the shade, and repaint the damn room herself after he finished all his projects.

Lydia swept the floor as Alfie pounced on the broom and re-scattered the dust. When she finally inflated the bed, the whistling sound and expanding mattress scared Alfie out of the room. Lydia opened the closet to unpack the two suit-cases of essential clothes she'd brought with her: five pairs of pants and some blouses and sweaters to wear while teach-ing, a couple pairs of jeans, two simple dresses, flats, pumps, boots, loafers.

Lydia was only partway through the second suitcase when she ran out of room in the tiny closet. Even though she'd left half her wardrobe for Audrey to sell, she still had boxes of clothes the movers were to deliver. Where would she put them all? Jamming one more hanger on the sagging rod, Lydia paused to listen to a noise downstairs.

Was that Alfie?

She went out in the hall to investigate. Down in the foyer, Alfie had found one of Viktor's paintbrushes and was chewing the bristle end.

"No, Alfie—drop it!" But that was a command Alfie hadn't mastered. Lydia had to chase the dog all through the downstairs to get the brush. Alfie's snout was stained yellow and so were Lydia's hands and jeans before she finally won the tug of war.

Lydia blocked off the room with the paint supplies and went upstairs to take a shower. Stepping into the small stall shower in the bathroom connected to her bedroom, Lydia felt an anemic spray of water sputter over her. She turned the faucets, but both were fully open.

She looked up at the shower head. This was a brand new fixture. Why wasn't the water pummeling her as it did in her shower in Palmer Ridge?

Then a niggling worry crept into her brain. Viktor had been trying to tell her something about water pressure two weeks ago. In his broken English, he said something about the supply line and how replacing it would require a master plumber and weeks of work. She'd told him not to worry about it.

Did that mean she'd be showering under this pissy little stream forever?

Lydia got out of the shower and put on clean clothes. A dull pain thumped in the back of her head. She gathered up her dirty clothes and headed down to the basement to do the laundry.

Twice she nearly tripped on the rickety, unevenly spaced steps. Alfie declined to follow her into the dark and waited at the top of the stairs. A bare bulb provided the only illumination in the chilly, damp basement. Against one wall, Mrs. Maguire's ancient washer and dryer stood next to a deep washtub sink. As she put her clothes in the washer, a tiny movement caught her eye.

Lydia looked into the washtub. There, curled in a corner near the drain, a snake darted its red tongue in and out.

Lydia screamed.

Dropping the laundry detergent, she stumbled up the stairs screaming again and again. Alfie ran away from her and cowered under the breakfast nook table.

By the time she reached the safety of the kitchen, her heart felt like it would explode from her chest. She hated snakes. She couldn't even look at them in a zoo or on a TV nature show.

She couldn't stay here with that thing, that reptile, in her basement.

A soft knock at the back door ratcheted her heart rate back up again.

"He-l-l-o-o? Are you okay? Do you need help?"

Lydia went to the back door. A middle-aged Indian woman stood on the porch. "Hello, I am Aastha Banerjee. I live there," she pointed to the house on the other side of Lydia's. "We heard screaming, and my mother-in-law said I must come to check on your safety."

Lydia shook her wet hair. "I'm so sorry to have disturbed you. I just discovered a snake in my basement. I guess it's silly, but I've always been afraid of snakes, and...." She trailed off, not sure what she wanted this poor woman to do about her problem.

Aastha's face brightened. "Oh, a snake. We were concerned that you were injured." As if by magic, an older woman in a sari appeared at Aastha's side. She explained the situation to her mother-in-law rapid fire in their native language. The old woman smiled.

"If you would like, we can come and take the creature away for you. My mother-in-law is fearless in this regard."

Grandma Banerjee grinned.

"You would do that?" Stunned by her neighbors' generosity and courage, she opened the door wide and ushered them in. "I'm Lydia Eastlee, by the way."

They shook hands, and the two Banerjee women headed down into the dungeon. Lydia followed, but stopped at the midpoint of the stairs. "It's in the sink," she directed.

Grandma Banerjee looked down into the depths and spoke solemnly.

"She says it's just a garter snake," Aastha called to Lydia. "Very useful in the garden."

The old lady's hand darted out, and a moment later she turned with the snake dangling from her fist.

The thing was at least a foot long. Lydia couldn't help herself. She screamed again.

Grandma Banerjee chuckled, while Aastha kept her distance. "Go upstairs ahead of us. We will release our friend in the garden."

Lydia raced upstairs and out the door. "Could you let him live in your garden?" she asked when they were outside.

Grandma's warm brown eyes crinkled with amusement. She apparently understood what Lydia said because she walked over to the fence and dropped the snake into her own yard, where it slithered into a flowerbed. She nodded in Lydia's direction and spoke a few words.

"My mother-in-law says you are very generous to give us the benefit of this hardworking creature," Aastha translated.

"You're welcome...I guess."

Grandma waved and returned to her house.

Lydia's heart finally slowed down. "Thank you so much. I know I'm being irrational, but I just—" She shuddered.

Aastha smiled and held her hands up to the trees. "God's creatures surround us. The walls of our homes are unimportant to them. We were happy to be of service." She began to walk toward her own house. "My mother-in-law was certain you were being attacked by a serial killer. She watches too many detective shows on TV."

"Does she speak English? She seemed to understand what I was saying."

"She declines to speak anything but Punjabi," Aastha tugged her ear, "but she understands English perfectly. So be careful what you say."

Aastha Banerjee left with a wink and a wave.

Lydia re-entered 43 Lilac Court and coaxed a trembling Alfie out from under the table. With his company, she hung the curtains on compression rods and hooked the mirror over the closet door. Lydia cleaned out one cabinet in the kitchen to hold a few dishes and mugs. All that was left in the Target bag were her four porch swing cushions—striped, polka-dot, flowered and paisley, each with a touch of lilac.

She fixed herself a cup of tea and grabbed a Milkbone for Alfie. "Come on—let's relax on our front porch. We've earned it."

With the cushions arranged, the swing was amazingly comfortable. It still squeaked on its rusty chain, but after a while Lydia found the sound rather soothing. With Alfie at her feet, she read her book, looking up occasionally to wave at people walking by.

"Isn't this nice?"

Alfie wagged his tail in agreement.

At five-thirty, an enticing aroma caught her attention.

She sniffed. Curry! Mrs. Banerjee must be making dinner.

Half an hour later, a car pulled up to the curb and two couples emerged. The women wore colorful saris and carried trays of food. The men toted shopping bags. As they advanced up the walk, the delicious smells grew stronger. The Banerjees' front door flew open, and Mr. Banerjee and the two women emerged all talking at once to their guests in a mixture of English and Punjabi. What a lively party!

The houses were so close here. Lydia felt like she was eavesdropping even though she couldn't understand the Banerjees and their guests. When her neighbors in Palmer Ridge had company, Lydia certainly hadn't noticed.

So she hadn't experienced envy.

Lydia felt rude sitting and pretending to read, so she called Alfie and they both went inside.

Now the microwavable Lean Cuisine she'd bought for her dinner seemed even less appealing. Luckily, Alfie was content with his kibble regardless of what the neighbors were eating. They ate and settled in the living room. The Vintage Visions chair was comfy, but Viktor hadn't painted in here yet. Surrounded by the ghostly outlines of Mrs. Maguire's art and the empty and now noticeably sagging bookshelves, Lydia's eyes pricked with self-pitying tears.

"I want to go home."

She startled herself—she hadn't meant to say the words aloud. Alfie lifted his head to look at her.

"I'm sorry. This place just doesn't feel like home yet. What do you think of it?"

Alfie raised his shaggy eyebrows.

"The neighbors are very nice—you can't deny that."

Alfie's tail swished across the floor.

"The wildlife situation is a little troubling. Maybe we need a cat to help you out."

Alfie edged backwards.

Through the open window—still no air-conditioning—the relentless beat of Indian music drifted in. To her western ears, the notes sounded high-pitched and whiny. When the song ended, the Banerjees yelled and clapped.

Nothing is louder than a party you haven't been invited to.

Alfie lay down and rolled onto his side.

"Here's the thing, buddy. Some Swedish executive and his family are moving into Palmer Ridge. We can't go back. We have no choice but to charge ahead."

Alfie released a long, shuddering sigh and closed his eyes.

Chapter 32

Two weeks later, Lydia awoke to the sound of hammer blows below her.

Groggily, she peered at her alarm clock: 7:15. She wasn't teaching until the afternoon and had stayed up late the night before grading papers.

Why was Viktor here so damn early?

She stumbled downstairs and entered the kitchen just as Viktor was about to take a crowbar to the built-in table and benches in her breakfast nook.

"No!" She lunged at his arm and deflected the blow.

"Today start kitchen. Table must go."

Lydia put her hands on her hips. "I distinctly told you I want to preserve this table. Work around it."

"Ni." Victor pointed to a crack in the plaster of the breakfast nook. "Gotta pull out so can fix wall nice. Put in Sheetrock. Nice and smooth."

"This table is solid chestnut. I'm not letting you destroy it so you can put in Sheetrock easier. Work around it."

Viktor tapped his temple with his forefinger. "You not use your head. You let me decide what is best."

Lydia grabbed Viktor's crowbar and tossed it toward the kitchen sink where it clattered to the floor.

Alfie growled.

"Get out," she hissed. "Get out of my house. Sit on the front porch and figure out what I owe you, and I'll write you a check."

"What you mean?" Viktor protested.

"You're fired."

Hours later as she walked across campus, Lydia still trembled with rage as she relived the moment when Viktor had tapped his temple as if she were some lunatic because she wanted to preserve the architectural details of her home. She was glad she'd fired him, glad to be done with the endless arguments.

But the fact remained: her house was only partially renovated. Now she needed to find another contractor, and anyone good would probably be booked for weeks.

On the bulletin board outside the cafeteria, amidst the garish jumble of ads for upcoming concerts and parties and hand-printed signs with tear-off fringes seeking roommates or ride shares, one flyer caught her eye. After all those years in advertising, Lydia could appreciate a well-constructed ad—clean lay-out, clear message, complimentary colors.

Wright Side Design

- Custom carpentry and cabinet-making
- Elegant storage solutions
- Original concepts and faultless execution

Three photos of lovely shelves, cabinets and a corner cupboard displayed the artist's work. A website address and phone number appeared at the bottom.

If he could design cabinetry as well as he'd designed this flyer, this might be a good candidate to replace Viktor. Lydia scrambled in her bag to find a pen, and then remembered to do what her students always did. She pulled out her phone and snapped a picture of the flyer.

After teaching her first class, Lydia remembered the carpenter's ad and pulled out her phone. First, she visited the Wright Side Design website, which contained even more pictures of beautiful carpentry projects as well as a quite poetic tribute to the virtues of hand-crafted wood. Convinced, she called the phone number. It rang several times, then rolled to voicemail. "Hey, it's Seth. I've got my hands full. You know what to do."

Hey, I've got my hands full? What kind of greeting was that? Well, she'd found Viktor too authoritarian. This fellow was clearly more relaxed. Lydia left a message describing her projects and ended the call.

Moments later, her phone rang, showing the number she'd just dialed.

"Hello?"

"Hey, it's Seth. You called me."

"Yes, did you get my message?"

"I never listen to voicemail. Just tell me what you said."

Lydia held her phone away from her ear and stared at it. But ultimately, she did as he instructed. "I have a few projects—a breakfast nook, some display shelves. I saw your flyer at Palmer Community College, and I wondered if you could come over and give me an estimate."

He hesitated before replying. "Mmm, yeah, I guess—today good?"

He sounded less than eager, despite having an open schedule. But she needed the work done. Why complain that he was available to do it? "Sure. I teach until five-fifteen, so any time after five-thirty."

"K. See ya."

———————⬤———————

A BROKEN DOORBELL WASN'T a problem with a dog like Alfie in residence. At five-thirty, he began barking like a horde of zombies was approaching, so Lydia had the door open before the carpenter tried to ring or knock. Struggling to restrain the dog, Lydia observed her visitor from the ground up: work boots, jeans, t-shirt....

Face.

That was some face! Lydia staggered back a step still in a crouch with her hand on the dog's collar. The young man looked down with vivid blue eyes under straight dark brows. He barely met her eye, seeming more interested in the dog to whom he offered the back of one long-fingered hand for a sniff.

Alfie stopped barking, broke away from Lydia, and put his paws on the visitor's chest.

"Alfie! No! Get down." Lydia moved to grab the collar again, but the carpenter scratched Alfie's ears, encouraging his terrible behavior.

"That's okay." Seth Wright kept playing with the dog, giving Lydia a chance to study him further. She knew him from somewhere. But where would she have met a carpenter in his twenties?

Then it dawned on her. This was the young man from that first class of Roz's that Lydia had observed, the kid who'd stormed out when Roz asked him about a late paper. He was a Palmer Community College student—that explained the presence of his flyer on the bulletin board.

"Come on in." She ushered Seth and the dog into the house, and Alfie ran off to find a toy.

Seth sized up the foyer with approval. "Nice chestnut," he said, running his fingertips over the newel post. "I love the houses in this neighborhood. Most of them were designed in the 1920s by a man named Harvey Caswell. He studied under Gustav Stickley, leader of the Arts and Crafts movement. He felt that working people deserved simple but beautiful designs that would last a lifetime."

It came back to Lydia that Roz said the kid's goal was to be an architect. He seemed to know a bit about the field. "Have you ever been to Craftsman's Farms?" Lydia loved the estate and museum devoted to Stickley's work.

"Many times." Now Seth took more interest in Lydia. His diffidence dissolved into a degree of enthusiasm. "Isn't it crazy that such a cool museum is right off of Route 10, tucked away between all the strip malls and superstores? Craftsman's Farm was more than a design studio. It was a philosophy of life." As he spoke, Seth became more animated, walking further into the house without waiting to be invited. He poked his head into the living room. "Nice! The original fireplace tiles and mantlepiece are still there. So many people have painted over the woodwork and pried up the tiles to modernize." He shuddered. "I could re-set those loose tiles for you and give this wood a light sanding to clean up the finish."

"That would be great." For the first time since she closed on the house, Lydia felt a surge of optimism. Finally, a workman who saw what she saw in 43 Lilac Court. "The really big project is back here in the kitchen." She led the way, explaining as she went. "I have to do some upgrades to make the kitchen functional, but I want to retain the original charm of the room. My contractor couldn't understand that. He wanted to gut the whole room down to the studs. We couldn't agree, so...." Lydia turned to face Seth. "He stomped off. Or I fired him. Depends on your perspective, I guess."

Seth offered a wide, relaxed smile. Lydia felt her heart rate kick up a notch. What the hell was that about? Technically speaking, this man was young enough to be her son.

He cocked his head. "So, you teach at Palmer Community? I used to go to school there."

"Yes, I just started last semester." Clearly, he didn't recognize her. She was just one middle aged woman out of many he passed in the halls every day. "So, you've graduated?"

He gave his head a quick shake. "Quit." Without elaborating, Seth prowled around the half-demolished kitchen, prodding studs with a penknife and shining a flashlight into dark corners. Then he pulled a notebook and a stubby pencil from his small backpack and dropped onto the sagging breakfast nook bench. His brows knit together as his hand sped across the page. After five minutes of sketching, Seth slid the paper around for Lydia to see.

She gasped. He'd managed to capture, in a few swift strokes, the vision of the kitchen she'd been trying to convey, fruitlessly, to Viktor. Cozy, yet functional. Contemporary, yet paying homage to the house's past.

"There's hardwood under this old linoleum. I'd rip that up and refinish the floors. I'd refurbish the table and benches here. You pick out the cabinets and counter tops you want, and I'll install them. You'll have to hire a plumber for the sink and the stove, but I can do the rest."

"Fantastic! When can you start?"

"I'll be here at seven on Monday."

Chapter 33

Lydia had started auditing Conrad McPartland's Intermediate Keyboarding class, which had the additional benefit, in her mind, of taking her to campus an extra day each week. She arrived in the classroom early, but Laquan, one of the three other students, was already playing, his head hunched, his long, dark fingers flying up and down the keyboard.

Even though she was only auditing the class, Lydia felt a twinge of competitiveness. She'd never be as good as Laquan, who clearly had a natural talent and a determination to improve. But she felt she was better than Samantha, a green-haired girl who pounded through their lessons cheerfully oblivious to her mistakes. The third kid attended only sporadically although Conrad never reproached him.

When Conrad entered, everyone sat up to attention. He greeted the class breezily, but it was clear to Lydia he commanded all the students' respect. Even the slacker seemed to crave Conrad's approval.

He began by demonstrating a tricky fingering in a Beethoven sonata, then had each of them play it. Laquan nailed it on the first try, Lydia on the second. The other two stumbled along until Conrad decided to move on.

The class continued in this manner for the full seventy minutes. At the end, Laquan stayed afterward to talk earnestly with Conrad while the other two students bolted for the door. Conrad made eye contact with Lydia over Laquan's head as if urging her to stay, so she sat at the piano, practicing softly until Laquan finally left.

When they were alone, Conrad slid onto the piano bench beside her and began to play without saying a word. Lydia recognized Joni Mitchell's "River." As she got lost in the poignant melody, she noticed a tear slipping down Conrad's cheek, but he kept playing.

When he finished, Lydia put her arm around him. She couldn't recall all the lyrics to the song, but she remembered the part about losing the best baby I ever had. Conrad had been alone the night they had sung at Blue Monday. She had no clue about his love life.

"What happened?" she asked softly.

"I met someone a few months ago who was very special. I thought he felt the same." Conrad shook his head. "But apparently not. He's younger. Has things to do that don't include me." Conrad faced Lydia on the bench. "I'm just so tired of looking, you know? I'm ready to settle down, but it's not happening for me."

He played a splashy chord. "I'm sorry for unloading on you. But I figured you were a safer bet than bursting into tears during Intro to Musical Theory."

Lydia squeezed his hand. "I'm happy to offer a shoulder to cry on." She played a few measures of "Just One of Those Things," keeping her eyes on the keyboard as she spoke. "It's so hard to get the timing right. One person's ready, the other's not. You compromise." She looked up. "Or you realize you can't."

———◈———

LYDIA ARRIVED HOME to a cacophony of sawing. But the table saw fell silent by the time she made it to the kitchen.

"Hi, how's it going?"

Seth did not look up from his measuring. Maybe he was focusing on remembering the measurement. Lydia waited.

He turned away from her and picked up a screw driver. That's when she noticed the tiny white ear pods. Naturally, like all kids his age, he was listening to music and totally tuned out to his surroundings.

"Seth." Lydia tapped him on the shoulder and he jumped. His eyes widened, then he smiled and removed the earbuds.

"Sorry, I didn't mean to startle you."

"That's okay. I was in a groove."

"What are you listening to?" Lydia believed music brought people together, but she expected Seth would be listening to hip-hop or metal or something else she'd never heard of.

"Miles Davis. I love *Kind of Blue*. It helps me focus."

Lydia was impressed. "You like jazz from the Sixties? I love Bill Evans. Most people your age have never heard of modal jazz."

Seth turned away with a scowl. "I could say most people your age don't want a persimmon kitchen, but I try not to make sweeping generalizations."

"Ouch. I deserved that. Sorry." Lydia realized she should be insulted that her contractor spoke to her so critically.

Instead, she found herself intrigued and wanting to make amends. "Do you play an instrument? I play piano. That's why I'm such a Bill Evans fan."

"I fool around on guitar, but I suck. And I used to play clarinet in the middle school band until I let other kids convince me it wasn't cool. I regret that."

"It's not too late to take it up again. I let my piano playing slide for a while, but lately I've been practicing every day."

Seth set down his screw driver and studied her with new interest. "Really? I don't see a piano here."

"I have my piano in storage because the renovation dust is bad for it. For now, I practice at school. I can hardly wait until the work is done, and I can bring my piano home."

"Cool. I'll try to make that happen for you." Seth turned back to his work, but Lydia didn't leave the kitchen.

"You told me the other day that you quit going to Palmer Community. Why did you decide to drop out?" Lydia kept her tone light as she sat at the dust-covered breakfast nook table.

Seth lowered his head over the frame he was building. "Because I got straight A's in all the courses I need to be an architect—calculus, computer aided design, drafting. But then I flunked some stupid grammar test on dangling participles and comma splices. And I couldn't be bothered writing dumb essays about the best vacation I ever took. Who the hell cares?" He pounded in a nail with a vicious swing of his hammer.

"I'm sure anyone who got an A in calculus can easily pass a grammar test."

"That's not the point. It's stupid, useless stuff. I don't have time for that shit."

Lydia waited until his agitated words faded away. She wasn't going to try to convince him of the relevance of writing clearly and grammatically. Not right now, at least. "So, you're not going to try to become an architect?"

Seth tossed his hammer into his toolbox. "I'm going to keep on doing what I do. I'm my own boss. I design things for people who want my skills. That's good enough for me."

Methinks he doth protest too much. But Seth would hardly appreciate a quote from Shakespeare.

He turned to look at her before he started on the next step of his project. "What do you teach at Palmer Community anyway?"

"English." Lydia smiled and left the room.

Chapter 34

Excitement around Halloween had been steadily building in Burleith. More and more houses sprouted decorations although none matched the lavishness of the Banerjees', where a ten foot inflatable Frankenstein's monster waved an ax at passersby. The community garden sponsored a pumpkin sale and jack 'o lantern carving festival on the Saturday before the big day. Lydia carved a grinning face into a twenty pound pumpkin, then had to persuade the Morrow kids to walk home so her jack 'o lantern could ride in their little red wagon. Lydia bought two big bags of Kit Kats and returned to the store for Skittles when Mrs. Banerjee told her she wasn't well prepared. "You must expect fifty children," she said. "Maybe sixty if the weather is fine." Grandma Banerjee nodded in agreement.

The parade of kids began the moment Lydia returned from work. The youngest ones arrived before it got dark, dressed as princesses and dinosaurs. Once the sun set, the more ferocious trick or treaters rang the bell brandishing fake swords and wands and other accessories of action heroes Lydia didn't recognize. Eventually, Alfie got used to the commotion and stopped barking although he supervised the distribution of treats with a keen eye.

Around eight-thirty the action slowed. A few teenagers who couldn't be bothered with costumes rang the bell, and Lydia gave them the last of her candy so she wouldn't eat it herself. Then she blew out the candle in the jack o'lantern and locked the door.

"Well, that was fun, wasn't it, Alfie? We never had a single trick or treater in Palmer Ridge. Those kids all went to private Halloween parties."

Alfie shook his head in disbelief, and the two of them curled up in the living room to read for a while.

The loud knock on the door at nine made both Lydia and Alfie jump.

Alfie ran to the foyer and Lydia followed. Surely kids weren't still coming this late when she had turned out the lights and the Banerjees had deflated their giant Frankenstein. She flipped the light switch by the door and pressed her eye against the murky old peephole, but could only make out that her visitor was a broad-shouldered man.

Alfie wasn't barking, but his ears pricked, and his tail stood straight up.

The man knocked again.

Lydia's heart beat a little harder. Anyone she knew would surely have called first before coming. She checked her phone to see if she'd missed a call or text.

Nothing.

She could shout, "Who is it?" through the door, but then the man would know she was in here. The house in Palmer Ridge, with its alarm system and securely locking windows and doors, seemed liked a fortress compared to rattletrap Lilac Court. Maybe she was being silly, but she felt vulnerable.

What if it was just a neighbor? Maybe a kid hadn't returned from trick or treating and a worried dad was looking for him.

If they'd seen her pull her car into the garage, they knew she was home and would think her refusal to answer odd and unfriendly. If only she could see the man's face.

He knocked again.

Lydia crept into the dark dining room, crouched on the wide window seat of the bay window, and pressed her face against the glass. In the brief illumination thrown by a passing car's headlights, she made out the man's wavy hair and familiar profile.

Tom Schilling!

Lydia jumped down and ran to open the door. "Hi, Tom! You startled me. What are you doing here?"

He grinned and crossed the threshold. "I was at a meeting a few blocks away and thought I'd pop by to see this house I've heard so much about." He bent to pet Alfie's head. "Hey, buddy! You're a fine fella."

Lydia's tension left her in a rush. "I thought you were a home invader. I should've known, they don't knock. Come on in, and I'll show you around. Would you like a drink?"

"That would be very hospitable."

"Everything's still disorganized because of the renovations," she explained as she led him into the living room. "My booze is in here, but we'll have to go into the kitchen for glasses and ice." Lydia laughed. "No bar with a mini-fridge and running water in this house—I'm roughing it now!"

Lydia found a bottle of scotch in the cabinet under the bookcases. She tucked it under her left arm as she pointed out the wonders of her fireplace, her book shelves, her decorative tile.

Tom smiled indulgently. "It's wonderful to see you so happy, Lydia. You're glowing."

"Aaaw, thanks. I'm really enjoying working on making this house my own. And I couldn't have done it without your help. You should've seen the expression on Mitchell's face when I told him I'd qualified for a mortgage based on my own resources. She grabbed his hand and tugged. "Come on and see the kitchen. It's a wreck now, but in a few weeks, it'll be perfect."

Lydia continued to chatter as she filled a glass with ice and poured on the scotch. "You're the first person from my old life to visit me here. Once I get all my projects finished and all the dust cleaned up, I'll have a party and invite everyone."

The words came out of her mouth without much thought. Would she do that? Invite people like Alton Finn and Betsey von Maur and Mitchell Felson to visit this cozy little house? Probably not.

Tom smiled at her, eyes glittering, as he sipped his drink. It occurred to her that this glass of scotch might not be his first cocktail of the evening.

"Well, I won't invite Mitchell," Lydia revised, "but I'll invite you and Madalyn."

"I saw a pile of construction debris outside. You must have finished at least one project. Where did all that wood and plaster come from?"

"The hall bathroom. Come upstairs and see how it turned out," Lydia gushed. "You have no idea what an ordeal this bathroom was. Viktor said I was days away from the bathtub falling through the floor into the foyer. I suspect that's one thing he was absolutely right about."

Tom followed her up the steps with his heavy tread. Alfie stayed in the foyer looking up at them. "Viktor said I had to have plain white, but I got a deal on this imported blue Italian tile." She threw open the hall bathroom door. "What do you think?"

Tom leaned against the door frame. "I think you're very persuasive." He drained his glass and tossed the ice cubes in the bathroom sink. "What other work have you done up here?"

"Oh, Viktor remodeled the second bath as well, but it's tiny. Not much to see there."

Tom prowled down the hallway, peeking into the three bedrooms. Lydia trailed behind him.

When he reached the door of her room, the only room with a bed, he turned to face her. "You're so beautiful, Lydia. Charles was a lucky man."

What?

Lydia stopped in her tracks, as startled as if Tom had started speaking in tongues.

He grabbed her arm and pulled her towards him.

Tom was strong, a much bigger man than Charles. Stunned, Lydia couldn't find the neural connections to make her body resist. Before she fully comprehended her situation, he had both burly arms wrapped around her and was pressing his scotch-scented lips against hers.

She whipped her head back and forth and managed to get one hand on his chest to push him away. "Tom! Stop! What the—"

"You know you want it." He tried to shove his tongue into her mouth but got her cheek.

"I don't want anything! You're married. Madalyn is my friend."

"You let me worry about Madalyn," he growled, and resumed his assault on her mouth.

Had she somehow encouraged him? Signaled to him that this is what she was after when she led him up here to see the remodeled bathroom?

No. She had been showing off her new house to an interested friend. And she got a gross sexual battering in response to her enthusiasm.

She lowered her chin and pushed her head away from his with her forehead. At the same time, she brought her right foot down hard on his instep.

"Ow!"

Her move surprised him enough that she was able to twist away.

Lydia's arms hurt where his hands had squeezed her. Her face burned where his late-day stubble had scratched her. Trembling, she backed down the hall toward the stairs, never taking her eyes off Tom. "What the hell's the matter with you? You're drunk. Or crazy."

"Oh, Lydia—for a beautiful woman, you can be awfully prissy. You must be lonely since Charles died. Let me help you with that."

Lydia had reached the top of the stairs. Alfie lay sprawled in the foyer.

"Alfie, come!"

Miraculously, the dog responded to her command and trotted to her side. Lydia felt braver with Alfie nearby. "Get out of here, Tom." She worked to keep her voice low and steady although her chest was heaving. "Go home right now."

She stepped back to allow Tom enough room to pass her and go down the stairs. Alfie stood with his tail held high and his head cocked, watching.

But Tom didn't follow her instructions. He kept coming toward her with his arms extended.

"Get away from me!" Lydia's voice rang out high and agitated.

Alfie leapt up and locked his jaws around Tom's right forearm.

"Augh!" Tom shook his arm, but Alfie held on. "Call him off!"

Lydia pointed downstairs to the front door. "Get out of my house, Tom."

Tom headed down the steps, dragging the dog with him. When she was sure he was headed out, she called, "Alfie, release."

Chapter 35

"I feel like such a fool."

Lydia and Roz sat at a corner table in the nearly empty college cafeteria.

"Don't blame yourself. That's such a woman thing to do." Roz ripped open a bag of Sun Chips. "Report the bastard to the police."

"It's not that easy." Lydia rubbed her droopy eyes. She'd barely slept last night, jumping at every sound she heard and falling into fitful dreams, from which she awoke fighting with the covers. "I invited Tom upstairs. He could claim I wanted it, and he had to push me away. He said/she said. He'll paint me as a hysterical, unbalanced woman reeling from her husband's death."

Lydia traded a stalk of celery she'd brought from home for one of Roz's chips. "But I did take a picture of myself last night." She slid her phone across the table so Roz could see.

"Jeez—look at those fingerprint bruises! That's proof he grabbed you and squeezed. And your face still has beard-burn. Call the cops. Don't let him get away with this."

Lydia reflexively stroked her own cheek. "It's not like reporting a man I barely know. I'm still stunned that Tom did this to me. Tom! Of the whole circle of friends Charles and I had, Tom and Madalyn were my favorites. Tom is—was—funny and easy-going. He helped me get my mortgage. And then last night, he turned into a totally different person."

"He never got frisky with you before?" Roz squinted at Lydia. "You know—wandering hands at the pool party, too eager under the mistletoe?"

"Never. He'd hug me. He hugged everybody." Lydia sealed and unsealed her snack bag. "He was a monster last night. I was genuinely afraid. Alfie performed brilliantly, though." Lydia grinned. "He's my hero."

"I hope you gave him a big treat."

"A huge hunk of rotisserie chicken. His service went well above the standard milk bone." Lydia gnawed on her lower lip. "I wonder how Tom explained the dog bite to Madalyn?"

"Probably told her he was attacked by some random stray. Men like that are always quick with a plausible explanation."

Lydia clenched her phone. "I should show Madalyn this picture. I'm supposed to spend the day at a training session with her later this week." She leaned forward, warming to her own idea. "That would punish Tom more than reporting it to the police. If Charles had been chasing women, I would have wanted to know."

"Ha!" Roz shook her head. "Don't count on her being grateful to you for pointing out her husband's a creep. Women married to men like Tom are always ready to defend their husbands' cover stories, even when they know they're not true. Especially when they know they're not true."

Lydia drew herself up straight. "That's not fair. You don't even know Madalyn. She's a good person. She's Tom's victim as much as I am."

Roz gave a pitying shake of her head, the kind she'd give a student who offered the wrong answer to a question the class had reviewed a million times. "Of course she knows. You think he's lived a blameless life for sixty years and suddenly went berserk last night? You think she's never smelled other women's perfume on him, seen the scratches from other wome—"

"Stop!" Lydia slapped the table, and a group of kids halfway across the room glanced at them in curiosity. She lowered her voice. "You're choosing to see Madalyn in the worst possible light. She'd never stay with Tom if she knew what he does to other women. I'm sure of it."

Roz looked up at the blinking florescent lights in the cafeteria ceiling and took a deep breath. Then she started talking. "I've never been married, but in my early thirties I lived with a man named Rob for three years. We each gave up our crappy studio apartments and moved into a nice one-bedroom. We bought a sofa together. We merged our book collections. I brought my special broccoli casserole to his family's Thanksgiving dinner and everyone loved it."

Lydia felt queasy at the direction she could predict this story was headed.

"After a year and a half, Rob started working late on Thursday nights, even though he hated his job. Then he started watching football with the boys on Sunday afternoons. Always at some unnamed bar. Then he had to go away for the weekend to some great-aunt's funeral." Roz locked her gaze with Lydia's. "I knew, Lydia. I knew he was cheating on me, but I chose to ignore it. Because breaking up meant more than just losing him. It meant moving out of a nice apartment I couldn't afford on my own. It meant losing friends we'd made together. It meant untangling every strand of our lives together."

"I'm sorry," Lydia whispered.

Roz snapped back to her smart-aleck self. "When the size extra-small thong panties showed up in our dryer, I had no choice but to kick his sorry ass to the curb. My one consolation was that the other girl dumped him, too."

Roz glanced at the perpetually inaccurate clock on the wall and began clearing up the trash on their table. "Sorry to bore you with my tale of woe. I just want you to realize Tom provides his wife with the life she's become accustomed to. She won't leave him out of solidarity with you."

Lydia took the crumpled chip bag and shot it into the garbage can. "Thanks, Roz. You really know how to cheer me up."

"Any time, girl."

———◆———

ALTHOUGH IT WAS EARLY November, the weather had turned from crisp to unseasonably warm. Lydia pulled up to the driveway of Lilac Court, but Seth's truck was backed in. No doubt he'd needed to unload something for the kitchen. She parked on the street and entered the house through the front door. No sound of hammering or sawing, but she could hear water running. Lydia walked back to the kitchen, but Seth wasn't there although the back door was wide open. She looked out the kitchen window.

Seth, coated white in plaster dust from head to toe, stood on the crooked brick patio with the garden hose coiled at his feet. He pulled off his t-shirt over his head and shook it.

Lydia stayed rooted to the spot as if she were watching a movie unfold on a screen. Seth's broad shoulders tapered down to a slim waist. His jeans rode low on his hips, the bones jutting out. Although his back was smooth, his chest had some brown hair above his decidedly six-pack abs. When he turned to pick up the hose, Lydia noticed the thin line of dark hair disappearing under the jeans' waistband.

Lydia felt a warm flush heating her chest. She shouldn't be watching Seth like this. Still, she couldn't look away.

As Seth extended his left arm, the muscles rippled under his tanned skin. He directed a stream of water up and down his arm, then moved the hose to the other hand and rinsed the other arm. Then he bent his head and ran the hose over his dusty hair. He straightened and shook like Alfie did after a bath.

The low afternoon sun made the droplets of water on his skin glisten.

A wave of desire swept over Lydia. She gripped the edge of the kitchen counter, lightheaded.

What was happening to her? She'd been numb to the very idea of sex since Charles had died. And the encounter with Tom had made the prospect totally uninviting. Where had that lust come from?

Lydia backed away from the window and slid into the breakfast nook bench, giving herself a shake. She was leering at a twenty-three year old kid like the kind of creepy, cat-calling construction worker she despised.

The back door banged open. "Hey! When did you get home? Sorry my truck's blocking the driveway—I had to load up some stuff." Seth chatted as he strode around the kitchen picking up tools. "I sanded the first coat of spackle. I'll do the second coat later in the week."

Lydia could barely bring herself to look at him. Seth would probably be revolted if he could read her mind. Or maybe he'd simply laugh uproariously at the thought of his old lady client lusting after him.

"What's the matter?" Seth paused with his arm stretched above his head as he checked his work.

Lydia averted her eyes. "Nothing. Everything looks great. You're making fabulous progress." She still felt warm and prayed she wasn't flushing.

"Okay, see you tomorrow." Seth's voice sounded puzzled, but Lydia couldn't bring herself to look up and smile.

Once Seth was gone, Lydia stared out the kitchen window at the wet splotch his impromptu shower had left on the patio bricks. Unbidden, a thought popped into her mind.

She was as much older than Seth as Charles had been older than she.

Chapter 36

Lydia stared at her calendar. "Training with Madalyn" flashed back at her. Each day this week she'd considered sending a quick text. "Sorry—something's come up. I have to cancel."

But each day she'd postponed doing it, until now, the day of the training session had arrived.

Why was she going? To maintain her friendship with Madalyn, whom she genuinely liked? To make Tom squirm, thinking she might say something to his wife? Or maybe to probe, to see if Roz was right, if Madalyn really did know the kind of man she was married to?

Lydia studied herself in her bedroom mirror. How about this? She was going today because she genuinely wanted to learn how to coach low income kids in writing their college essays. She didn't want to wait six months for the next training session. She would never allow herself to be alone with Tom again. But she wasn't going to give up things she wanted to do to avoid Madalyn.

As she turned away from her own image, she saw the glint in her eye.

She would also do a little digging.

GETTING TO THE TRAINING session took less time than she'd estimated, so Lydia chatted with another volunteer until Madalyn arrived. "Sorry I'm late," she whispered in Lydia's ear. "A little crisis with my daughter, but it's all resolved now." Madalyn smiled at the other volunteers near them, and the training session began.

The leader rolled through her presentation, and Lydia focused on taking notes. But occasionally, she shot a sidelong glance at Madalyn.

Unlike everyone else, Madalyn wasn't using the handouts they'd all received to follow along with the lecture. Was she tense? Distracted? Or just confident that she knew how to handle the task at hand?

"Okay, everyone. Let's break for coffee and Danish, and we'll come back and do some role-playing," the leader announced at ten.

Lydia and Madalyn walked to the refreshment table. "The presenter is very good," Lydia observed. "Very well organized."

"Mmm." Madalyn pulled out her phone and frowned at the screen. Then she sighed and closed her eyes for a beat as if praying for patience.

"What's wrong? Is your daughter okay?"

"Ginny is struggling with getting her driver's license renewed. Because of her autism, she has trouble advocating for herself, talking to strangers. Normally, I'd go with her, but I had this commitment."

"Couldn't Tom help her?" Lydia asked. A prickle of sweat emerged on the back of her neck as she brought his name into the conversation.

Madalyn put a big cherry and frosting covered Danish on her plate. "Tom refused to go. He says I baby her too much."

Lydia gauged her response carefully. Before what she now thought of as "the incident" she might have taken Tom's side, suggested that Ginny might benefit from muddling through on her own. Instead she said, "What do you think?"

Madalyn had sunk her teeth into the rich pastry and merely shook her head. Maybe that meant she couldn't talk with her mouth full. Or maybe it meant she didn't want to continue that discussion.

By the time Madalyn had chewed and swallowed, some of the other volunteers had gathered around and the conversation shifted to what they'd learned so far. They talked about readiness for college and whether the kids they would be helping were all good candidates.

"If I think a kid's not cut out for college, I won't hesitate to suggest he study plumbing," one of the tutors in training said. "There's a lot of opportunity there. You can't find a decent plumber these days."

"That's for sure!" Lydia agreed. "After I fired my first contractor, I had a terrible time finding a plumber to finish the work in my kitchen."

"How's the remodeling going?" Madalyn asked.

"Almost done. Tom stopped by to see it on Halloween. Didn't he tell you?"

The words were out of her mouth before she had time to reconsider.

Madalyn paused a beat before answering. "Maybe he mentioned it, and I forgot. We've both been so busy lately—like ships passing in the night."

After the coffee break, they separated into small groups for role-playing. Madalyn and Lydia were paired with two men, one retired, one in his thirties. They were to take turns playing student and tutor.

"I'll go first as the student," the young man volunteered. "Who wants to play my tutor?"

"I'll do it." Lydia stepped forward.

They went back and forth, with the guy in the student role throwing up obstacles and Lydia working to patiently overcome them.

"What I'm interested in is video games," the guy playing the student insisted. "I want to write my college essay about how many people I've killed in *Call of Duty*."

"Whoo, boy—let's see you turn this around," the older guy said to Lydia.

She grinned and took the challenge. "That's certainly a possibility. What good qualities about yourself does your skill in *Call of Duty* display?"

"I have a really quick trigger finger." Lydia's role-playing partner mimed shooting.

"So, you're telling me you have excellent hand-eye coordination. What are some other ways you use that skill in your life?"

Madalyn and the other observer grinned and clapped. "Smooth move, Lydia—great technique in moving him away from an inappropriate topic."

Lydia took a small bow. "Distraction. It's a technique I learned from my dog trainer—always offer your dog a squeaky toy when he's chewing your shoe."

The two men in the group laughed and gave a thumbs up. But Madalyn had a funny look on her face. "I forgot you have a dog now."

After the role playing exercise, the temperature in the meeting room seemed to go up by ten degrees. "Am I having a hot flash?" an older woman asked. "Or is it stifling in here?"

Another woman laughed. "It's not you. I'm hot, too." She pulled off her sweater.

Lydia followed suit, sliding off the silky cardigan she wore over a sleeveless shell. As she draped it over the back of her chair, she froze. The fingerprint bruises were still faintly visible on her upper arms. Would anyone notice? How would she explain them away?

But if the others in her group noticed, they were too polite to comment.

The final hour of the training wound down and they all clustered around saying good-bye and trading phone numbers.

"Don't forget your sweater, Lydia." Madalyn plucked it from the back of a chair and held it out, but her gaze stayed fixed on Lydia's upper arms. "It matches your shirt so well."

Chapter 37

When Lydia got home, the temperature was still balmy as she walked Alfie, but the weatherman had predicted a drop and the possibility of snow. "Don't believe it, Alfie," Lydia said to the dog as they passed the Morrow house where orange and yellow chrysanthemums still bloomed. "I know you're eager to experience your first snowstorm, but you may have to wait. Those forecasters love to get themselves worked up this time of year."

Alfie glanced up at her and nodded. Lydia could always count on him to agree. When they turned the corner into the alley behind Lilac Court, she saw her back door was open. Seth had arrived.

She and Alfie entered the kitchen just as Seth shouted, "Fuck off, Dad!" into his phone. His face was flushed, and his hand trembled.

Lydia couldn't pretend not to have heard. She didn't know anything about Seth's family situation except that he had grown up in Palmyrton and now shared a house with a couple other guys.

Breathing heavily, Seth stared at Lydia and Alfie.

"Would it help to talk?" she asked gently.

He jammed his phone into his back pocket and picked up a screwdriver. But his hand still trembled with anger and the tool slipped out of the screwhead.

"Sit down." Lydia headed to the coffee pot. "Have a cup of coffee and a muffin with me. You'll feel better."

Seth slipped into the breakfast nook bench and cradled his head in his hands. Lydia set a coffee mug in front of him and rested her hand lightly on his shoulder. "Sometimes we get angriest at the people we love."

Seth snorted. "My parents got divorced when I was in high school. My mother got remarried right away and moved to Connecticut. My dad made it clear staying in Palmyrton with me was a big sacrifice. He expected me to go away to college after I graduated high school, so he could move to a golf community in North Carolina. When I started working as a carpenter that summer and changed my mind about college, he got mad. He sold the house out from under me and moved. Figured that would force me to go to college."

Lydia smiled. "I can see you're not an easy person to force. Why did you change your mind about college?"

Seth flung himself backward and gazed up at the ceiling. "Because I hated high school, and the thought of sitting in classrooms for four more years depressed me. And I didn't want to go to frat parties and football games." Seth spat the words out with contempt. "My father didn't care about what I wanted. He only cared about how my decision affected him. He left me here when I was eighteen and didn't even know how to write a check. And now, after I've been supporting myself for five years and paying my own way through Palmer Community, he still thinks he can control me and push me to do what he wants."

Like finish up at Palmer Community and transfer to a university. Lydia guessed Seth's father knew about his son's decision to drop out one course short of his associates degree. What father wouldn't be disappointed by that? And what about Seth's mother? Why wasn't he mad at her? "So your father is upset that you quit Palmer Community?"

Seth scowled. "My mother told my sister who told him. He's an accountant. My mom's a nurse. I'm a big disappointment to both of them. They never expected they'd have a blue collar son."

"Or maybe," Lydia suggested, "they know how smart you are and think you'd be a great architect." She slid a plate of muffins toward him. "After all, you chose that goal for yourself. Just because it would also make your parents happy doesn't mean it's a bad direction for your life."

Seth ripped apart a muffin. "My dad is trying to bribe me to go back. He wouldn't give me a penny these last five years. Now he's trying to control me by dangling tuition money in front of me. Well, screw that!"

Lydia knew she was only hearing one side of the story. If Seth's father were sitting across the table from her, she'd probably be hearing about how the impetuous son went out of his way to reject all offers of assistance. How he was immature and temperamental. And she'd have to agree. "Maybe your father is impressed by how much you've accomplished on your own. Maybe he just wants to help you finish up. Parents tend to want their kids to succeed."

"You don't know what it's like to have someone trying to control you with money!" Seth pushed away from the table and went back to his tools.

"Actually, I do." The very softness of her reply made Seth turn around with interest.

The words had escaped her without forethought. Now she had no choice but to continue. "My husband and I had never discussed his will when he was alive. After he died, I learned that he put terms in his will that would work to influence my future decisions. It was upsetting. His lawyer friend assured me Charles did it to protect me. But there's a fine line between protection and control." There—she'd said it. She hadn't told Madalyn, or Roz, or her sister, or Kathleen, but she'd told this twenty-three year old carpenter how her husband had tried to control her from beyond the grave.

"Yes, exactly. Now you see what I mean." Seth stood before her with his hands jammed in his pockets. "Sure, helping your kid with college tuition seems like a nice, responsible thing for a parent to do. But not if the money is given and taken away all according to what the giver wants." Seth took a step closer. "So what exactly did your husband put in his will?"

How had she gotten this personal with her contractor? But Seth wasn't just someone she'd hired; he was a young man struggling with a big decision. Lydia really didn't want to share the terms of Charles's will, but if she could show him she understood his dilemma, maybe he'd be more flexible about letting his father help him with college. "He left me some money, but he worried I'd be a target for gold-diggers. So he put it in his will that I wouldn't get all the money if I remarried. But it doesn't really matter, since I have no intention of getting married again." Lydia heard herself talking faster and faster as Seth's eyes widened in amazement. "It just...hurt...that he would think I didn't have good judgment and needed restrictions placed on me after he was gone."

Seth ran his fingers through his hair. "Jesus, Lydia—that sounds like something out of an old movie. What are you going to do?"

"I'm going to live my life the way I want to and use the money he left me the way I want to. I bought this house, which I know he wouldn't have approved of. I fired Viktor, who was my husband's favorite contractor, and hired you. I'm not letting him hold me back, but I'm also not making any grand gestures and refusing to touch a penny of his money."

Seth's dark brows drew down. "You think I'm making a grand gesture telling my father to screw off? I'm not. It's not just about the money. I don't want to go to college any more. I'm committed to my carpentry business. That's what I told him. He needs to accept my decision."

Seth left the kitchen and walked out to his truck.

Lydia got the message. She needed to accept Seth's decision, too.

Chapter 38

The next day, emerging from the classroom building, Lydia was knocked back by a frigid blast of wind. The temperature had plummeted thirty degrees since she'd entered the building this morning. The predicted November snowstorm, which had seemed preposterous during the balmy days that had started this week, had arrived with a vengeance. Lydia pulled her scarf up around her face and struggled against the stinging snow toward the parking lot. These weren't fat, fluffy flakes drifting down from the sky. They were nasty little snow-ice pellets shot from a malevolent heaven. When Lydia finally reached her car, through the snow she saw a shadowy outline further down the line: a raised hood and a hunched figure.

Was that Roz?

Lydia dumped her bag onto the front seat and walked down the row of cars to investigate.

"Roz? What's wrong?" she called when she recognized the dented Hyundai.

"Damn battery's dead." Roz aimed a flashlight under her hood and jiggled some wires.

"I'll call Triple A." Lydia reached for her phone, but Roz intercepted her.

"I don't have Triple A. Your policy won't cover me." Roz pushed back her wooly green hat. "I just need a jump. Can you bring your car down here beside mine?"

"Yes, but I don't know how to jump start a battery."

"I have the cables. I'm an old hand at this."

When Lydia came back with her car, Roz had the green and red cables connected to her battery. Lydia frowned as she opened the hood of the Subaru. "Are you sure we won't blow up both cars?"

Roz elbowed her out of the way. "Perfectly safe. I suppose you don't know how to change a tire either." She connected the cables to the Subaru's battery and directed Lydia to her car. "Start your engine, but don't rev it."

Lydia did as she was told. She realized it was remarkable she'd made it so far in life without ever having to deal with car trouble. But Charles had kept their vehicles in perfect working order, anticipating problems, checking air pressure and fluid levels, keeping meticulous maintenance records. So maybe her ignorance of emergency procedures wasn't so surprising after all.

She sat in her car as icy snow pelted the windshield. Occasionally, she heard the grind of Roz's battery trying to turn over and sputtering into failure.

This was hopeless, and the snow was getting worse. Could she offer to pay for a tow truck? Her friend could be prickly about money, always insisting on splitting checks, even in the school cafeteria.

A gust of wind rocked the car, and Lydia reached for her phone. They couldn't fool around any longer. But at just that moment, Roz's engine coughed and sputtered to life.

"Yay! You go, baby!" Roz shouted. She signaled Lydia to turn off her engine and went to disconnect the cables.

The engine hardly sounded like a purring race car. Lydia followed Roz to her trunk as she stashed the cables. "I'd better follow you home, just to be safe."

Roz waved her off. "Nah, I'm fine. But thanks a lot for the jump."

"I insist. If the car dies again, no one will stop to help you in this storm."

Roz put her hands on her hips. "The car is running. I don't need more help."

"It could stall again. Better safe than sorry."

Roz yanked her ugly hat down over her ears. "I don't need you playing Little Miss Guardian Angel. Go home."

"Doesn't matter what you say," Lydia pivoted. "I'm following your car all the way home."

Roz got into her car and gave the door a ferocious slam. She took off with a lead foot, and the Hyundai fishtailed across the parking lot.

Lydia pulled out cautiously and followed Roz at a safe distance. Why did the woman have to be so ornery?

They made their way down the long, slippery college drive and edged out onto the deserted main road without having to stop. Lydia held her breath when they coasted up to the first red light, but Roz's car stayed running and pushed off again when the light changed.

Lydia's hands gripped the wheel as she slipped and shimmied down the unplowed, slushy road. She hated driving in the snow. Often Charles would come to pick her up at Imago when a storm started in the middle of the day. Now that Roz's car seemed to be holding up fine, Lydia began to regret her generosity. But she wouldn't peel off now. She'd said she'd follow Roz home, and she intended to go the distance.

Eventually, Roz signaled and turned off the main road. Lydia followed her along a dingy two lane street that was even more poorly maintained than the county road. Then Roz signaled again, and Lydia followed her into a parking lot surrounded on three sides by two-story yellow brick apartment buildings.

Fresh snow had a way of making everything look clean and peaceful.

But the snow wasn't working its magic here. The scratched metal doors of each apartment unit contained numbers, some self-adhesive, some painted on, some screwed in. Bulging bags of garbage slumped against an overflowing Dumpster. A wheel-less bike was chained to a rusty No Loitering sign. On the second floor, someone had rigged a makeshift clothesline out a window, and two huge, frozen brassieres blew in the wind.

Home sweet home.

No wonder Roz hadn't wanted Lydia to follow her here. Now Lydia had succeeded in embarrassing her friend when all she'd meant to do was help. She should have listened when Roz told her to go home.

Roz parked her car and gave a brusque wave in Lydia's direction. Then she stomped up the unshoveled walk to a dark apartment on the ground floor.

A moment later, a light came on behind pulled-down shades.

Lydia turned her car around and headed to Lilac Court.

⸻❧⸻

THE NEXT MORNING, LYDIA awoke to noise coming from next door. She peeked out her bedroom window. Manish Banerjee clung to a ladder struggling to string Christmas lights along his roof while Grandma Banerjee stood on the porch shouting instructions in agitated Punjabi.

Christmas! There were still over two weeks until Thanksgiving. Lydia was looking forward to spending Thanksgiving with Kathleen and her fiancé in Pittsburgh, but she hadn't even contemplated how she would survive Christmas. Maybe she could join Roz in the Jewish tradition of Chinese food and a movie, but Roz might not welcome her shiksa friend after last night's incident.

Lydia went downstairs and started the coffee. Then she pulled on her down coat and boots over her flannel pajama pants and went out on her own porch. "Can I help you, Manish?"

"Ah, good morning, Lydia!" Manish waved from the ladder. "I am sorry we are making so much noise. My mother feels I am spreading the lights too thin. She wants them closer together."

Grandma Banerjee nodded emphatically. Then she pointed at Lydia's bare roof and furrowed her brow.

"I won't be having lights this year," Lydia explained to Grandma. "I'm just not in the mood."

Manish spoke sharply to his mother in Punjabi, and she nodded sadly.

Lydia didn't like where the half-spoken conversation was headed. She looked out at the yard where Santa and his reindeer awaited inflation. A glittering star of Bethlehem hung from a tree. "You're sure going all out for Christmas, Manish. Aren't you guys Hindu?"

Manish draped another strand of lights from the porch roof. "Why would we want our house to be the only dark house on the block? It is un-American!"

Grandma's face registered deep disapproval. She opened the front door, hiked up her sari, and dragged two more large cardboard boxes labeled XMAS out onto the porch.

Manish climbed down the ladder and accepted another string from his mother. "We Hindus celebrate Christmas not as a religious holiday, but as an expression of peace and love and light. That is a good thing, no matter what your faith, don't you think?"

Lydia smiled. "Absolutely."

Leaving the Banerjees to their project, Lydia went back into her house. She had no energy for Christmas this year. Halloween at Lilac Court had been fun precisely because she and Charles had never celebrated that holiday. Thanksgiving with Kathleen would be a cozy, turkey-fueled reunion. But Christmas loomed like an iceberg threatening to sink her fragile happiness.

Hauling the artificial tree and the ornaments out of the attic had been Charles's job. He took great pride in how realistic their fake tree was (except for its lack of scent, of course). He would set it up in the living room directly in front of the window, and spend hours stringing the lights in a perfect distribution. Then he would call for Lydia and they'd hang the ornaments together.

She had left the tree and ornaments in Palmer Ridge to be sold by Audrey Nealon.

While walking Alfie, Lydia noticed that the Police Athletic League was sponsoring a Christmas tree sale in the community garden. She had considered buying a live tree there, but watching the burly cops wrestle huge trees onto the roofs of SUVs made her heart heavy. How could she manage erecting a big tree single-handedly? Lydia remembered how her parents had squabbled every Christmas as her dad tried to screw the tree into the stand straight. They would yell and curse and then collapse in laughter into each other's arms.

Lydia blinked back tears.

She and Charles threw a big Christmas party every year on the third Saturday of December. Caterers brought in the food and a string quartet played Christmas carols in the foyer. Then on Christmas Eve they'd attend the midnight service of lessons and carols at St. Peter's. Christmas morning they opened their presents. Among their other presents, they'd developed a tradition of giving each other several books—never anything from the bestseller list, but obscure books that they'd each researched for the other. Then they'd spend the day reading their books and listening to Christmas carols and picking at leftovers from the party.

No family arguments. No stressful cooking. Just a cozy day in front of the (gas) fire.

Maybe it wasn't loud and exciting, but it was their family tradition.

And it was gone.

Lydia looked at an empty corner in her living room. Maybe she could buy a tiny Charlie Brown Christmas tree at the supermarket. Isn't that what all the lonely old widows did?

Chapter 39

Lydia had only one day of teaching left before the Thanksgiving break. She crossed paths with Roz briefly, and her friend gave no indication she was still annoyed about the snowstorm incident, so Lydia guessed they were agreeing to forget about it. They wished each other happy Thanksgiving—Roz rolling her eyes at the prospect of turkey with her cousins in Brooklyn—and Lydia went off to teach her class. To her students' surprised delight, she dismissed them ten minutes early.

She could hardly wait to get home herself.

Her piano would be delivered today.

Yesterday, Marta and her partner had blasted through 43 Lilac Court, vacuuming plaster dust, sweeping nails and wood shavings, mopping and polishing. Seth still had to install the kitchen cabinets, but he assured her that wouldn't create much dust.

Lydia flexed her fingers in anticipation. She'd tried to keep up her practice on the pianos on campus, but that was no substitute for daily practice on her own instrument.

Shortly after Lydia got home, the piano movers entered the house. "Where's it goin'?" the fatter one asked.

"In here." Lydia ushered them into the living room.

The taller one scratched his head. "You measure this space?"

My god, what was with these men, constantly question-ing her every statement? "Of course, I measured it!" Lydia snapped. "It fits."

"Okay, if that's where you want it. You're the boss."

First they brought in the piano's legs. Then they went out to the truck for the guts. Lydia was so excited, she couldn't bear to watch the delicate process of maneuvering through the front door and into the living room. She went into the dining room to wait until the men called her and said her Steinway was ready to be played.

In twenty minutes, the call came. The tall guy stuck his head into the dining room. "We're ready to go, if you're sat-isfied."

Lydia ran into the living room.

The men had indeed set up her piano exactly where she told them to.

Her Steinway engulfed the right half of the room. The soundboard pressed against the far wall. The bass end of the keyboard touched the back of the sofa. The bench was shoved all the way under the instrument. The piano looked like a buxom matron crammed into a skinny teenager's sun-dress.

"Want us to move anything else for ya?"

Lydia shook her head, shoved a twenty dollar tip into the mover's hand, and hustled him and his partner out the door.

Then she sat on the steps and cried.

How could she have been so stupid? Yes, she'd measured the piano and measured the room, but she hadn't allowed for the other furniture. The position of the fireplace and the windows meant that the sofa could only fit in one spot: jammed up against the piano.

This is what came of rejecting all guidance and insisting on doing everything herself. She'd had a vision of her cozy living room—curling up by the fire to read a book, then moving over to the piano to play. Having friends over for intimate gatherings. Ha! They'd be wedged in like riders on the A train at rush hour. She should have known she couldn't execute that vision. She had terrible spatial relations skills. She should have hired a decorator.

That miserable Mitchell Felson was right: modest little Lilac Court wasn't big enough to hold her most treasured possession.

She'd have to sell the baby grand and replace it with an upright.

Or sell the house.

Both options made the tears flow harder.

Eyes bleary, she stumbled to the kitchen for a paper towel to blow her nose. On the way through the empty dining room, she paused.

Maybe she could put the piano in here. Make the dining room a music room.

But that would mean letting go of the fantasy of big cheerful dinner parties like Monet used to throw.

Oh, who was she kidding? She barely had enough friends to fill a booth at the Palmyrton diner. If she wanted to invite Roz and Conrad for dinner, they could eat in the breakfast nook. They didn't need to be impressed.

Dining room into music room was a solution she could live with, even if it wasn't ideal.

The back door slammed. "Hey, did your piano come? I thought I'd enter to the sound of you playing."

Lydia spun around, wiping the last of her tears with the hem of her t-shirt.

"Lydia?" Seth came through the dining room and saw her sitting on the bay window seat, her swollen eyes and red nose impossible to conceal. "Hey, what's wrong? Did your piano get damaged?"

Lydia gestured mutely toward the living room. Exposing her mistake to another person brought her down all over again.

Seth entered the living room and uttered a low grunt. He stayed in there for a while, then emerged with his tape measure in his hand. He walked past Lydia without comment, heading back to the kitchen.

Lydia felt annoyance mingling with her disappointment. Seth could at least acknowledge her problem. Sometimes this "man of few words" routine got a little old.

She rose and followed him, talking as she went. "I'm going to move it into the dining room and make that a music room."

But when she got to the kitchen, the room was empty.

Seth emerged from the back hall. "How attached are you to that mudroom?"

"It's handy for wiping off Alfie's paws after a walk. Why?"

He waved her into the rectangular room between the kitchen and the back door. "This wall," he tapped below the hooks where her coat and Alfie's leash hung, "backs up to your living room. I could take this wall out and make an alcove for the piano."

Lydia's brow furrowed. "How would it—"

Seth pulled her back to the kitchen, sat at the table, and sketched out his design. She watched him the way she'd once watched her mom sew the arm back onto her teddy bear, breathless with the combination of tension and hope that Seth would come up with a solution that wouldn't mean losing her dining room. In a few minutes, Seth slid the drawing over to her. At the top of the page, he'd rendered the living room with a new alcove on the wall perpendicular to the bookcases. He'd even drawn in the piano to show how it would fit, and show how there would be enough space to walk around the sofa.

The bottom of the page held a picture of the modified back hall, now narrower, with some cubes next to the door to hold the bare necessities.

Lydia studied the picture in wonder. Her gaze lifted and she stared into Seth's blue, blue eyes. "How do you *do* this? How do you see the potential in the space?"

He shrugged. "I dunno. It's easy for me. I have a knack for picturing how stuff fits together."

Lydia grabbed Seth's wrist and pinned it to the table. "No. It's more than a knack. You have a rare gift, Seth. It's something you were born with, the way my friend Conrad was born with perfect pitch. The way Michelangelo could see a statue in a particular hunk of marble. You should be an architect, a creator, not just a carpenter who executes other people's plans."

Seth yanked his arm away. "Don't start on the school stuff again. I'm not cut out for sitting in dull classes, wasting my time."

Alfie yipped in support.

Lydia knew better than to go another round on the value of English composition. But the dog's agitation made her think of Jim and his theories. "When I first got Alfie, he used to nip at me if I got too close to his food. He'll still nip if he perceives a threat. You know what his trainer says? Jim says that Alfie nips when he's insecure. He says that anger is the flip side of fear."

"You're comparing me to a dog?"

"Yes, I am." Lydia stood and paced around the kitchen. "Whenever I bring up architecture, you get angry. I think you're afraid. You're afraid you're not actually good enough to make it as an architect. You're afraid you'll meet people just as talented as you, maybe even more talented. That's why you get angry when anyone tries to push you to continue your education."

"I don't need a piece of paper to give me permission to design."

"Oh, yes—you're an *artist*, a free spirit." Lydia gave a woo-woo wave of her hands. "But remember Seth, you're not an artist who only needs a canvas and some paint. To design big, beautiful, dramatic houses, you need raw materials: granite and teak and stone and tile. That means you need rich people to underwrite your work, Seth. And I know from rich people." She tapped her chest. "Rich people aren't going to hire a community college dropout to design their ski lodge or their beach cottage or their town house. They're going to hire an architect. A certified, registered architect."

She walked over and tapped him on the chest. "Not a carpenter."

Seth pushed past her and slammed out the back door. A moment later, his truck gunned out of the driveway.

Lydia looked around at the raw holes in her kitchen where the cabinets should be.

Had she just fired another contractor?

Chapter 40

The evening stretched ahead of her, empty and unwelcoming. She took Alfie for his walk and fed him his dinner, but there was nothing in the fridge for her to eat. She couldn't face pizza or carry-out Thai food again.

She wanted to be in the company of other humans.

Alfie laid his head on her knee. "Sorry, buddy. You're just not doing it for me tonight."

Whom could she call? Roz was teaching her evening class at Essex. She peeked out the back window at the Morrow's house. All dark.

An idea popped into her head. She could go to the Blue Monday and eat a burger at the bar. At least she'd be surrounded by light and noise and energy.

She twisted her fingers together. Could she walk into a bar by herself? She'd never done that, not even as a single girl in her twenties.

Lydia gave herself a shake. She wasn't going to some sinister, drug-fueled dance club. Sitting among the cops and frustrated musicians with a beer and Blue Burger would lift her spirits.

Lydia grabbed her keys and a folder full of essays to correct, and drove to the Blue Monday. She wouldn't have to talk to anyone—the essays were her electric fence against unwelcome advances by obnoxious drunks. But she could at least feel like part of the human race.

Arriving at seven, Lydia found the bar pretty quiet. The grab-a-beer-after-work crowd was dispersing, and the party-all-night crowd hadn't yet arrived. Hoping she looked confident yet casual, Lydia hopped on an empty stool, placed her order, and pulled out her essay folder and red pen. Around her, cops discussed the arrests of the day—"blood from the stolen steaks was dripping outta her purse!"—while sports fans shouted at the TV—"you call that a foul?!"

The juicy Blue Burger arrived and Lydia realized she hadn't had a hot meal with red meat all week. That made her think about her own kitchen, so far away from being a functional space in which to cook food. Why had she felt the need to nag Seth about his education? If he didn't want to finish his degree, what business was it of hers?

Lydia dragged a French fry through the ketchup but left it dangling in her hand. Because she liked Seth. She didn't regard him as hired help. Yet he wasn't quite a friend. And he hadn't asked for advice.

She of all people should be sensitive to the dangers of unwanted advice. She'd certainly rejected all guidance in her pursuit of 43 Lilac Court.

A second beer appeared in front of her almost empty plate.

"I didn't—"

The bartender thumbed over his shoulder and kept walking. Lydia squinted across the bar, lit only by the glow of the TV above her head. Two burly cops argued about the Jets' prospects. A young woman tossed her blond hair and stared nervously at the door. A thin man sat with his head bowed reading a book.

She knew that hair.

Hair that looked short, but was actually pulled into a pony tail. Was it...?

Jim. Jim, the dog trainer.

She finished the last bite of her burger, picked up her folder of essays and her fresh beer, and moved around to his side of the bar. "Hey, you come here often?" Lydia slid onto the stool beside him.

Jim looked up from his book and smiled slightly. "Often enough."

"Why didn't you come over and talk to me?"

He squirmed in his seat. "You seemed engrossed in whatever you were doing. I know sometimes I'm not in the mood for company."

"I hope tonight's not one of those times. I could use some conversation."

He brightened. "How's Alfie?"

"Much better. He has some occasional backsliding, but I trust him enough to give him the run of the house while I'm out."

"Have you gotten him a crate?"

Lydia wanted some pleasant conversation. "Yes," she lied. And then she moved on quickly. "I've moved completely into the house in Burleith, you know. But it's still a work in progress."

"Tell me about that."

So Lydia spun out the whole tale of her clashes with Viktor and her discovery of Seth with all his contradictions.

"So," she ended, "I used some of your dog psychology on him, and I'm afraid it backfired."

Jim sat in silence for a moment. Eventually, he turned to face Lydia and spoke. "I think your assessment of Seth's problem is probably correct. Why did you feel the need to challenge him with it?"

"Uhm...I don't know. But somehow, I suspect you have a theory on that."

Jim gave his funny little half-smile again. "Well, Lydia, I'd say your challenge to Seth also displayed some anger. Do you think your anger is associated with fear?"

That question knocked her back. Something about the way Jim never spoke hastily made it easy to sit and think before answering his question. "I guess...I guess maybe I'm afraid *for* him. Afraid that he'll make the kind of mistakes I made when I was his age."

Jim arched his eyebrows as his only encouragement to keep talking.

"I nearly dropped out of grad school without finishing my master's degree. I discovered I didn't really care for academia, but it would've been a mistake to quit with only two classes and a master's thesis to go. And I thought I didn't possess any marketable skills. But I did. I was good at writing ad copy."

Lydia edged forward on her stool, wanting to tell Jim the whole story. "I was kind of stuck when I was Seth's age—not able to move forward, not wanting to leave what was familiar. I suspect that's where he is, too."

"Perhaps you should share your own experience with him next time you see him. Instead of telling him what to do, lead by example."

"If there is a next time."

Jim offered his slight, twitchy smile again. "Oh, I imagine there will be. When friendships die, they most often fizzle out from lack of interest. Where there's strong emotion, there's life."

He tossed a twenty dollar bill on the bar and slid off his stool. "Goodnight, Lydia. Maybe I'll see you here again sometime."

Lydia watched him walk toward the door. As he passed under the light of the Yuengling Beer sign, she noticed he was wearing a green shirt.

Her shoulders tightened. In her mind, she reeled back to the open mic night here at Blue Monday. Was Jim the man that Roz claimed had been staring at her? The bartender called him the guy in the green shirt. She suspected Jim didn't own very many shirts. Had Jim sent them drinks anonymously? Why hadn't he come over to talk to them? Had Jim heard her singing? Why hadn't he mentioned it tonight?

What an odd man.

Nice, but odd.

Chapter 41

When Lydia got back to Lilac Court, Seth's truck sat in the driveway.

An interesting development. Jim was some kind of psychic.

She parked behind the truck and walked slowly toward the house thinking about what she'd say. Certainly, Seth wouldn't have come back at night and sat around waiting for her if he intended to yell at her and quit.

She hoped.

She went in the front door and followed the glow of a lamp to the living room.

Seth sat on the sofa with the baby grand looming over him.

She dropped onto the cushion beside him. "Hey."

He sat quietly, watching her.

Was he waiting for her to apologize? She wouldn't. She wasn't sorry for speaking the truth, just for the harsh way she'd presented it. She recalled how skillfully Jim had drawn her into a long conversation simply by asking a quiet question and waiting.

"What made you come back?" Lydia asked.

Seth's long dark lashes—lashes any woman would kill for—brushed his high cheekbone. "Wanted to prove how brave I am."

"You could try taking a steak away from Alfie. That requires a Green Beret's courage."

Seth didn't smile at her joke. His gaze searched her face. Lydia reached out and took his hand. "I think you're tremendously talented and you'd make a great architect. I hate to see you running headlong away from success. That's why I said what I did. I didn't mean to hurt you."

"I know. But I already screwed up, so I can't apply to architecture school now. It's too late." He pulled away from her.

How melodramatic he was! But she knew better than to say that.

"Seth, it's one flunked course, not a homicide conviction. You can fix this." Lydia grabbed her laptop from the coffee table and pulled up the Palmer Community College website. "There's a late-start, on-line Comp 1 class that you could start next week and be done in seven weeks. Once you pass it, the failed class won't count in your GPA. And you have a fabulous portfolio. Any university would be lucky to get you."

"But the failed class will still be on my transcript. I checked. I need to do more than just get accepted to an architecture program. I need a scholarship."

"So you write a truly compelling application essay. I'll help you. And I'll nag you through your Comp 1 homework as well."

"If I start architectural school this fall, I won't finish until I'm twenty-eight."

"Seth, in four years you'll be twenty-eight no matter what. You can be twenty-eight and an architect, or twenty-eight and still a carpenter."

He sat silently, staring at his nicked and callused hands.

"Grandma Moses was seventy-six when she first picked up a paintbrush. Julia Child was in her fifties when she got her TV show."

"Who's Julia Child?"

She kept forgetting how young he was. "Never mind. J.K. Rowling—you know who she is, right? Thirty-two before *Harry Potter* started selling."

Seth squinted at her. "How do you know all this?"

"Because I thought my life was over at twenty-four, too. My husband helped me to see that my life was just beginning. He saw something in me that I didn't see in myself. And then I thought my life was over again when he died, and I had given up my job in advertising. Now, I'm starting over again, too. It's hard. It really is. It's easier to just slog along in the same old safe path. But to live, you have to take risks."

Seth scrutinized her. "What's the last risk you took?"

Lydia knew Seth wouldn't be impressed by the riskiness of buying this house or starting a new job teaching. "I sang at Open Mic Night in a bar."

Seth sat up out of his slouch. "No way!"

"Way. And I was pretty good, too. People bought me so many drinks that I was still drunk when I woke up the next morning."

Now Seth was truly impressed. "I want to hear you sing."

Lydia rose. "Move the sofa a little so I can slide out the piano bench."

Seth did as instructed, and Lydia sat down at the Steinway. Her fingers drifted over the keys playing a few chords. Then she took a deep breath and began to sing and play "One Fine Day." Seth stood beside the piano and watched.

When the last note died away, he sat back down on the sofa, pulled the laptop onto his knees, and looked at the course selections. "You really think I can pass Comp 1 this time?"

"I know it."

Chapter 42

Thanksgiving weekend passed quickly. Lydia had spent hours pouring out her heart to Kathleen. But oddly enough, by the time Sunday rolled around, Lydia had been ready to come home to Lilac Court and Palmer Community College and especially to Alfie, who'd been frantic with joy when she picked him up from Happy Tails doggy day care.

On Monday morning, Lydia entered the adjunct office with a spring in her step.

"How would you pronounce this name?" Roz greeted her by sliding a class roster in front of Lydia with a first name highlighted: C-E-R-Y-N-E

"Serene?" Lydia guessed.

Marty looked over her shoulder and offered his wager. "Ser-*inn*?"

"Karen." Roz said. "The kid tells me her name is Karen. Honestly, I understand that parents might want to give their kids an unusual name. Go ahead: name your kid Aphrodite Abramowitz or Birchbark Benitez. What I don't get is why you'd want to give your kid a perfectly ordinary name and then *spell it wrong*."

"How do you get 'Karen' out of that combination of letters?" Marty protested.

"Exactly. New parents in the maternity ward should be required to pass a phonics test before they're allowed to name their baby," Roz grumbled.

"Be grateful the name doesn't contain any random apostrophes," Celine, the French teacher, chimed in. "I once accidently flunked a kid by leaving out her apostrophe in the grading program."

Lydia tried to tune out the "can you top this" stories of the other adjuncts. She'd wanted a job with an active water cooler culture, and she certainly got it. Still, sometimes she missed the peace and quiet of her big corner office with a solid wood door at Imago. It was hard to focus on grading papers with so much background noise.

The familiar opening trill of "Bad to the Bone" sounded several times in a row.

"Roz, answer your damn phone," Marty complained.

Roz trotted back from the copier across the room. "Hello? Yeah. How much?"

Lydia had been listening with half an ear. Suddenly, the tone of Roz's voice changed.

"What! No way! Can't you just patch it together? A whole new transmission. No, no—I'll have to get back to you."

By now, everyone in the office was listening.

Roz jammed her phone in her pocket and ran out the door.

Marty met Lydia's gaze and shrugged. "Sounds like her car trouble is worse than she expected."

Celine swiveled back to her computer. "Wasn't Roz's car in the shop just last month?"

Lydia got up and followed Roz out the door. She saw her friend striding toward the ladies room, and caught up with her as she entered.

Roz's face was streaked with tears.

Lydia extended her hand. "What happened?"

Roz jerked away. "Nothing. Just give me a little space, wouldja?" She ducked into a stall and slammed the door behind her.

"Roz, answer me," Lydia shouted through the metal door. "How much did the garage say the repair would cost? I have a good mechanic. He can probably do it for less." Lydia knew Roz was too proud to take a loan from her. But if Roz would take her car to Lydia's garage, Lydia could arrange to pay for part of the repair.

"It needs a whole new transmission. The repair would cost more than the car is worth, no matter who does it. I'm screwed." Roz's voice shook. She sounded more than upset; she sounded terrified.

Lydia rapped on the stall door. "Roz, come out of there. Talk to me. Let me help you."

The door slammed open. Roz's bloodshot eyes bulged wide with fear. "I'm broke, Lydia. My credit cards are maxxed out. I have nothing...zero...zip in the bank. I live paycheck to paycheck. I thought I'd have the full-time job by now, but then that damn Chester Renault—" she kicked the stall door shut—"decided he wasn't ready to retire after all."

Roz scrubbed her tear-streaked face with a wet paper towel. "How am I going to survive without a car? How can I get to work? Today, I took the bus here. A five mile trip took an hour and fifteen minutes. My choice is to come two hours early or fifteen minutes late. But who's going to take me to freakin' Essex Community College? I doubt I could get Uber to pick me up there at ten at night. Not that I could pay Uber. And I need that second job. I can't pay my rent without it."

Lydia pulled Roz's trembling body close to hers. "Calm down. I have a solution. You can borrow my car, and—"

"Are you listening?" Roz's voice grew shrill with panic. "I have to leave here at four on Tuesdays and Thursdays to make it to Essex by five-thirty. You're still teaching at four."

"Hush! Let me finish. I never got around to selling my husband's car. It's in my garage. I'll drive that car and you drive my Subaru."

Roz pulled back and stared at Lydia. "You have an *extra* car? Just sitting around? Collecting dust?"

Lydia certainly wasn't going to tell her friend the truth—that she and Charles had always had an extra car. That she'd sold his Jaguar, but had made a conscious choice to keep both the Subaru and the BMW. That having two cars for one person had never, until this moment, struck her as excessive. "I've had a lot on my mind. Selling Charles's car wasn't a top priority. The insurance was paid through the end of the year, so I figured there was no rush."

Roz was still breathing as if she'd narrowly survived a knife attack.

Lydia kept talking. "So now I'm glad I didn't sell it. You can use the Subaru as long as you need to. Take your time—save up and buy a decent car."

Roz looked at her incredulously. She seemed incapable of speech.

"Wash your face." Lydia nudged Roz toward the sink. "Come back to the office, and I'll give you my keys so you can drive to Essex this afternoon, and I'll take an Uber home."

"I can't. It's too much—"

Lydia turned her back. "It's not too much. This is what friends are for."

Chapter 43

No sooner had Lydia returned from teaching than a knock came at her front door. After the incident with Tom Schilling, she had ordered a sturdy new door with a deadbolt and a clear, functioning peephole. She looked through and saw Aastha Banerjee on the front porch. A few snowflakes clung to her shiny black hair.

Lydia opened the door and pulled her neighbor inside. "Come in, Aastha—you're freezing out there."

"I do not mean to disturb you, Lydia. But I see that you have no lights or tree this year, and I know this holiday must be very difficult for you."

Lydia stood with a wan smile on her face. *Please, God, don't let her offer to put an inflatable Santa in my yard.*

"So I have come here to ask you to join us for Christmas," Aastha continued. "I said to my husband, 'Manish, maybe Lydia will feel better to come here and eat curry and samosas and pakora with us.' It will be a good option for the very reason that it is so different from what you have done in the past. No comparisons!"

No "Silent Night", no egg nog, no pine cones. Lydia could practically smell the cloves and cardamom and cumin of Grandma Banerjee's curry. Her eyes welled with tears at the pure kindness of her neighbors.

Lydia flung her arms around Mrs. Banerjee's neck. "Yes, I'd love to come."

With the Christmas conundrum solved in such an unexpectedly positive way, Lydia sat down to tackle all the end-of-semester papers she had to grade before the holiday break. Alfie insisted on sitting beside her on the sofa with his head in her lap, which made writing comments on the papers a little awkward. But poor Alfie couldn't get enough of her after four days apart, so Lydia indulged him.

As she worked, she could hear emails pinging into her in-box, but she forced herself to finish one stack of essays before she paused to check her phone. Amid the many offers of rock-bottom Christmas sales, one email stood out: "You're Invited to the 35th Annual Schilling New Year's Eve Blast!"

Ha! No way was she going to that. The last thing she needed was to be cornered by a drunk Tom Schilling when the ball dropped at midnight.

She quickly checked "sorry, can't make it" on the Evite, and returned to correcting the next batch of papers.

Seconds later, her phone rang.

Madalyn.

Shit.

She could hardly let it roll to voicemail when she'd just responded to the RSVP. Obviously, she was home.

"Hi, Madalyn."

"Lydia, I know it's rude to grill someone about why she's declined an invitation..."

Yes.

"...but I just want to make sure you're not saying no because you think it will be awkward to be a singleton at the party. I have quite a few bachelors and bachelorettes coming this year. Not that I'm trying to fix you up, or anything."

"No, no—I truly appreciate the invitation, Madalyn, but I...er... got invited to a party being thrown by a colleague at work, so I said yes to that."

"That's nice. But everyone has been asking about you—they want to see you. So here's an idea—stop by our house early, and then move on to your second party. That way, you can see everyone here and still have fun with your new friends."

Good lord, Madalyn was persistent. Lydia's brain spun to think of another excuse. "Well, uh, that won't work because, uhm, I'm driving to the party with someone else."

"Lydia, you're a lousy liar," Madalyn said with a chuckle. "I know you think it will be strange to come to our party alone after all those years of coming with Charles, but you *must* come —Betsy and Regis, and the Finns, and our daughter—everyone wants to see you. Please say yes."

As horrible as it was to disappoint Madalyn, it was even more horrible to contemplate being with Tom at a party where people were expected to kiss one another. Halloween came back to her in a rush, and she could feel Tom's meaty tongue forcing its way into her mouth and his thick fingers pressing into her flesh. Lydia shuddered.

"No, Madalyn. I'm sorry, but I simply can't come this year."

"Hmm—you leave me no choice but to call out the heavy artillery," Madalyn said. Then she hung up.

Ten minutes later, Lydia understood what that meant.

Tom was calling.

She stared at her phone's screen.

She could refuse to answer.

Or she could tell that prick exactly why she wasn't coming to his damn party.

Lydia hit "accept." "Hello, Tom."

"Hi, darling." Tom's jovial voice rang in her ear. "What's this I hear you're not coming to the New Year's Eve bash? You're breaking my wife's heart."

He could seriously say that? Act like nothing had happened between them?

"*I'm* breaking her heart? No, Tom—I'm protecting her, so we don't have another episode like we had on Halloween when you sexually assaulted me."

"Heh, heh." Tom gave a nervous chuckle. "No need to worry about that."

Lydia suspected that Madalyn was right there listening to her husband's end of the conversation. She lowered her voice. "You listen to me, Tom Schilling, and you listen good. I haven't forgotten that you attacked me, would've raped me if not for my dog. I won't be able to avoid you forever. So I'm warning you—the next time we meet, you keep your distance. Or there will be hell to pay."

"Okay, Lydia. I understand." Tom sounded like he was struggling to maintain his salesman's congeniality. "I'll let Madalyn know I couldn't change your mind about the party."

Lydia ended the call while Tom was still saying goodbye. Her hands trembled, but her heart felt strong. She got out her best stationary and wrote Madalyn a gracious note thanking her for understanding just how difficult holidays could be for the recently bereaved.

Chapter 44

With the end-of-semester frenzy in full swing, every desk in the adjunct office held a red-pen- wielding professor. People worked silently, eager to get their grading done and call the semester a wrap.

"Whoa, Lydia—you made the news." Marty broke the room's quiet industry.

"What are you talking about?" Lydia swiveled away from her own computer and rolled toward Marty, who, as usual, was perusing social media instead of correcting papers.

"Your picture is on PalmyrtonNow.com."

A picture of Roz, Lydia, Jim, and Jim's friend, whose name Lydia had forgotten, filled Marty's screen. "Yeah, that was taken at my neighborhood block party last summer. Why are they running it in PalmyrtonNow months later?"

"It's in a round-up of community events that make Palmyrton great. Whenever the website publishes too many clickbait trash stories, the advertisers pressure them to write something upbeat." Marty zoomed in on the photo. "You're keeping some pretty exalted company."

"What's that supposed to mean? I ran into Jim, who helped me train my dog. And that other guy is his friend." Marty could be funny, but sometimes his nonstop commentary got annoying, and his jokes depended on arcane references.

"That," Marty pointed to Jim's friend, "is Peter Ahlberg."

"Yeah, Pete. That's how Jim introduced him. Why, do you know him?"

"I wish! Lydia, Peter Ahlberg is on the Fortune 500 List of the country's richest tech executives. He was one of the co-founders of SoftGraph. And then he sold that and bought Attune and totally turned it around. I hope he paid for that ice cream you're eating in the picture."

Lydia rolled closer to the computer and squinted at the picture on the screen. She looked pretty good in her flowered sundress. Roz grinned with Alfie at her feet. Jim stood on one side of her in his perpetually baggy khakis, and his friend stood on the other side, laughing and waving off the photographer. He wore a black t-shirt and a backwards baseball cap. "Seriously—Jim's friend is rich and famous? He didn't act like he was anyone special. And why would he come to the Burleith neighborhood block party?"

"Slumming, I guess."

Lydia grew more perplexed as she stared at the picture and its caption: "Tech Star visits Palmyrton neighborhood festivities." She rolled back to her own computer and Googled Peter Ahlberg. As she scanned his Wikipedia biography, a sentence jumped out at her. "Ahlberg founded SoftGraph in 1998 with his Stanford college roommate, James Fontaine, of Palmyrton, NJ. In 2004, the duo sold SoftGraph, and Ahlberg went on to buy Attune." Lydia didn't care what happened to Ahlberg after that. Instead, she Googled James Fontaine. A shorter biography popped up, along with a picture of a much younger Jim, but unmistakably her dog trainer, Jim. She realized that she had never known Jim's last name. He'd never told her. His dog trainer's business card didn't have his full name.

She started to read Jim's bio. "James Fontaine was born in Palmyrton, NJ, son of Delia and Vincent Fontaine. After serving two years in the Army, he graduated from Stanford University, where he majored in computer science and economics. It was at Stanford that he met Peter Ahlberg, with whom he would go on to co-found SoftGraph." Lydia skimmed over the part that described how revolutionary the software product they developed was. But her interest picked up when she got to the end of the bio. "Fontaine and Ahlberg sold SoftGraph in 2004 for an estimated $30 million. Ahlberg remained active in the San Jose hi-tech community, going on to buy Attune and invest in many smaller start-ups, while Fontaine returned to Palmyrton, where he has avoided the spotlight."

Lydia sat staring at the screen, but picturing Jim at the dog shelter, Jim at her house with Alfie, Jim at Blue Monday. Why had he hidden his background from her? True, she couldn't expect him to announce his net worth upon being introduced. But he'd never even mentioned he was a software developer. He'd let her believe he was an under-employed dog trainer, scraping by with an old car and even older clothes.

Lydia felt oddly betrayed.

Then she gave herself a shake and went back to grading papers.

Chapter 45

Christmas day with the Banerjees had been delightful, and Lydia returned home with enough leftovers to feed herself for a week. The rest of the holiday season dragged, but Lydia worked hard to stay busy.

She repainted her bright yellow bedroom herself, and got the entire upstairs at Lilac Court decorated and organized. The tutoring organization that had trained her and Madalyn called with some winter break projects, which Lydia eagerly accepted. Roz had daytime and nighttime gigs teaching SAT prep, so Lydia only saw her a few times for drinks.

Seth suspended work on the kitchen for a week while he visited his mother in Connecticut, but returned after New Year's and plunged in with renewed vigor.

Finally, the spring semester began.

When Lydia entered the adjunct office for the first time in mid-January, pictures of used cars filled Roz's screen. "As soon as we get paid this month, I should be able to swing a down payment on a car, so I can finally return your Subaru."

"Roz, I've told you a million times—there's no rush. Drive it as long as you need to. Wait until you have enough saved to buy a reliable used car."

"Driving your car is making me a nervous wreck. Some old lady let go of her shopping cart in the ShopRite parking lot the other day. I caught it two seconds before it crashed into your fender. And leaving it in the Essex parking lot worries me to death. I need to return that car to you before something terrible happens to it."

"It's insured. And I'm not some car fanatic." *Like Charles was.*

Roz ignored her and returned to scrutinizing the cars on the screen. Lydia peered over her shoulder. "A Honda Civic with a hundred thousand miles on it? That doesn't seem like a good choice."

Roz's shoulders tensed. "Well, Lydia, I'd love to get a quality pre-owned Mercedes from German Motors of Palmyrton, but that's not in the cards."

Lydia retreated. Once again, she'd managed to put her foot in her mouth on the subject of Roz's financial situation. She'd seen the banner headline on the website Roz was perusing: Bad Credit? No Problem! Roz couldn't afford to look for the best deal on a car. She needed to buy from a place like this because she couldn't qualify for a loan anywhere else. All she had for a down-payment was the cash she'd gotten from scrapping her beater and what she'd earned from teaching SAT prep over Christmas break. She'd end up paying much more for a used car than someone like Lydia would with an all-cash transaction.

The poor always paid more than the rich. And Lydia knew if she hadn't married Charles, she might be in the same place as Roz right now: underpaid and never able to get a leg up on her debts.

Lydia wanted to help her friend, but Roz wouldn't let her.

There had to be a way. Lydia decided that on the way home, she'd stop by the garage that had been servicing the Eastlee cars throughout her marriage. Maybe Jonathan, the owner, would have an idea.

———◆———

JONATHAN FARADAY, OWNER of Prestige Auto Maintenance, always wore a crisp white button down shirt and sharply creased navy Dockers. His hands were as clean as a brain surgeon's. Yet he knew all about the inner workings of cars even though he seemed never to touch them. No wonder Charles had loved working with the man.

"Mrs. Eastlee—how nice to see you. What can I do for you today? Trouble with the BMW?"

Another point in Jonathan's column was that he never treated his female customers as too dumb to understand their own cars. He'd helped Lydia sell Charles's Jaguar and had reviewed with her every detail of the car's value before setting a price and finding a buyer. "No, my cars are running fine. But I need your advice for my cousin."

Lydia had already decided that Jonathan might find it strange that she was making such an effort for a friend, so she'd upgraded Roz to a relative.

"Certainly. How can I help?" He leaned forward with his hands folded on the counter, ignoring the clank of tools and the hum of the lifts out in the service bays.

"She needs to buy a reliable used car. Her resources are...er...limited, but she's very proud. I'd like to help her buy a car without her realizing."

"So she'd pay some and you'd pay the rest." Jonathan clarified the situation without changing his facial expression. How refreshing not to have a man offer his unsolicited advice!

"Exactly. She was looking at a Honda Civic on that website, Kars 4 Keeps."

Jonathan's eyes widened in alarm. "Oh, no. Never, ever buy from those scumbags. I know about a sweet Honda Civic with reasonable mileage. Bring her in here tomorrow, and we'll arrange the title transfer. She'll write me one check, and you'll write me a check for the balance later." He offered Lydia a conspiratorial wink.

"Perfect, Jon." Lydia squeezed his hand. "I knew I could count on you."

Lydia turned to leave, then doubled back. "So how much is that Honda?"

"He's asking twelve grand, but I can get him down to ten."

Lydia gulped. She hadn't bought a used car since she used her summer lifeguarding money to buy a jalopy back in Ohio. Well, there was no turning back now. She had to keep reminding herself of the obscene amount of money she now possessed. Charles had left two million to his high school. She could think of this as an endowed chair for her favorite professor.

She thought Charles might even approve.

"Fine. I'll bring my cousin in tomorrow."

Chapter 46

E very workday when Lydia picked up Alfie from Happy Tails doggy day care, the workers would tell her he had been a good boy who played nicely with the other dogs. But as soon as Lydia got him home, Alfie would tear around the house like a lunatic. Apparently, the effort of behaving pushed him to his limit, and he had to release his pent-up joy at being back on his own turf and king of all he surveyed.

"Alfie, give that back," Lydia shouted as the dog zoomed past with one of the shoes she'd just kicked off. She chased him down and retrieved the shoe, playing tug with one of his toys to distract him. But as soon as she turned her attention to making dinner, Alfie was up to mischief again. When she turned around to get the butter she needed to sauté her chicken, the butter dish was empty and Alfie sat in front of the counter licking his lips.

"Oh, Alfie, no!" Lydia looked in her fridge, but she had no more butter and no milk for breakfast either. She hadn't been grocery shopping all week. "Fine! Now I have to go to the market. You stay here."

She left her unremorseful dog chewing a Nyla Bone and drove off to Whole Foods. When she returned forty-five minutes later, Alfie didn't run to greet her.

Odd.

"Alfie, I'm back," Lydia called, "and I bought you some liver treats even though you don't deserve them."

The dog didn't answer.

"Alfie?" Lydia went into the kitchen. Alfie's bed was empty although his bone was still there.

Uneasily, Lydia entered the dining room, still calling. By the time she reached the living room, her heart was pounding. She switched on the light, and there lay Alfie beside the fireplace. His tongue lolled out of his mouth, and as she ran to him, his body spasmed. Falling to her knees beside him, she smelled a pungent odor and saw a pool of liquid and an overturned can. Alfie had gotten into the oil Seth was using to restore the wood on the fireplace mantle and trim.

Alfie's eyelids flickered as he panted rapidly. My God, someone else she loved was going to die right in front of her just as Charles had.

Lydia reached for her phone to call 911, and then realized they didn't send out an ambulance for dogs.

She grew frantic. What to do?

With shaking fingers, she scrolled through her contacts until she found the vet, but of course she got their voice-mail—it was nearly eight o'clock.

Alfie moaned and his body shook again.

Jim! Jim would know what to do. Luckily, she'd entered the number from his business card into her phone.

Please, please pick up.

"Hello, Lydia." Jim's voice was calm and mellow, as always.

"It's Alfie. He's eaten something poisonous and he's having seizures. What should I do?"

Immediately, Jim's voice changed. "Take him to the 24-hour animal emergency room, and bring what he ate."

Jim gave her the address. "I'll call ahead to warn them and meet you there."

——◆——

THE NEXT THREE HOURS passed in an alternating whirl of panic and relief: panic when she got stuck at a long red light on the way to the vet, relief when Jim was there to meet her, panic when the vet said Alfie needed IV medication, relief when he emerged from the examining room and said the dog would be fine, but they would keep him for a day for observation.

Shaking with emotion, Lydia leaned on Jim as they walked back to their cars in the parking lot.

"Thank you so much for helping me," Lydia said as they stood beside Jim's battered SUV.

"No problem. But how did Alfie get access to those chemicals?"

"He got into my carpenter's supplies while I was out at the supermarket."

Jim's brow furrowed. "You should keep him in his crate whenever you're out as long as this repair work is going on."

A sob choked Lydia. She should've gotten a crate. Why had she been so stupid?

"How does he like his crate?" Jim persisted. "Do you need me to help with crate training?"

Lydia couldn't take any more. "I never got him a crate," she confessed. "I didn't think we needed one."

Jim looked puzzled. "But that night at Blue Monday, you told me you did get a crate."

Lydia looked at the ground. "I didn't feel like arguing."

Jim drew his shoulders back. "I'm stunned that you would lie to me, Lydia."

This was too much. Her emotions were already frayed to the breaking point. She didn't need Jim's criticism heaped on top of her own guilt. "Well, you lied to me, too!" she lashed out. You never told me you were Jim Fontaine. *The* Jim Fontaine, software entrepreneur."

"I most certainly did not lie." Jim didn't raise his voice, but he was emphatic.

"You lied by omission. You let me believe you were some poor schlep barely surviving as a dog trainer."

Jim arched his eyebrows. "No, Lydia—you leapt to that conclusion. You saw my clothes and my car and assumed I was broke, not that I was practical. You never asked me about my life. If you had, I would have told you the truth."

Was that true? No—surely she'd asked him how long he'd been training dogs. "You told me you'd been training dogs since you were in your twenties. Your business card intentionally omits your last name."

"I have been training dogs since I was young. I just didn't do it professionally." Jim paced between their cars. "It's true I don't want to use my full name on my cards. I left Silicon Valley because I wanted a complete break with that phase of my life. After Pete and I sold our company, we both stayed in San Jose. All day long, people were hitting me up with investment opportunities in high-tech start-ups or wanting me to give them technology advice. I couldn't escape my history. Then my mom got sick, and I came back home to Palmyrton to help her out. I discovered I wasn't famous here, and I tried my best to keep it that way. But my life story has always been a simple Google search away."

Jim opened the door to his SUV and looked back over his shoulder. "For those who cared to look."

Chapter 47

The next morning, Lydia arrived at Pet Emporium before the store even opened. She bought a crate and spent the morning watching YouTube videos on how to train the dog to accept it.

She certainly couldn't ask Jim for help.

Whenever her mind wasn't otherwise occupied, thoughts of Jim and the scene in the vet's parking lot rushed in. Jim had gone out of his way to help her, and she had behaved badly in return.

But why did he have to take that tone of high moral indignation when she admitted she'd lied about the crate? It was the tone Charles took when he discovered a client had lied under oath.

But what she'd done wasn't a felony; it was only a white lie she'd told to avoid an unwanted conversation.

And had she really been so self-absorbed that she'd never bothered to ask Jim about his life? That charge felt unfair to Lydia. Jim had a talent for deflecting questions and turning the conversation in a different direction. Was she supposed to interrogate him?

She pushed those thoughts out of her mind when the vet called to say Alfie was ready to come home.

A subdued and chastened Alfie greeted her at the vet. At home, she showed him the crate.

He sniffed it and walked right in when she gave him a treat.

"You can stay in there with the door open now. But when I go out, I have to close it. It's for your own good."

Alfie pulled the tail of his new stuffed squirrel and settled down to rest.

Lydia snapped his picture in the crate and texted it to Jim.

Thank you so much for helping me last night. I'm sorry I was so unreasonable. I hope you'll accept my apology.

Lydia waited, but there was no response. Much later, when she picked up her phone, the words "no worries" had appeared.

Lydia left Alfie in his crate when she went to campus to teach her one late afternoon class. Seeing Roz in the adjunct office after class reminded her what she'd been doing before the whole drama with Alfie started.

"I happened to have my car at my mechanic's for a tune-up and he told me about a car that came to him through a relocation company," Lydia said to Roz's back.

"Mmm." Roz continued circling errors in an essay with vicious swipes of her red pen.

"When big corporations transfer executives overseas, they hire companies to sell the executive's house and cars and stuff so he can get where he needs to go quickly. The executive gets the payout upfront, and then the relo company worries about selling the stuff."

"A fascinating look at how the other half lives, Lydia. I don't see what it has to do with me."

"Jonathan, my mechanic, picked up this car for a song. A Honda Civic with only 60,000 miles, but it had a big dent that Jon fixed. Now he wants to sell it quickly."

"I don't have cash upfront—I need financing."

"Not for this car, you don't. You can get it for your down-payment money. Jonathan was supposed to be scrapping the car because of the dent, but instead he fixed it and whatever he gets for it is extra money in his pocket. He can't advertise it. He needs to sell it privately." Lydia knew she was talking in circles, but she had to trust that Roz was willing to believe a corporate fairy tale. Her friend had no idea how relocation deals worked—why couldn't they work like this?

"Sounds sketchy."

"Jonathan has the title. You pay him two thousand bucks, you get the title. If there's anything sketchy, it's between Jon and the relo company. Come on." Lydia tugged on Roz's arm. "Let's go look at it."

An hour later, Roz was the proud owner of a low-mileage, late model Civic. She kept shaking her head in amazement as she wrote the check for two grand. Meanwhile Jon winked at Lydia over Roz's bowed head.

She might be a bad pet owner, but she was a good friend.

She'd pulled off her subterfuge without a hitch.

Chapter 48

Later that week, Lydia stood in front of her open fridge mournfully considering her dinner options: a gloppy mound of left-over Pad Thai, an on-the-verge-of-slimy bag of salad greens and a frozen solid block of ground turkey. When her phone vibrated in her back pocket, she grabbed it, hoping it offered a solution to her sad dinner options.

I agreed to do a set of old standards at Blue Monday tonight. It would be better with you on harmony. Meet me there at 8??

Lydia felt pleased beyond the content of Conrad's three short sentences. A professional musician valued her ability—okay, not a famous musician, but still.

I'd better practice. What's our playlist?

When Conrad sent her a list of four songs, Lydia's appetite evaporated. She needed to practice and soothe her throat. She settled on heating up a can of low sodium vegetable soup, and headed to her piano.

At seven-thirty five she decided she was as ready as she'd ever be. She debated whether to drive or take an Uber. She couldn't stay late and she couldn't drink—she had to teach in the morning. Still, she knew she'd likely end up drinking something. Blue Monday wasn't the kind of place where a woman could order a Diet Coke.

When Lydia's Uber dropped her off, she was relieved to see the parking lot half empty—she lacked confidence for a packed house. As she made her way to meet Conrad at the tiny platform that served as a stage, she darted a few glances at the crowd around the bar. No signs of Jim or of Bryce Salazar—just a few cops and firemen.

She relaxed a bit.

Lydia was a little rocky on the opening measures of "You Oughta Be With Me," but she soon found her groove. Soon she and Conrad had the crowd singing along with the refrain of "Proud Mary". They sang two more songs together, and Lydia turned the stage over to Conrad.

Once again, Lydia's performance earned her many offers of free drinks. More cautious this time around, she accepted one glass of wine to soothe her throat. But the cabernet went to her head. Too late, she remembered she'd only had a bowl of soup for dinner. Unfortunately, there was no such thing as a healthy snack on the Blue Monday menu. She ordered a plate of fried mozzarella sticks—she couldn't leave before Conrad's set ended—and perched on a bar stool waiting for them to be delivered.

One thing led to another. When the chesty red-haired cop and her girlfriend struck up a friendly conversation about music, of course she had to respond. And when a few other cops joined the group, Lydia somehow ended up with another glass of wine. Then Conrad finished his set, but before she could plow through the steadily growing crowd to say goodnight, the jukebox came on and one of the cops saw her swaying to "Rock and Roll all Nite" and pulled her onto the dance floor.

Lydia hadn't danced to a rock song since the party at Gwen's house. Charles had been an excellent ballroom dancer—he'd taught her the fox trot, merengue, and swing. But he declined to participate in the exuberant free-form shimmying that was required for a song by Kiss. The big cop who'd pulled her onto the floor was surprisingly agile. He shimmied his shoulders and bounced his hips and Lydia mirrored his movements.

It was fun!

Then Conrad found her and everyone started dancing to "Love Shack".

Lydia glanced at her phone. Ten forty-five—how had it gotten so late? She had to teach tomorrow morning.

She left the dancers and paid for her food at the bar. But when Lydia tried to head for the door, she got pulled onto the dance floor again. Conrad was teaching three big cops and their girlfriends how to swing dance, and he needed a partner. She couldn't say no—she was quite good at swing dancing. After Conrad twirled her across the floor a few times, her filmy dress billowing around her legs, other dancers closed in. On her next twirl, Lydia bumped into someone standing next to the bar. "I'm so sorry," she gasped as she turned around.

She found herself face-to-face with Seth Wright.

He put out his hand to steady her and grinned. The song ended, and the sudden musical silence made the room seem quieter than it was.

"Good night, Lydia," Conrad called with a wave, and headed for the door.

"Your boyfriend?" Seth asked with a raised brow.

"Just a friend. He's gay," Lydia added, not sure why she felt it necessary to make this clear to Seth. Lydia picked up a napkin from the bar and pressed it to her sweaty brow.

Seth continued to watch her as if she were an exotic wild animal with fascinating habits.

Her throat was parched and the mug of beer he held looked so refreshing. "I'm thirsty, but I don't want another drink. Can I have a sip of your beer?"

He held out the mug to her and she took a sip from the opposite side of the rim, suddenly aware of how intimate it was to share a glass with someone.

Seth took another gulp of beer before speaking. "I'm surprised to see you here. Blue Monday doesn't seem like your kind of place."

"Why? I'm too old?"

Seth flushed. "No, not at all. You're too—"

"Uptight?"

He laughed. "I was going to say 'classy.'"

"Safe to say, I shattered that image."

Seth took a step closer, looking her up and down as if truly seeing her for the first time. "That's a good thing."

Lydia found herself acutely aware of Seth's arms—the way his soft, plaid shirt sleeve was rolled up to reveal the tendons in his forearm, the almost delicate bend of his wrist, the way the beer sign light above them illuminated the golden hair above his hand.

"You're here alone?" she asked, to stop herself from staring.

"Yeah—I don't normally feel comfortable going to bars solo. But this place is friendly, right?"

"Yeah, there's a cozy vibe." Seth didn't mention her singing, so he must've arrived after that. "You like the music?"

Seth grinned. "It's old school. I can feel it, though."

Lydia knew she should go, but she didn't want to. Her papers were graded, her lesson planned. So what if she rolled into the classroom a little short on sleep? She was a morning person. The tiredness wouldn't hit her until late in the afternoon.

A man stood before the jukebox feeding in coins. Lydia had had enough of loud music. But the song that came on was Willie Nelson's "You are Always on My Mind."

"I love this song." She and Seth spoke the words in perfect sync.

"Well, then—we have to dance to it." Seth took her by the hand and led her onto the dance floor.

Only two other couples joined them. At first, Seth held her as if they were going to waltz, with enough space between them to fit a third person. But as the verses continued with their soulful lament of underappreciated love, Seth pulled Lydia in closer. By the last verse, he had both arms around her waist and she had her arms around his neck.

Lydia breathed in his unadorned scent. He smelled clean, like clothes straight from the dryer.

She could feel the prickly shaved hair on the nape of his neck.

She could feel his heart beating against her breasts.

She could feel him harden against her thigh.

Lydia knew she should pull away, but her power to move had drained away. How long it had been since she'd relaxed into a man's embrace!

The fingers of Seth's right hand traced up and down her spine.

Lydia thought her knees might buckle right there on the dance floor.

As the last notes of the song faded away, Seth whispered in her ear, "Let's get out of here."

Wordlessly, she followed him out of the bar, her fingers interlaced with his.

Outside, the cool night air refreshed her, but didn't chill her desire. Seth strode toward his red pickup truck, parked in the far corner of the almost empty lot. Lydia scurried to keep up with him.

They both knew what they intended to do. No need for words.

Seth pressed the unlock button on his key fob from ten feet away. He yanked open the passenger door and pulled her in on top of him.

They tumbled across the large bench seat. Seth stroked her thigh under her dress as she fumbled with his belt buckle. Her desperate need consumed her, pushing every rational thought aside.

When he entered her she arched her back in pleasure, giving herself a view of bar patrons tumbling out of the Blue Monday. Laughing and gasping she collapsed on top of Seth.

"You're crazy," he murmured in her ear.

She knew he was right, but she didn't care. This brief interlude wasn't enough.

"Come home with me," she whispered.

Chapter 49

A distant chime pierced Lydia's consciousness.

Her alarm. She had an early class to teach, but she couldn't bring herself to open her eyes. Why was she so tired?

Why were her thighs sore?

Alfie lay beside her, but his breathing seemed louder than usual.

She reached out a hand and felt...skin.

Not fur.

Lydia's eyes flew open.

Seth sprawled uncovered across three-quarters of her queen-sized bed, his gorgeous ass pointed toward the ceiling, his long lashes skimming his cheek.

Lydia knew damn well she didn't look as good as that in the morning.

She had to make it to the bathroom before his eyes opened. She couldn't be here when he recoiled in revulsion at where a couple beers and a jukebox rendition of "You are Always on my Mind" had landed him.

Lydia slid her left leg toward the edge of the bed.

Seth's lashes fluttered open.

He lifted himself on one elbow. A grin spread from his mouth to his eyes.

He rolled onto his back, and damn if that flag wasn't flying again!

He pulled her towards him with a moan.

She was going to be really late for Basic Skills.

———————◆———————

LYDIA RUSHED STRAIGHT to her classroom. Crossing the threshold at three minutes after the hour, she started babbling about apostrophes before she even set her bag down.

An hour and twelve minutes later, she escaped and staggered into the Adjunct Office, mercifully unoccupied except for Roz.

"What happened to you?" Roz knocked back the last of her Diet Coke and tossed the can in the recycling.

"What do you mean? Nothing happened to me." To her own ears, Lydia's voice sounded high and sharp.

Roz narrowed her eyes. "Oh, yeah—something's up. You look like the cat who ate the canary."

Lydia felt the blood surging to her face and tried to force it back into her heart where it belonged. Roz didn't know what had happened last night with Seth. All Lydia needed to do was keep her mouth shut and her head down.

Roz started laughing. It began with a snort, climbed to a chuckle, and escalated to a full-throated roar. "You sly bitch! You got laid last night, didn't you? Who's the lucky guy?"

How could Roz possibly know that? Lydia worried she still smelled like sex. Or maybe she was walking lame. "Shut up! People will hear you."

"C'mon." Roz grabbed Lydia's arm and hauled her into an empty classroom across the corridor. She locked the door and crossed her arms across her chest. "Give."

Lydia knew she should be outraged by her friend's brazen behavior. But the truth was, she wanted to talk. She felt about ready to explode. Maybe that's what had clued Roz in.

Lydia double-checked the door and sat in a student desk next to Roz. "Oh. My. God. I can't believe what I did. It's crazy. It's irresponsible. But oh, God it was fantastic."

Roz's eyes lit up like a kid watching the opening credits of a superhero movie. "Last night was Tuesday. Where the hell did you pick this dude up?"

"I didn't pick up a stranger in a bar! Gross. It's someone I know."

Roz scrunched her face in thought. "I hope you didn't change your mind about Rapist Tom."

"Yuck." Lydia pushed Roz's leg with her foot. "It's not any of Charles's old fart friends."

"Hmm. Someone younger. Wait—you had an enemies-to-friends experience with that Bryce Salazar character."

"No-o-o! It's someone you know. Someone you like. Or did like."

"I give up. Just tell me, for God's sake."

"Seth Wright."

Roz could not have looked more shocked if Lydia had told her she'd slept with Prince Harry. "Are you crazy? He's a student!"

"He dropped out, remember." She didn't mention that Seth had re-enrolled in an online course. That hardly seemed relevant. "And he was never my student. He's been working on my kitchen. I told you that."

"So how did this progress from 'baby, lay my floor tile' to 'baby, lay—"

"I went to Blue Monday last night. Conrad texted me and asked me to come sing with him. I would've called you to join me, but I knew you were working at Essex. Seth showed up and we had a beer together. People started dancing to the jukebox around ten. He asked me to dance, and well...."

Roz stared at her. "Wow. Seth Wright. I gotta hand it to you, Lydia—that's some score."

"It's not a *score*. You're making it sound so, so...sordid." And that was without her even knowing about the parking lot escapade.

"Well, what is it, then?"

As always, Roz cut to the chase. Lydia raked her fingers through her hair. She hadn't thought ahead until this moment. What did she want from Seth Wright? Was last night a one night stand? "I don't know."

Chapter 50

B y the time she drove toward home that afternoon, Lydia's hormone-fueled high had cooled. After their morning interlude, Seth had, predictably for a man, fallen back asleep. So Lydia still hadn't had a coherent conversation with him since the moment he'd run his hand down her back dancing to "You Are Always on My Mind."

Normally, he'd still be working on the kitchen when she got home from school. One part of her prayed that Seth would be gone.

Tools packed.

Sawdust swept.

Kombucha out of her fridge.

But she knew that wasn't a solution. She owed Seth money for the work he'd done. Even if he didn't want to continue, she couldn't stiff him for his labor.

And she'd promised to help him with his architecture school applications.

She wanted to help him. He might never finish if she didn't give him a nudge.

Waiting for the traffic light to change, Lydia rested her head against the steering wheel. Why had she been so reckless?

When she pulled onto Lilac Court, she could see the back of Seth's red pick-up in her driveway.

Okay, so they'd do this face-to-face. She wouldn't have to deal with the anxiety of calling or texting and having him ghost her. Seth must have realized he couldn't afford to walk away without getting paid. They'd settle up like adults, and that would be that.

Lydia took a deep breath and walked through the back door.

She found Seth engrossed in holding a level on a cabinet he'd just installed. The ever-present ear pods drowned out the sound of her arrival. But when Alfie came bounding to greet her, Seth turned around.

A flush spread from the neck of his t-shirt to his hairline. The level clattered to the floor.

He pulled out his EarPods. "Hey."

"Hey, yourself."

They stood staring at each other.

"Look—"

"I'm—"

They both stopped.

Seth yanked a fistful of his thick hair and started talking in a rush, his eyes focused on the floor. "I'm so sorry for the way I acted last night. I...I think I hurt you. I was too— I mean, it's been a while since I— And I just want you to know I'm not usually like that."

Lydia took a step backward. Was she hearing this right? Was Seth apologizing for being too rough? Jeez, she was the one who acted like a crazed alley cat in heat. And what was "been a while" for a twenty-three year old guy—two weeks? She could tell him about *a while*. "No, Seth, that's not the problem. You didn't hurt me. Far from it."

Seth looked up with a hopeful light in his eyes. "Really? Because this morning it seemed like...well, maybe...you know..."

Lydia laughed nervously. "Yeah, well, it's been a while for me too, so I am a little, uhm, sore, but it's not your fault. Not at all."

Seth reached out and took her hand. "I want you to know, just because we got started in a bar—that's not my M.O. I...I have to connect with a woman before I can...." He dropped her hand and turned back to his work. "So anyway," he muttered. "It's not what you think."

So what was it?

Seth's words stunned Lydia into silence. She had entered the kitchen looking for a way to get out of this entanglement with her dignity intact. Now it seemed Seth wanted forgiveness, not an escape hatch.

She touched his back lightly. "You have no reason to feel bad. We both got a little carried away, that's all." She waited a moment. "Still friends?"

"Of course."

And then, by the grace of God, Seth's phone rang. He answered it immediately. Lydia clipped on Alfie's leash and took the dog for a walk.

A long walk.

By the time she returned, Seth's truck was gone.

He left a note on the kitchen table in his meticulous printing. "Will finish bottom cabinets tomorrow."

Lydia went upstairs to take a long bath. Alfie rested his head on the edge of the tub and watched her.

"What are you looking at?" she asked the dog. "Haven't you ever seen a naked slut before?"

Alfie blinked.

"Oh my God, Alfie—I did something really irresponsible. What if someone had seen us in the truck at Blue Monday?" Lydia stared at her aquamarine Italian tile. "And you know what? I'm not sorry. I keep looking for regret, but I'm not finding it."

She turned the tap to add more hot water to her cooling bath. "Things might be a little awkward with Seth for a while." She extended one slender leg out of the water. "But I think I showed the kid a good time."

Chapter 51

A week later, Seth popped his head into the living room. "I'm knockin' off a little early. I have a paper to write for my class."

"When's it due?"

Seth examined the side of his work boot. "Midnight."

"I see. And have you started?"

Seth rammed his fists into his jean pockets. "N-o-o-o, Lydia—I haven't started."

"What's the assignment?"

"Three pages. Compare and Contrast. Maybe I'll compare Stickley and Frank Lloyd Wright."

Lydia shook her head. "Too big and it requires research. Compare something that you already know about. Something to do with your work now."

Seth groaned. Rolled his eyes. Pulled his hair. "I dunno. I hate this shit. This is why—"

"Stop. I'm not interested in hearing the Comp 1-is-pointless rant again. You're just wasting time." Lydia paced around the living room when her gaze fell on her mantle-piece. "Last week you were telling me why hickory was better for certain projects and chestnut was better for others. Write about that."

Seth's face relaxed as he thought. "Hmmm. Maybe."

"Write the first two paragraphs here. Dinner in forty minutes."

She left the living room to the sound of him heaving a sigh. But she soon heard the click-clack of typing.

Lydia made four grilled chicken breasts, thinking she could eat the leftovers for lunch tomorrow. But she ate one and Seth ate the other three. Ah, to have a twenty-three year old's metabolism!

She pushed the plates aside. "Let's see what you've got."

Seth rubbed his eyes with the heels of his hands. "It sucks."

"I'll be the judge of that."

She read the introduction: a mixture of pointless platitudes and meaningless generalities.

But the second paragraph, when he started warming to his subject, was quite good.

"This paragraph," Lydia highlighted the introduction. "This was your warm-up paragraph. It's like when Alfie circles his bed three times before he lies down. Now, we can get rid of it." She hit delete and vaporized five sentences.

"Hey! It took me twenty minutes to write that," Seth objected.

"The effort's not wasted. By the time you got to this paragraph, you hit your stride. Write three more paragraphs like that, and then we'll go back and work on the introduction."

When Lydia returned again, Seth had four paragraphs. "What's your thesis statement?"

Seth shrugged. "Beats me."

"Every essay needs a thesis statement. Hasn't your professor gone over that?"

"Sounds kinda familiar."

Lydia forced him to meet her gaze. "You've been winging it this far, haven't you? Sliding through by relying on your obvious intelligence without actually learning what you need to know to do this right."

Seth leaned back in his chair and gazed at the ceiling. He didn't say, "blah, blah, blah," but he may as well have.

Lydia switched direction. "Do you ski?"

Seth's eyes lit up. "Love to ski. And snowboard."

"So, anyone can get down the beginner trails and even some of the intermediates just by doing a snowplow. But if you want to ski the double black diamonds, you have to learn the proper technique, right?"

Seth scowled at her. "Is that some teacher thing? Engage your student by making a sports analogy." He spoke in an advice-giving sing-song.

"Resist all efforts of assistance—is that a bad-boy carpenter thing?"

Seth scoffed. "I'm not a bad boy."

"Then stop acting like that's your aspiration in life."

They glared at each other until Seth finally backed down. "Okay, fine—help me with the thesis statement thing."

After that stand-off, Seth plugged away steadily. At eleven-thirty, Lydia returned for the final edit. She pulled the laptop to her side of the table and read the essay straight through. "Okay, this is quite good. Now, let's fix the punctuation."

Seth's face switched from pleasure to fury in a flash. "Lydia, come on! It's nearly midnight. I'm tired. Can't you just stick the damn commas in where they need to go?"

"I'm not going to be riding on your shoulder your whole life, whispering in your ear 'use a semicolon there'. Learn to do it right."

Seth threw his hands up in the air. "It's good enough, for chrissakes."

"It's not. You're this close—shoot for the A."

"I'm happy with a C," he muttered.

"I've watched you tear out a drawer three times to get it to slide just right. You're a perfectionist with your carpentry. Be a perfectionist in your writing."

He glared at her.

She tapped the screen. "Comma or semicolon?"

"Semi."

"Correct. Here?"

"Comma."

"Here?"

Seth squinted at the screen. "That doesn't need anything at all."

Lydia beamed and clapped her hands. "Perfect. You see—you do understand punctuation."

Seth banged on the keyboard, hitting "save" and "send." He slapped the laptop shut and leaned across the table. "You're a royal pain in the ass, Lydia."

"So are you." She held her glare until she burst out laughing.

Seth pulled her out of her chair. His lips found hers and her arms went around his neck. His knee pressed between her legs.

They edged across the room without breaking their embrace and tumbled onto the sofa.

Alfie trotted over to investigate.

"I'm okay. Go away," Lydia whispered.

Chapter 52

The reignition of the flame with Seth put Lydia in a euphoric mood. She no longer dreaded the loneliness at the end of her teaching day. Instead of leaving after a quick conversation about the progress of his work building the alcove for the piano, Seth hung around to talk about architecture and art and music and literature.

Lydia loved his idealism. The ideas were all new to him, and she listened to him patiently, sometimes challenging him; sometimes letting him slide. She wondered when she'd allowed critical thinking to suck the joy out of her passions.

The assignments for his Comp 1 course got more challenging just as the deadline for the architecture programs drew closer. More evenings than not, Lydia cooked dinner for them both. Seth admitted he focused better on his schoolwork and his applications when he worked on them at Lilac Court, away from the temptation of TV, video games, and texts from friends.

And then there was the sex.

Seth was never too tired. Or too preoccupied. Or too lazy.

Lydia gave him a fresh toothbrush to use at her house.

Then Seth brought over a couple t-shirts to change into after his dusty construction work ended.

Soon his electric shaver appeared in Lydia's bathroom, and his boxer shorts tumbled in the dryer with her sheets.

One Wednesday, Seth had gone back to his own house, which filled Lydia with an odd mix of melancholy and relief. Sometimes she needed a break from the intensity. Shortly after ten, Lydia's phone chirped the arrival of a text.

Roz.

Turn on Channel 12. Quick.

Lydia fumbled for her remote. Channel 12 was the local news station, offering up a combination of fiery car crashes and heartwarming human interest stories. But Roz wouldn't be alerting her to *Bear Rescues Toddler From Smoldering Wreckage*.

When she got the TV on, Tom's face filled the screen. A headline crawled along the bottom: Palmyrton entrepreneur arrested for sex assault.

Lydia's hand gripped the throw pillow on the sofa.

The reporter came on with a backdrop of the Palmer County courthouse. "Tom Schilling denies the charges and claims his accuser has a history of mental instability. We'll be following this story closely. Back to you, Katherine."

Immediately, Lydia's phone rang.

"That's your guy, right?" Roz asked.

"Yes." Lydia choked out the word. "What did they say at the beginning of the story? What did I miss?"

"Tom and this young administrative assistant were working late. He cornered her in the copy room. The reporter called it 'unwanted touching.' Groped her, I guess. She screamed and the custodian heard her."

"So she has a witness."

"I don't know. They didn't interview the custodian. Maybe there will be more information in the paper tomorrow."

"You were right, Roz. He must do this all the time."

"What're you going to do?" For once, Roz sounded puzzled, like she had no good advice to offer.

Lydia didn't have an answer either. "I don't know. I have to think."

After she hung up with Roz, Lydia sat in the cozy glow of her reading lamp letting her mind roam free. What would Charles advise? Lydia had been married to a lawyer for eighteen years; she had learned to think like one. True, Charles was a corporate litigator, not a criminal defense lawyer. But he lived by certain axioms.

Minimize risk.

Never lie.

By the first axiom, she should keep her mouth shut and her head down.

Lydia had done that after Tom attacked her and look at the result—he'd quickly gone on to hurt another woman. If she had spoken up, she might have spared this young woman the pain she was going through now.

Lydia twisted on the sofa. Who was she kidding? If she'd pressed charges against Tom, they would never have stuck. She had no witnesses except Alfie. And Tom counted as friends all the same lawyers that she did.

With whom would Alton Finn and the rest of Charles's partners side?

She had a sinking feeling they'd support their own.

One of the boys.

Lydia grabbed her phone and pulled up Twitter. In her advertising days, she had monitored the social media platforms of her clients. Since leaving Imago, she'd happily left Twitter behind, but it could be useful for following news in real time. She searched for Tom's name.

Yes. Hundreds of tweets already. Most of them attacked Tom and ended with the hashtags #believeher and #metoo. But there was some pushback. Tweets defending Tom that ended in #falseaccusation and #MRM.

What did that mean? Lydia had to Google it: men's rights movement.

Oh, please!

The ridiculous thing was, none of these social media warriors knew either of the people involved, but they were more than willing to weigh in with their opinions.

This is what she'd be wading into if she spoke up.

Lydia curled into a ball on the sofa.

If Charles were here, he would defend her. Protect her.

But he wasn't here.

Lydia was on her own, and she had to fight this battle herself.

But she couldn't afford to be impulsive, emotional. She wasn't adopting a dog or buying a house. This would affect more than just her.

———— ◉ ————

AFTER A RESTLESS NIGHT, Lydia was grateful for Alfie's wet nose on her cheek. She got out of bed and walked him in the breaking dawn light, then returned to the house to eat her breakfast in front of the TV.

Sure enough, Tom had managed to get himself on the early morning New Jersey chat show, *Sunrise with Dave and Jenna*. Lydia had suspected that Tom would act to get out ahead of the story instead of laying low. He sat on a sofa across from the morning show hosts looking somber yet confident.

And beside him sat Madalyn.

She looked like shit.

The makeup on her cheeks and lips stood out like slashes of gore against her pale skin. Someone had poufed and sprayed her hair into a rigid helmet. She stared blankly into the camera while Tom spoke earnestly. "This is a terrible misunderstanding. I had agreed to give this young woman an entry level position in my company as a favor to a friend. But she has not been working up to our standards. She's very insecure, while at the same time having unrealistic career expectations. I had asked her to revise and recopy part of a proposal, and she simply lashed out at me. The custodian heard her raise her voice. But I never laid a hand on her."

Dave and Jenna listened intently, Jenna with her head cocked to one side like an alert robin. "But the custodian said your accuser's clothes were …uh…in disarray."

Tom opened his eyes wide. "She got so agitated about having to revise her work that she clawed at her own blouse and a button popped off."

Occasionally, the camera would leave the close-up of Tom's face and draw back to show both Tom and Madalyn. Madalyn continued to stare straight ahead, her eyes dead with pain.

She looked like all those politician's wives who'd been forced to stand beside their husbands in a show of solidarity while the men tried to squirm out from under career-ending charges: Governor Jim McGreevy, Congressman Anthony Weiner, Governor Eliot Spitzer.

It had ended badly for all of them. And eventually the women had all come to their senses and divorced the creeps.

Lydia leaned toward the TV screen and scrutinized Madalyn's face. Roz was right. Madalyn knew. She must have even more dirt on Tom than Lydia did. The poor woman was reeling, and her husband had succeeded in hustling her into this public appearance while her defenses were down.

But Madalyn was the weak link in Tom's defense, Lydia was sure of it.

She wished there was a way to break that link. She and Madalyn might both be better off for it.

Chapter 53

After the news appearance, Lydia sent Madalyn a text. *I'm sorry for your trouble. I'm here if you need to talk.*

Lydia wasn't necessarily expecting an answer, but Madalyn surprised her.

Thanks. I'll be there in an hour.

When Madalyn arrived, she looked even worse than she had on TV. Her Talbots slacks had a stain on the knee. Her blouse was untucked. The wind had blown the part out of her hair. Her face looked wan because she'd scrubbed off the make-up she'd worn for the cameras.

Lydia took Madalyn's hand and pulled her across the threshold. "Let me fix you a cup of tea." Lydia guided Madalyn toward the kitchen.

"Gin," Madalyn demanded. "I need a martini, but gin on the rocks is close enough."

The clock hadn't yet struck noon, but Lydia wasn't about to stand on ceremony.

Madalyn sat silently staring at the wall until the drink appeared before her.

Neither of them said the words that would be expected between friends in this situation.

I can't believe it....a terrible mistake....the truth will come out.

Lydia certainly wasn't going there. She waited patiently for Madalyn to make the first move. *Listen*, she advised herself. *Ask questions.*

Her friend took a gulp and made eye contact with Lydia. "Tom says this girl is unstable."

"What do you think?"

Madalyn's gaze drifted to a spot over Lydia's shoulder. "She's young. These kids who go to fancy schools aren't used to anyone ever criticizing their work."

Lydia stayed silent although it required superhuman effort.

Madalyn rattled the ice cubes in her drink, and Alfie scrambled off his bed in the corner of the kitchen to investigate the sound.

"This is your dog?" Madalyn stretched out her hand to pat Alfie, but he jumped back.

"That's Alfie. Sorry, he's skittish around strangers. Just let him sniff you."

Madalyn stared at the dog. "He's bigger than I imagined. Somehow I thought you'd gotten a little Shi-tzu or Maltese."

"No little fluff-balls for me. Alfie's a tough guy, aren't you?"

The dog gave his best guardian bark.

Lydia hadn't thought Madalyn's face could get any grayer, but it did. "Does he ever bite?"

"He can be nippy. He's very protective of me."

Madalyn's eyes widened. "Tell me the truth. Did your dog bite Tom?"

Lydia met her friend's gaze without blinking. "Yes."

"You had fingerprint bruises on your arm at the same time Tom had a dog bite on his hand. Tom and you have been avoiding each other ever since." Madalyn's breathing grew ragged. "Something happened on Halloween night. Tell me what it was."

This was it. Madalyn was asking for the truth. Lydia reached for her friend's hand, but Madalyn jerked away. "I struggled with whether to tell you at the time it happened. Tom dropped by unannounced saying he wanted to see the house. It never occurred to me to not let him in. I showed him around, and when we were upstairs...." Lydia paused. There was no need for the gruesome details. "Alfie saw me struggling, and bit Tom's hand. He left after that."

Madalyn's eyes narrowed. "You should have told me."

"He'd had a couple drinks. When it first happened, I thought it was an aberration. I thought other people would blame me because I invited him upstairs to see the bathroom renovation."

Lydia remembered the conversation she'd had with Roz. The one where Roz said the wife always knew and turned a blind eye. "Has there ever been any other incident? A time when you suspected something?"

Madalyn plopped back into her chair and cradled her head in her hands. "God forgive me," she whispered. She lifted her tear-stained face. "When our oldest daughter, Maggie, was in college, she invited her best friend to join us on a family vacation in Cape Cod. We'd rented a big house. There was plenty of room for all the kids' friends. Three days into the trip, Maggie's friend, who was very beautiful, very feminine, suddenly announced she had to leave. After that, she never visited us again, even though she and Maggie stayed friends."

"It's hard to doubt your husband—"

"Tom showed unusual interest in her from the moment he met her. Kept talking to her, telling her he could help her get a job in broadcasting. He sat beside her at every meal, planned little outings for him, Maggie, and her. One night, a big group of us had a bonfire on the beach. This girl—I can't even remember her name now—got up to go get a sweatshirt from the house. A few minutes later, I noticed Tom was gone, too. The next morning, the friend left. Tom and Maggie both said they had no idea why."

"You think Maggie suspected?"

Madalyn shook her head. "What young woman wants to think her father is capable of hitting on her friends? But I suspected. I saw how he looked at her. There's a certain type he's drawn to."

Lydia's stomach turned. How could she be the same type as these young college girls? "What do you mean? In all the years I've known Tom, he never did anything like this before. That's why I was so shocked."

"He wasn't interested in you when Charles was alive." Madalyn crushed an ice cube with one bite. "After Charles's death, after you'd left your job, you seemed fragile, vulnerable. That's what Tom is drawn to."

Madalyn gave a bitter laugh. "Not his sensible, sturdy, no-nonsense wife." She banged her glass on the table. "But now he wants me to stand by him. To be his character witness. This girl at the office isn't backing down. Tom has scratches on his neck. The custodian is a witness. This isn't going away."

Lydia leaned across the table. "What are you going to do?"

Madalyn crumpled. "I don't know...our kids, our house...."

"What about you, Madalyn? Do what needs to be done for you."

Madalyn took a deep breath and raised her head. "I'm going to divorce that bastard. And I'm going to call the police and tell them I know of at least two other of my husband's victims. Will you tell them what happened on Halloween?"

Lydia squeezed her hand. "I have a picture of my bruises. I'll talk to the police if you want me to. But don't act out of revenge, Madalyn. Make sure you're doing what's best for you."

"No!" Madalyn's loud protest roused Alfie from his bed again. "That's how I ended up in this position, Lydia. By overlooking Tom's sins in the name of financial security for me and the kids. But the kids are all launched now. I have to give up my vision of being the grand matriarch in the big house, hosting every holiday surrounded by tumbling grandchildren." She began to sob. "It's a sham. All a sham."

Lydia stroked her friend's arm. "You can do this. I'll help you."

Madalyn grabbed a paper napkin from the table and blew her nose. "Tom totally misjudged you. You're much tougher than you look."

Chapter 54

The next three weeks passed quickly.

Madalyn told Tom she was leaving him. And she told the police what she knew and what she suspected.

The police invited Lydia to the Palmyrton Police Department to tell the story of Halloween night. They were very interested in the photo.

Tom hired the best criminal defense lawyer Alton Finn could recommend. There was talk of a plea bargain.

The spring semester ended in a flurry of grading for Lydia and a flurry of paper-writing and scholarship applications for Seth.

He got a B+ in Comp 1.

Neither of them noticed when their weeknights together sometimes stretched into weekends.

But Lydia was careful not to let Seth totally take over her life. Periodically, she shooed him back to his own house or encouraged him to go out with his buddies so she could spend time with Roz and Conrad and Madalyn and her neighbors.

There was no point in trying to fit Seth into her new circle.

They wouldn't understand him; he wouldn't understand them.

This affair was temporary.

Intense, but temporary.

So on a rainy Sunday afternoon the day before the summer semester was to begin, Lydia urged Seth to go to a sports bar to watch basketball with his friends while she made plans to see a movie with Roz.

Alfie announced Roz's arrival before the doorbell rang. "I'm back in the kitchen," she shouted as Roz walked in.

Roz shook her wet curls and hung up her raincoat by the door. "It's miserable out there. Mind if I make a cup of tea?"

"Help yourself. The tea bags are in that cabinet over there." Lydia pointed. "I finally have this kitchen organized the way I want it."

Roz turned on the tea kettle and crossed to the breakfast nook. "Seth really did a great job refinishing this wood. It's so nice and smooth."

"Just push those papers aside. I was sorting through stuff that's been piling up during the renovation." No sooner were the words out of Lydia's mouth than she remembered what paper was on top of the pile she'd just told her friend to move.

The invoice from Prestige Motors for the Honda she'd bought for Roz.

Lydia moved toward the table.

Too late.

Roz's eyes widened in disbelief as she held up the invoice. "What the hell is this? It says balance owed for Honda Civic, eight thousand dollars. The guy charged me two thousand."

Lydia snatched the paper away. "None of your business. That's between me and Jonathan."

Roz stamped her foot. "I knew that deal was too good to be true. You tricked me into buying a car I can't afford. Now

I'm eight thousand dollars in debt to you." Roz hurled the Honda keys on Lydia's table.

Lydia crumpled the invoice. "You don't owe me anything. I don't want your money."

"And I don't want your charity."

"It's not charity. It's one friend helping another." Lydia held out her hands in appeasement. "Look, Roz—I know I overstepped my boundaries. I know I shouldn't have tricked you into taking the car. But you know, you bear a little blame here, too."

"Blame!" Roz's eyes narrowed. "I'm to blame because you're an interfering busybody?"

"You make it impossible for anyone to help you." Lydia paced around the small kitchen. "You could have driven the Subaru until you saved up enough money to buy a decent car. But you insisted on giving it back early. I couldn't sit back and let you take out a car loan from those extortionists. You're so damn proud, you'd rather cut off your nose to spite your face than accept a helping hand."

Roz scowled. "What kind of lame-ass mixed metaphor is that?"

"All right—I'm a bad friend and a bad English teacher. Just heap the abuse on me until you feel better. And then take the damn car."

Roz whirled around, her eyes fierce. "What part of 'no' don't you understand? I'm not letting you buy me a car like you'd buy me a beer. I don't want to be beholden to you."

This line stunned Lydia. She softened her voice. "You're not beholden to me. I'm giving you the car, no strings attached."

"Money is power, Lydia. You of all people should under-stand that." Roz wagged a finger at Lydia. "Your husband is still controlling you with his money from beyond the grave. You bought this house to spite a dead man. I want no part of that game."

Wha-?? Lydia had no time to evaluate this turn in the discussion. "Look, Roz—I inherited a crap ton of money I didn't earn. I got it because one day when I was a broke grad student working in a restaurant—just like you—I accepted a date from an older man. And that one action changed my life, both for the better and for the worse."

"You were his wife for eighteen years. You did things for each other, made sacrifices for each other." Roz pulled a flower out of the vase on the table and stripped it of its petals. "The money is your joint property, Lydia. You earned it, even if you'd like to pretend you just found it lying under a tree."

"I didn't earn it. I lucked into it. And even Charles didn't truly earn it."

Roz stepped backward into Alfie's water dish and kicked it out of her way. "Now you're going to claim he stole it, and you're Robin Hood, giving it back to the poor?"

"Of course he didn't steal it. My husband was very ethi-cal. Charles was smart; so are you. He was hard working; no one works harder than you. So why don't you have what he had? Because he was born into a well-to-do family. He had every advantage. His parents had the connections to get him into the best schools. He graduated without a penny of debt and waltzed into a great law firm position because his father knew one of the partners. Yes, he worked hard and invested well. But who couldn't win with the hand he was dealt?"

Roz wouldn't back down. "I've seen people lose with a straight flush."

Lydia back-tracked. "I don't mean to imply Charles didn't do anything to earn his success. He played his hand well. But what if he'd had to support his sick mother? What if he'd had to search for a job by mailing in his resume with hundreds of others?"

Lydia leaned closer to her friend. "This car is every letter of recommendation from a powerful friend of your father's that you never got." Lydia shook the Honda keys in front of Roz's nose. "It's every unpaid internship you could never afford to accept. It's every string that never got pulled, every door that never got opened. Take the damn car, Roz. You're not accepting charity. You're striking a blow at The Man."

Roz stared at her. Like an iguana, she held the gaze without blinking. But a twitch of a smile played at the corner of Roz's mouth. "You're such a spin doctor, Lydia. Your talents are truly wasted teaching Basic Skills at Palmer Community."

"I'll take that as a compliment." Lydia tossed the Honda keys to Roz, who caught them. "Let's go get a pizza and decide on a movie. You drive."

Before they left, Lydia clapped her hands and pointed. "Crate."

Alfie trotted in and lay down to wait for her return.

Chapter 55

Lydia pulled a long string of melted mozzarella off her pizza. "Do you really think I bought Lilac Court only to spite Charles?" Now that the thrill of victory had worn off, Lydia found Roz's shot in the heat of battle paining her.

"Let's see," Roz held up a hand to tick off items, "you gave up an attached garage, central air, walk-in closets, and fifty fully functioning triple-glazed windows for a house with pretty tile around the fireplace. Uh, yeah—I'd say there were some emotions at play in your decision."

"Okay, okay—I know I was being defiant. I bought the house to piss off Mitchell. And of course, Charles would hate this place, but—"

"But what?" Roz popped a slice of pepperoni in her mouth.

"Spite is a strong word, Roz. That makes it sound like I hated Charles. I didn't. I loved him."

"But you were angry with him."

"Angry for the restrictions in the will. Angry because I quit my job for him and then he went and died on me."

Roz chewed. "I think you've been angry for a while, Lydia. Years."

They eyed each other, but Roz declined to say more.

Lydia thought before she began to speak softly. "It's not all Charles's fault. I'm angry at myself. I let him rescue me when I was young. But then I never insisted that we change as we got older. In the back of my mind, I knew that clause was in our pre-nup, but I never challenged him on it. I never asked about our finances. I never said I didn't want to quit work."

"How come?"

Lydia took a drink of beer before she answered. "Because I was safe. The house in Palmer Ridge was like Alfie's crate—a secure space to retreat from the world. Most times, I didn't mind being in it."

Roz nodded. "Nice cushion and a couple chew toys and you're all set."

"But a creature can't live in there, Roz. Then the crate does become a prison."

"So you broke out."

Lydia grinned. "Big time. I've been working on getting back everything I gave up: funky house, bohemian friends, low-paying job."

"Hot young lover. Let's not forget that one." Roz reached for another slice. "So what are you doing about him?"

"The affair is nearly over. Seth has applied to five architecture programs. He's bound to get into one—he's really good. And he'll leave. The tempestuous fling I should have had in my twenties will be over, and normal middle-aged life will resume."

Roz cocked her head. "You really think it'll be that easy?"

"No. I'll cry. I'll miss him. But I learned to sleep alone once. I can learn to do it again."

Roz frowned. "I meant, do you really think it'll be that easy *for him*?"

Chapter 56

When Lydia walked into the house the next day, she found Seth leaning against the kitchen counter with a shell-shocked look on his face. Before she could even ask what was wrong, he held out his phone with an email showing on the screen.

Congratulations! You have been accepted to the Rice University Architecture Program as a New Horizons scholar.

Lydia shrieked with delight. "Oh my God—fantastic! I knew you could do it. Your first choice. And a scholarship, too." She wrapped him into a hug. "Why aren't you more excited? Still in shock?"

Seth pulled her close and murmured in her ear. "I don't want to leave you."

Lydia pulled away. "You have to accept. You got a full scholarship to one of the best architecture programs in the country. You can't pass that up."

Seth grabbed her hands. "Come with me. There's nothing holding you here."

But there was. Her house. Her job. Her new friends.

But there were bigger reasons Lydia knew she wouldn't go with Seth.

She'd be reliving her life with Charles in reverse.

Scenes of a hypothetical life together flashed through her mind. She wouldn't want to live in some grungy student apartment, so she'd pay for a nicer place and then Seth's student friends would find it awkward to visit.

He would stay up late doing homework and sleep until noon. She would go to bed early and wake up early as she always did.

She would pay for dinners out and vacations and new clothes. He would chafe at the power over him her money provided.

They would make each other miserable, and the love they felt right now would cough and sputter and finally flame out in anger and recriminations.

Seth grabbed her hands, interpreting her silence all wrong. "Marry me."

Lydia felt light-headed. Yes, sometimes in the heat of their passion they'd murmured "I love you" to each other. She did love him in those moments. But had she really led him to believe they were heading for a lifetime commitment?

She found her voice. "Seth, no. You don't understand what you're saying. That would never work."

Seth's eyes flared. "Don't say it. Don't tell me you're too old for me. You're beautiful and I love you and I want you. That's all that matters."

"I believe you. And I know how lucky I am. I love you too, Seth. That's why I can't do anything that would hurt you. Building a life with another person starts with love, yes, but it requires more than that. If we could make these last few weeks last our whole lives through, yeah, that would be perfect. But we can't. You're going to need to take chances, move, explore. When I married Charles, I skipped right over that part of my life. Because he'd already done it. And he didn't want to do it again."

She stepped away from him. "I've spent this past year living the stage of my life I missed. I'm caught up now. It's your turn to go out and live your twenties. Really live the hell out of them!"

Seth's eyes darkened. "That's an excuse. You won't marry me because of the money. You don't want to lose your inheritance."

His words struck Lydia like a slap in the face. "Don't be ridiculous. I'm not saying this because of the money. I'm trying to do what's best for you. You'd be miserable with me within a year."

Seth rushed to the back door, but turned before he left. "I was so stupid. You used me. And now you're glad I'm leaving, so you can go back to your rich bitch life."

He slammed the door. "Enjoy it!" she heard him shout from the porch.

Chapter 57

The week after Seth left passed in a constant churn of agony.

Lydia had always known their affair would end, that Seth's departure would leave a hole in the fabric of her life. But she hadn't imagined it like this. She'd pictured a fond, melancholy farewell; she got a blast of fury and heartache.

She knew Seth was sensitive and impetuous. But in her heart, she figured a twenty-three year old man certainly wouldn't want a woman twenty-two years his senior for long.

Even though Charles had never had a moment of hesitation that she would want him.

But an older man with a younger woman was a time-honored tradition.

A younger man with an older woman was the stuff of porn fantasies.

That's why she thought she couldn't possibly hurt Seth.

Lydia longed to call him to try to explain, but she knew she'd make matters worse. She hoped Seth might calm down and call her, but he never did.

Instead, he came to the house when he knew she was at work and took back his clothes and toiletries and books. The only thing he left behind was the toothbrush she'd given him. It hung beside hers in the bathroom, a talisman of their intimacy. She didn't throw it out. Couldn't.

In the long, lonely evenings, Lydia found herself thinking more and more of Charles. There were things she wanted
to tell him.

I understand your need to protect.

*I see now why you worried about how money changes rela-
tionships.*

I forgive you.

Lydia played "River" over and over on the Steinway that
now fit perfectly in her living room.

———◆———

FAR IN THE DISTANCE, a man and a dog walked down
the sidewalk toward Lydia and Alfie.

Instantly, Alfie went on high alert.

"Easy." Lydia shortened Alfie's leash and kept him close
by her side.

As the two grew closer, Alfie's tail began a mad wag, and
he strained to walk faster.

Lydia squinted. Was it...?

Yes. Jim and Harley.

Just what she needed. Another man who hated her.

Jim raised his hand in a lukewarm greeting. "We walked
to the dog park, but there was no one there. Harley was disappointed."

"Oh, that's where we were headed. Alfie won't want to
stay if there's no one to play with."

They looked at each other and at the dogs excitedly sniffing.

Jim pivoted. "Come on, Harley. We'll go back so you can
run with Alfie for a while." He stopped addressing the dog

and spoke to Lydia without making eye contact. "Harley has been cooped up all day because I was in Newark."

"Oh? What took you there?" Lydia was determined not to say a thing about herself and instead draw Jim into talking about something personal.

"I volunteer with an organization called Born to Code. We teach low income kids how to code and expose them to the possibilities of tech careers."

"That sounds like a really worthwhile effort. Do the kids embrace that topic, or do you have to reel them in?"

Jim spoke for a while about using video games as a hook, and then broadening the kids' understanding of coding. He grew more animated as he explained the challenges, but he still didn't reveal much about how he felt about the kids.

Dirty green tennis balls littered the beaten down grass of the dog park. Jim picked one up and threw it for Harley and Alfie. The dogs took off in a flash.

"You have quite an arm there. Did you play baseball in school?"

"Little League and Babe Ruth, but I quit the high school team. I loved the game. The guys on the teams, not so much."

Lydia was about to wisecrack that Jim wasn't the type to snap towels in the locker room, but she caught herself. That would be the kind of stereotypical assumption Jim seemed to think she made about him.

On the other side of the dog park fence, two teenage boys played a rowdy game of Frisbee. Lydia noticed Jim's gaze following them. "Does your son play baseball or Ultimate Frisbee?"

Jim's body stiffened. Lydia could feel the tension radiating off him. Was her question that prying? Had she crossed some boundary? But Jim had mentioned during Alfie's first training session that he had a son. Was it wrong to enquire about the kid's interests?

"I don't know what sports my son enjoys playing these days. He's very...guarded...with me."

"Does he live here or in California?" Lydia asked.

"California. With his mother. She doesn't share much information. And now that Travis is eighteen, I can't compel her to provide it."

"Not knowing is hard," Lydia agreed. Every day she worried that after all the work he'd done to get accepted to Rice, Seth would use their breakup as an excuse not to go. "Sometimes what you imagine is far worse than reality."

Jim gazed at the horizon. "True. My visions tend to be gruesomely vivid."

Lydia reached out and squeezed his hand. "Keep letting Travis know that you care. He'll come around."

⸻ ◉ ⸻

WHEN LYDIA GOT HOME, the sight of her laptop on the table sparked an idea fueled by all that talk about coding and computers and privacy. Seth had frequently used her computer. If she checked the browsing history, would she be able to see his accepted student account at Rice University?

She flipped open the Mac and scrolled down the list of recently visited websites. When she clicked on Rice, it prompted her for a password. But sure enough, Seth had used the "remember me" option and stored his Rice password on her computer, so he wouldn't have to reenter it.

Lydia's hand trembled above the keyboard. She knew she shouldn't do this. But she just had to know if he had followed through with his enrollment.

And what if he hadn't? What would she do? What could she do?

She couldn't drag him there.

But at least she would know, good news or bad.

She clicked.

A new screen opened:

Welcome Seth Wright

In the corner, a little green bar flashed status: enrolled.

Below the status bar, a checklist of things to do to complete the enrollment process. A happy green check appeared next to each item.

At the bottom of the screen Lydia read, Transfer student orientation—August 15. We look forward to meeting you!

Lydia closed out of the account and sank back in her chair. A rock of worry rolled off her chest.

Seth had enrolled. He was going. That's all that mattered.

Chapter 58

A week later, Lydia looked up from her gardening when Alfie charged to the fence, put his paws on the pickets, and began barking like a maniac.

Harley sat calmly on the other side.

With one hand signal, Jim got Alfie to sit and stay while he opened the gate and ushered Harley in.

"Hi, Jim." Lydia rose and pulled off her garden gloves. He looked different. She walked all the way around him while the dogs frolicked in the yard. "You got a haircut. Your ponytail is gone."

Jim rubbed his close-cropped head. "Yeah. Figured it was time to lose the old hippie look."

You can say that again!

"I like it. You look like Ewan McGregor."

Jim's eyebrows knotted in puzzlement.

"The actor. *Star Wars*? *Trainspotting*?"

"Ah. Thanks. I guess."

An awkward silence descended. Lydia gestured toward the wrought iron chairs on her crooked little patio. "Would you like a glass of iced tea? Some cookies?"

"No. No, thank you." Jim waved off the offer. "I, uhm, have a little, uhm, favor to ask you."

"Sure—anything." Lydia smiled her encouragement.

"Uh, I may have mentioned I'm involved with this charity, Born to Code, to teach low income kids how to code."

"Yes, I think that's great." Lydia wondered how she could help with that. Maybe he wanted her to write some promotional copy for the organization.

"So-o-o-o, they've decided to give me this award. It's silly, but—"

"Not silly. Congratulations!"

"Well, I mean, the work isn't silly." He shifted his sandal-clad feet and looked down at the grass. "I just meant—I don't need an award, but they have it all planned, so I have to go. There's a party, a fundraiser, actually."

Oh, that was it—he wanted a donation. "Sure, I'll be happy to contribute. Let me get my checkbook."

"No!" Jim lunged at her arm to stop her. "I...I don't want your money. I...I—" His face was flushed. He actually had a bead of sweat on his forehead. Why was he so upset? Lydia had never known him to be so inarticulate.

"It's like a, a gala." Jim fluttered his fingers. "There's a dinner, and dancing, and—"

Finally, Lydia understood. "You want me to go with you? Be your date?"

Waves of emotion passed over Jim's face—relief that he'd made himself clear, and horror that she now realized what he wanted of her. "If you wouldn't mind. I mean, I totally understand if you're busy, and these things are boring so you probably don't—"

"Yes."

"And I know it's an inconvenience but—"

"Jim, yes. I said yes. I'd be happy to go with you."

"Really?" He looked like a man double-checking the numbers on his winning lottery ticket. "But, listen—it's black tie."

Lydia howled. "Black tie? You're going to wear a tux?" Oh, God—she was making assumptions again. But she couldn't help picturing Jim in a tux with saggy trousers, black Birkenstocks peeking out from beneath the too-long cuffs.

"Well, yeah." He seemed a little miffed by her outburst. "Don't worry—I won't show up in some rented prom tuxedo with a floppy bow tie and a pink vest or anything. I own a tux."

Lydia accepted the tennis ball Alfie brought her and threw it for the dogs. "You're a bundle of surprises today, Jim."

"And you have to wear—" Jim ran his hands up and down.

"A long dress. No problem."

"I figured you might have something like that."

Lydia grinned. "So that's why you asked me and not Elise from the dog shelter?"

Jim started to protest, then realized she was teasing him. His shoulders lost their tense hunch. "It's on September 9. At the Metropolitan Museum of Art. The Temple of Dendur, after the museum is closed."

Lydia's eyes widened. "No way! I thought it would be at some catering hall in New Jersey, next to a big Italian wedding."

Jim shrugged sheepishly. "Some of the ladies on the Board of Born to Code are into this society sort of thing.

They mean well. And the money all goes to buy equipment to teach the kids. I make sure of that."

"I'm sure you do. The organization is lucky to have you."

Jim whistled, and Harley ran immediately to his side. "Thanks, Lydia. I appreciate this. I'll see you on the ninth then."

Lydia watched as Jim walked to his Jeep in the driveway. He did look like Ewan McGregor, if Ewan McGregor were kind-hearted and awkward with girls.

Chapter 59

The Burleith Block Party was rolling around again. This year, Lydia was planning an after-party at her house. Conrad and his new boyfriend were coming, and so were Roz, Celine and her family, and Marty and his wife. Madalyn had been helping her plan the food, and Jim promised to contribute some Irish whiskey.

Lydia stood in front of the kitchen window as she prepped an appetizer platter for tomorrow. The sound of a vehicle in her driveway made her lift the curtain to look out.

Seth's red pickup sat there, the cargo area loaded and covered snugly with a tarp.

She smiled. He was leaving for Houston.

The driver's door opened, and Seth emerged. He stood beside the truck, hands jammed in his jeans pockets. Lydia's throat tightened. This was the pose she'd remember him by. Whenever he was puzzled, whenever he was thinking, whenever he couldn't decide how to proceed, he stood like this.

She went outside to make his task easier. "Hey."

He offered a half-smile. "Hey, yourself."

"Looks like moving day."

He turned and stared at the back of his truck. "Somehow, I thought it would never come to this."

She longed to take his hand but was afraid to touch him. "I'm glad you came to say good-bye."

"I'm sorry for the way I acted the last time we were together." Seth spoke still keeping his eyes focused on the truck. "It was just...hard."

"For me, too."

She saw his Adam's apple bob as he swallowed. "Come inside. I have a little gift for you."

He followed her through the back door. Lydia picked up the small package that had been sitting on the shelf in the back hall since it had arrived in the mail last week. She had ordered it not knowing if she'd ever have the occasion to give it. In the kitchen, Seth opened it.

He smiled as he shook out a navy blue and gray Rice University t-shirt. "Thank you."

"I could have ordered one with the school mascot. It's an owl. I thought that might be a little too rah-rah for you."

"Yeah, I gotta take this whole college thing one step at a time." He shifted uneasily. "I wish I had something for you."

"Actually, you do." Lydia tugged at the hem of the faded Bob Marley t-shirt he wore. "Take this off. I want it."

"This? Why?"

"Because it smells like you."

His gaze held hers for a long moment. Then he reached down and pulled the shirt over his head. When his face was covered by the fabric, Lydia took in that long, lithe torso one last time. He shrugged out of the shirt and handed it to her.

Lydia buried her face in the soft, faded fabric, still warm from his body. It smelled of soap and skin and fresh sawdust and a tiny overtone of turpentine.

Seth.

He pulled her into his arms. She rested her cheek on his bare chest and they swayed in a long embrace.

When at last she pulled away, his eyes were wet and so were hers. She tossed him the new shirt and turned away as he put it on. "You know I'll always be here for you. But I think it's probably better for both of us if you don't call or text too much in the beginning. Until we get...adjusted."

Seth sighed. "Right."

Lydia turned around. "But maybe in six months or so, after your first semester, you could email and let me know how school is going."

He nudged her foot with the tip of his sneaker. "I'll send you my report card."

Silently, they walked together to his truck. Seth got in, and before he closed the door, Lydia spoke. "Thank you, Seth."

"For what? I haven't given you anything."

"Oh, my dear, you have. You have."

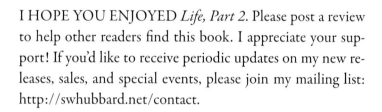

I HOPE YOU ENJOYED *Life, Part 2*. Please post a review to help other readers find this book. I appreciate your support! If you'd like to receive periodic updates on my new releases, sales, and special events, please join my mailing list: http://swhubbard.net/contact.

COMING SOON, *Life, Upended: Roz's Story*. Until then, read all the Palmyrton Estate Sale Mysteries, available in paperback, Kindle, and audiobook:

Another Man's Treasure
Treasure of Darkness
This Bitter Treasure
Treasure Borrowed and Blue
Treasure in Exile
Treasure Built of Sand

———◆———

If you've read all the Palmyrton Estate Sale mysteries, it's time to try the Frank Bennett Adirondack Mountain mystery series:
The Lure
Blood Knot
Dead Drift
False Cast
Tailspinner

About the Author

S.W. Hubbard writes the kinds of mysteries she loves to read: twisty, believable, full of complex characters, and highlighted with sly humor. She is the author of the Palmyrton Estate Sale Mystery Series and the Frank Bennett Adirondack Mountain Mystery Series. Her short stories have also appeared in *Alfred Hitchcock's Mystery Magazine* and the anthologies *Crimes by Moonlight, Adirondack Mysteries*, and *The Mystery Box*. She lives in Morristown, NJ, where she teaches creative writing to enthusiastic teens and adults, and expository writing to reluctant college freshmen. Visit her at http://www.swhubbard.net.

Made in United States
North Haven, CT
31 March 2022

17707332R20209